IN THE SILENCE THERE ARE GHOSTS

IN THE SILENCE THERE ARE GHOSTS

A NOVEL

JAMES CALVIN SCHAAP

Baker Books

A Division of Baker Book House Co
Grand Rapids, Michigan 49516

© 1995 by James Calvin Schaap

Published by Baker Books
a division of Baker Book House Company
P.O. Box 6287, Grand Rapids, MI 49516-6287

Printed in the United States of America

All rights reserved. No part of this publication may be reproduced, stored in a retrieval system, or transmitted in any other form or by any means—for example, electronic, mechanical, photocopy, recording—without the prior written permission of the publisher. The only exception is brief quotations in printed reviews.

Library of Congress Cataloging-in-Publication Data

Schaap, James C.
    In the silence there are ghosts : a novel / James Calvin Schaap.
        p.   cm.
    ISBN 0-8010-8381-8
  I. Title.
  PS3569.C33I6   1995
  813'.54—dc20   94-42286

I

Even though others felt it more than Emily Doorn did, there was an admission of failure in her coming home to Neukirk. Most people thought that if anyone was ever going to leave town and make it big time, the youngest daughter of Ben and Vivian Doorn, a girl brimming with talent, could and would. But she didn't.

Don't misconstrue. The story of Emily Doorn (who married a man named Forcier but never took his name) is not simply an updated, Neukirk version of the prodigal son. She didn't throw her life away by working the seamy corners of Los Angeles before seeing the light and returning to the farm. Nor was there a farm to return to—thus, no fatted calf either. Her parents were in their forties when they had her, their second daughter, almost fifteen years after their first, so by the time she returned home, thirteen years after leaving for the bright lights, her father was already gone and therefore incapable of throwing any kind of party. Her mother, even before her father's death, had been made an invalid by a stroke, and her sister, as everyone in town old enough remembers, died in a tragic car accident.

Neither was there a golden ring. Emily's California wealth, in fact, far surpassed the limited means of her father's Iowa estate. With her two children, she drove into town in what became Neukirk's only BMW. Dr. Forcier, an eminent surgeon whom we've all seen occasionally on Ted Koppel, became renowned as a medical ethicist; and when he politely told her that he didn't feel they had any future as husband and wife, he didn't leave her penniless. He was, and is, a gentleman, who, unlike many of Neukirk's wandering husbands, has never been a day late with alimony and child support.

Emily's failure is not only a story of thwarted ambitions—as an aspiring actress she never really rose above a few nationally televised commercials for Proctor and Gamble—it's also a story which is not atypical of the failures registered by Neukirk's more eminent émigrés. That is, it's not a story of dissolution; most of those who leave town with a backpack full of dreams do not end up in some crack house, perhaps because they carry too much of Neukirk's righteousness away with them.

Cocaine has bagged a few, however, because most of those who leave town, like Emily, are dedicated upwardly mobile types. They tend to be Neukirk's best and brightest, so when they fail, their losses often can be attributed to wealth, not poverty. In that sense, Emily's failure is not so uncommon a story.

As she herself explains it, her marriage to Dr. Benjamin Forcier (the same name as her father, except her husband wanted to be called "Benjamin") collapsed because of wealth and religion. I've already established Forcier's eminence as a physician and ethicist by alluding to his appearances on "Nightline" whenever Koppel chose to report on some daring experiments in genetics. He was—they were—wealthy; wealthier, in fact, than anyone in Neukirk. And by a long shot.

That religion would play a role in the demise of that marriage came as no surprise to anyone in town, since it had been whispered years ago, when the impending marriage was announced, that Forcier, then a flashy young intern at a La Jolla hospital, was Jewish.

Emily claims his Jewishness didn't really matter back then, but over the years of their marriage her husband went through a kind of reformation. At the time of their marriage he may well have been more of a prodigal than she ever was, but he grew back into his Jewishness in a way that alienated her and, she claims, ended their relationship. (She uses the word *relationship* herself, having lived in California for all those years; Neukirk people are more stubborn about conceding the word *marriage*.)

But no matter. What we're talking about here is a victim. Emily Doorn, someone who elicits sympathy even though she drives a BMW. What's important about her homecoming, however, is that Neukirk people did not see her as someone who, by some kind of moral vagrancy, designed her own demise. Quite simply, and traditionally, they blamed the Jew.

The problems between Benjamin and Emily were a bit more complex, of course, and I don't mean to spend all my time going over exactly what happened to ruin what seemed, for a year or so, a wonderful match. This story, like other secrets of Neukirk, takes a little time to tell. Let me just say this in summary. Emily, despite the fact that she was well-schooled in the importance of motherhood, was not herself given to staying home and caring for the children.

As happens in many marriages today, the kids became not so much the source of the problem as its most obvious focal point. Both Benjamin and Emily would stay at work long after normal office hours, refusing to be the one to pick up the kids from day-care or pre-school. Both of them actually tried to be away from home as often as they could to push the burden of the work on the other, not because either of them was lazy—not at all; and not because either of them couldn't handle children—they both could. In fact, when they were with the kids, they logged considerable quality time (another Emily word).

It was a simple power struggle, the desire for independence on both sides eventually tearing away at whatever desire and affection had brought them together in the first place; and in the balmy California climate, divorce began to look like the most sane solution.

Neukirk never knew all of that, and, to their credit, people in town never forced explanations from Emily once she came back. Besides, it was much easier, as I've said, to blame the rich doctor—and his religion, of course.

I don't want to beat this to death, but let me say once more that in most ways we're not talking about the return of the prodigal here. In the town where she grew up and the town she returned to, Emily's seen as a victim; she's got loads of money, she's been on national TV, and she's maybe the most beautiful woman in town, in the prime of life, I believe—33 years old. Every tribe and race has its beauties, but most folks in Neukirk are of Dutch blood, and thus tall and blonde, with skin that is tanning handsomely by early spring. There is ugliness here too; Neukirk certainly isn't paradise. But there are really handsome folks in Neukirk, lots of them, men and women. But none of them hold a candle to Emily.

Somewhere back in California, people who are paid to spot such things told her that she had a perfectly oval face with high cheekbones and graceful chin, the kind of face that will stop traffic if long hair is drawn back gracefully and worn up or back. You might say hers is a calculated beauty; but the fact is, she always was drop-dead gorgeous.

All of which begs the question. If Emily was stubbornly independent about her own career, if she has money and connections, if her beauty is legendary, and if she left Neukirk with an eye on a film career, why did she come back?

The answer, really, seems quite simple. In one way, at least, she is the prodigal son. And it's important to understand that her version of Benjamin's return to his Jewishness is not just a convenient excuse. Dr. Forcier has, in fact, become more "Jewish" in his expression of religion, and that movement did, in fact, create significant tensions in the marriage.

Once again, the children became the battleground. Once Benjamin "saw the light," he wanted his children to be reared Jewish; Emily, who had slowly but inevitably given up the ritual of weekly church attendance, refused to go along with change—not because of some passion for the devout Protestant Christianity in which she was reared, but because she refused to give any ground.

Thus, Benjamin's change brought about Emily's counter reformation, and she began attending a sprawling evangelical church in Anaheim as a counter to her husband's new sense of heritage. She soon found, however, that attending worship provided something she hadn't really identified as missing. She fell into a Bible study and even found some guidance when her marriage continued to fall apart.

None of which, of course, was any benefit to "the relationship." What her new-found Christianity did was galvanize her own independence, give her a moral cause as personal as Benjamin's, and reinforce her attitudes toward him with a long list of New Testament scriptures—all of which made her anathema to Benjamin's own revitalized Jewishness.

Old hymns sung by a thousand strong revived the kind of solace and comfort she remembered feeling as a young Christian girl. She found something "meaningful" about bringing her children into that wonderful, happy church, something that made her feel as if the Lord himself was smiling on the way she was— at long last—doing the right thing.

I have to get on with this, I know, but let me just say this about Emily's parents. In Neukirk there are lots of people who don't always want to go to church, but no one really hates it. There are no comic book hypocrites here, which is not to say there are no hypocrites. In Neukirk, people go to church for one of three reasons: one, because they love to—usually old people; two, because they always have, and, in attending, they satisfy their need for ritual; or three, because they feel it is necessary. The latter being the old and common cod liver oil argument: it's good for you, even though it tastes bad.

Everyone who ever knew the Doorns would have considered Ben and Vivian unpretentious Christians, the kind Tolstoy would have loved, undoubtedly "number ones." Ben would have been as unable to neglect church as he would have been unable to stifle his enthusiasm for spring planting. Vivian, people said, always was a saint, even before the death of her older daughter.

Type two and three churchgoers tend to be the most self-righteous, of course, and the most demanding as parents. Ben and Vivian never really spoke much about how important it was to them that their daughter love Jesus, and when she determined that she wanted to be an actress and move to California, they let her go. They feared for her all right—their only daughter, after the death of Emily's older sister—but they trusted her and they trusted God. Believe me, they prayed a lot, but then they'd always prayed a lot.

Her parents' influence, as much as anything else, led to Emily's return to faith after her father's death. And even though she didn't return to Iowa immediately after her marriage finally died, in that time she began more and more to see herself as a child of her believing parents—a believer, a child of God.

So she moved back to Neukirk for several reasons, not the least of which was her mother's condition. But also important was her belief that here in Neukirk her kids would be raised with neighbors who held Christian values. She saw her return as an experiment of sorts, because she was old enough and smart enough to understand that she might not be able to make the adjustment smoothly, having been away so long. But she wanted her children to grow up with a sense of heritage, not all that different from Benjamin's desire for the very same kids.

It was an angry divorce. Both of them wanted to pass on to the children their separate traditions; thus, both of them wanted custody, something neither of them seemed to care about before all the fireworks. Emily won. There was, after all, another woman.

And that was another reason she came home. The divorce was horrible, and she needed somewhere to hide.

She bought an old house on Main Street, and immediately people wondered why anyone with her kind of money would want to live so close to all the downtown hustle and bustle. What was even more strange was that she bought it sight unseen, which is simply not done in Neukirk. But people generally conceded that while blindly choosing such a central location was odd, what was laudable was the fact that she'd picked an unpretentious

10

place, a house that, rumor had it, was quite a steal. Frugality does not go unnoticed around here.

Her story was well known, of course, even before the North American Van Lines fourteen-wheeler hunched its way backwards up the front sidewalk. People knew she was rich. And her choice of the old Van Voorst place was in itself an indication of character, a moral choice (in Neukirk, the public choices other people make are quite regularly considered to be moral choices).

They knew she could have afforded the doctor's mansion for sale on the east side of town. By choosing the Van Voorst place she was showing her desire not to appear as high-brow as she might have, and that, they concluded, spoke well of her character.

She had no right to be snooty either, having trudged back home to middle America, where people really couldn't turn her away. Her ex-husband's several television appearances and her own prime-time commercials notwithstanding, she was returning with no real triumphal reentry; she came home, after all, having lost. To take the mansion would have signified some refusal to see herself and her situation realistically.

In short, Neukirk, self-righteous and smug but duly concerned about all these things, looked at the whole story and liked what it saw. Humility, after all, is Christlike.

The only person in town to know the exact day of her return was the realtor. I take that back. Emily's mother knew, but she hasn't said anything since her stroke; and, of course, Nancy Greiman, the nurse who reads Vivian Doorn the letters she receives from Emily. But Nancy is a professional; she told no one but her husband, who long ago swore he would never repeat anything she told him from her job.

So Nancy was furious when she heard the date mentioned at her card club. She thought it was her husband who'd leaked the information. Once she'd fished around, though, she discovered that the moving day had been announced at Emily's church, that the pastor had asked if anyone would like to help and mentioned that Marty Kamphoff was stringing together a squad of volunteers to help Emily feel at home in the old town—a Neukirk welcome wagon.

There'd be a women's group to help her put away things in the house and a men's group to unload the van. The pastor said Marty had already set up his own kids to baby-sit Emily's children. "If anyone would like to help," Marty told the congregation when the pastor asked him to stand, "he or she should call me or my wife."

"Did Emily tell someone?" Nancy asked her friends. "I mean, did she ask for all this help?"

No one seemed to know.

It was just another one of those perfectly righteous missions of mercy Neukirk people pride themselves in, one of those things no one could fault because it seemed so much like the Christian thing to do, even if some did wonder about the propriety of setting up the whole affair without even consulting Emily.

Administering this kind of operation was not out of character for Marty Kamphoff, who constantly seemed to be running for some office or other. But others were there as well. A few retired gents to help with the lifting, plus a couple schoolteachers unemployed during the summer months, and six women in scarves, jeans, and sleeveless blouses, armed with buckets and brushes.

One of the men was Norm Visser, who is, as everyone would admit, a man with a good heart and entirely capable of helping out whenever and wherever needed. I don't believe anyone questioned his being there that morning, even though at least some of them remembered that it was Norm who drove the car that Margaret, Emily's sister, died in twenty-five years ago.

Marty's squad was there when the van arrived—four cars and two pickups—Marty himself in an aqua summer coverall and a Victor Soap cap, six other men, and about that many women. Hennie Dortmans had brought a big aluminum coffee urn from church, ready to be plugged in.

The truck driver and his wife who stepped out of the van looked like they might have been from town themselves. His only distinguishing feature was a pair of old-fashioned, black-rimmed glasses, and his wife, who might have outweighed him by forty pounds, wore a cut-off sweatshirt over a red blouse, and what seemed to be men's Levis, cut with a bit more than "a skoosh more room," as the ads say.

"So where's Emily?" Marty said. He met them at the curb once both of them were out of the truck.

"I thought she'd be here," the driver said. "Who're you?"

"We're here to help her move in," he said, proudly.

"You family? I didn't think she had family."

"We're friends," Marty said.

The trucker's wife pulled on garden gloves. "She told us we might have to hire some kids to help," she said. "She didn't say anything about people being here."

"She doesn't know," Marty said. "This is just the way we do things. We're from the church."

The husband and wife looked at each other suspiciously.

"You don't have to worry," Marty said. "We all know who she is."

"Does she know who you are?" the woman said, not angrily.

Marty took off his cap and smoothed back his perfect hair. "We're a kind of welcome wagon," he said.

"Just the same, I ain't starting until she gets here," the trucker said. "It's a policy with the company."

"We're just volunteers," Kamphoff said. "We just want to help—she's been through a lot." The three schoolteachers stood behind him and the women behind them, huddled around the front steps.

"Emily Doorn? I got the right place here?"

"You got it," Kamphoff said.

From the perspective of most lifelong Neukirk residents, Emily had been through a lot. All the trucker knew was that he was toting the goods of one perfectly beautiful and very rich dame out of a California home, the likes of which you'd have to search half the state of Iowa to find.

Traffic stopped on Main Street when the trucker pulled his

rig into the middle of the road and pushed the back end up the curb and toward the front porch. It was all a matter of mirrors with him, of course, his wife waving him back like someone with earphones and a pair of batons standing on a runway. The women swept up their stuff and moved up on the porch, out of the way, and everyone watched as this huge van backed stiffly up over the sidewalk and aimed its posterior at the front door.

So no one saw Emily when she stepped out of the BMW for the first time in her old hometown. No one saw the way she stood there for a minute in the shade of the maples a few houses down from the one she'd bought, sight unseen. No one watched her pin up her hair quickly, straighten the collar on her blouse, and, with dignity and stiff composure, take a deep breath.

She walked up to the house with her children.

"I can't believe I'm here," she said, almost out of nowhere, as everyone stood watching the truck. "I can't believe that I'm back in Neukirk for real."

Marty swung around quickly, and for one of the few times in his life registered little but silence. She wore nothing more dramatic than a short-sleeved white blouse and a pair of jeans and tan canvas shoes with no socks. She was dressed for work, but her mere presence silenced him.

Neukirk people, men and women, know beauty when they see it, but they don't know pampered beauty. Even Marty Kamphoff, whose beautician wife has cut his hair perfectly for years, felt suddenly boorish, white and lumpy.

"Bring it back, Larry," the trucker's wife said. "Twelve feet."

By that time, of course, traffic was stopped up and down Main Street, and the rubbernecks were in full bloom—to mix a metaphor.

"We're here to help you," Marty told Emily. And the odd part, the really strange part to anyone who didn't know Neukirk history, was that he didn't even introduce himself—never thought of it, in fact, and, of course, didn't need to. She knew who he was the moment she saw him.

Nothing, not one line on her face, even cracked; but inside

Emily knew, at that very moment, that she was back home. Not because she felt something comfortably familiar in the air, but rather because she felt, all of a sudden, thrust back into the kind of publicness she'd nearly forgotten in the anonymity of Los Angeles—the oddly embarrassing sense that anything less than a polite and politic smile can, and will, be read by everyone as publicly as a loved one's last will and testament.

"I hope you aren't put off," Marty said, raising a hand. "We're here to give you a good Neukirk welcome—a welcome home."

She slid her fingers into the front pockets of her jeans and smiled. "I didn't expect anything like this—"

"If you don't want us, we can go somewhere and drink coffee," Marty said, jokingly. "But we got some women along here to help inside too." He pointed up at the porch, where the women smiled politely. "We figured that since you'd be alone, you'd need some help."

"That's very nice of you—that's so nice of you, really. I never dreamed that there would be people here to help." She looked around suddenly, as if she'd just that moment remembered that the house she was standing outside was hers. "I have no idea what it looks like inside," she said, "whether it needs a cleaning or not."

"That's what we figured," Marty said. "That's why we got the women here."

Her two children stayed close to her, the little boy edging up behind her, even though his eyes were busily assessing everything around him—the weeds in the flower bed, the swing on the front porch. The little girl seemed on the verge of tears. Both had their father's darkness, his thick curly hair.

"I got my son coming," Marty said. "He can look after your kids there." He pointed. "I know it might be strange to have a boy baby-sitter, but he loves it—"

"That's very kind—"

"He'd rather baby-sit than do anything." Marty swung around to look at the street. "I don't know where that kid is—

he's kind of a dreamer really. I told him to be here, and he will in a while."

Being met at the front step by an entire church committee struck Emily instantly on two levels. As someone returning to a tradition and a tribe, she found the unexpected welcome almost overwhelming, a kind of verification of everything she'd gambled her returning would prove—that in Neukirk people care deeply. But she also found it a bit stifling. Suddenly she had to wear a public face she hadn't put on for years.

She'd purposely stayed in Brooks, a town twenty miles down the road, the night before, because she didn't want her kids to rough it their first night in a new house in a new town, to sleep in a place without beds or maybe even power. She didn't want them to notice anything that might make them fearful, that might increase their anxiety about leaving the only home they'd ever known.

Now if the women who scrubbed that morning are to be believed—and they are—what followed was Emily's first tour of her own house with Marty leading, fawning over her as if she were his key to glory. He told her, for instance, that a new deck on the back would be simply perfect, that he could get her a deal on paneling from the Co-op if she wanted to cover the cracked mortar walls in the front room, and that a cathedral window on the south side of the dining room would be simply gorgeous and would not destroy the architectural integrity of the old house at all. Her two kids crowded her as if this place was some new planet with adult-sized aliens.

"I'm sure we can get some women from church to help you throw up some wallpaper in here," he said upstairs, at the doorway of one of the kid's rooms, "maybe something with teddy bears or whatever."

She nodded graciously, her daughter Rebecca's long legs dangling from under her arm as she lay against Emily's shoulder.

"The porch off this room is decorative only," he said. "Sometimes people did that in the old days—put on a porch just for show. Stupid, isn't it? We could put a door in the wall there so it would be functional, but I don't know if you'd want that."

"There's so much to think about," Emily said.

"Well, you know how it is," Marty told her. "It's like I said, if you need anything at all, just call."

Although she never once signaled it to anyone, Emily did find him cloying—as do most people in Neukirk. But he's nearly fifty, so she didn't see him as threatening in any way; he was simply a man who tried a bit too hard, but whose heart was in the right place.

"I'll have to get the water turned on," she said when they stood at the small upstairs bathroom. "I don't know who to call—"

"I've already taken care of that," Marty announced, and he walked up to the stool and flushed it as a demonstration. "And I called Ed Meester over at the phone company, just to find out if you'd contacted him. He said he hadn't heard from you yet. Somebody'll be here yet this afternoon."

She put Rebecca down, but her daughter stayed glued to her side. "I don't know how to thank you," she said. "I never expected this kind of thing—"

"Your father was a fine man, the kind who always helped out whenever he knew a hand was needed," Marty said. "I guess we all felt a little sorry for you—going through everything you did and then coming home all by yourself. I got a business I can leave every once in a while, especially when there's a damsel in distress."

She looked for, but found no note of irony. So she accepted the remark as something merely quaint.

"So, what say we start getting stuff in here?" he said. "I think the best plan is for you to station yourself on the front porch and just tell us where to bring the stuff. I got it figured that you really don't have to raise a hand for a while at least, not until we got all the boxes in. If I know women," he said, "you'll have to have everything just so eventually, and as long as you got the men here, you better take advantage of us."

The women thought Marty's constant attention rude, but typical. He should have allowed Emily her own initial tour. This was her house, a place she hadn't seen, a place she'd chosen to call her home. She deserved the privacy of her own thoughts. Instead, in that first quarter-hour tour, and really all morning long, Marty Kamphoff acted like a realtor. But, typically, no one dared tell him so.

Emily stopped him only once. It happened later, close to noon, in fact. He was down on all fours putting her bed together while she was in the closet hanging clothes.

"You looking for a job?" he said.

She let it pass, pretending she didn't hear. To say no would be to sound lazy, she thought, or risk seeming too independent. Of course, she wanted to find something. But to say yes would prompt a response she was afraid she didn't want—"I can get you something," he'd say.

"I said, 'Are you looking for a job?'" he said again from the other side of the box spring.

"I don't know," she said. "Eventually, I suppose, but for right now I just want to help my kids make the adjustment."

"I can help you," he told her, never looking up. "I don't have anything for you myself right now, but I got some pull around this burg, and if you ever decide to try to pin something down, just let me know."

"I'll have to think about it," she said, putting boxes of shoes away. "I'm really grateful for everything you've done—I really am."

Even as she said it, she knew it was her first Neukirk lie.

Norm Visser had, the entire morning, stayed in the background, not uncharacteristically. Norm is single, the same age as Emily's sister would have been—more than a decade older than Emily, twelve years to be exact, which would make him forty-four.

Some people claim he's really never gotten over the death of Emily's sister, the girl he was going with at the time of the accident—"were they in love?" Margaret was only a senior in high school. But there's an additional story about Norm that people in Neukirk certainly didn't overlook.

He married in college, even though no one in town ever met his wife. She was a soprano, he a tenor in the University A Cappella Choir. She sang, as did he, at their wedding in a suburb of Chicago—at least according to the article Norm himself wrote for the Neukirk News back then. She was going on to some fancy music school in Rochester, New York, the article said. Norm was going to be a teacher.

The marriage lasted six weeks, just long enough for there to be a picture of the bride and the wedding write-up in the local paper. The next week it was over—annulled.

Some people say, albeit quietly, that Norm was impotent.

You may wonder about the source for such an explanation. Norm and his wife lived in an apartment close to the university for those six short weeks, right next door to a house full of guys who rarely, summer or winter, shut all their windows. One of the guys was from a town just across the Minnesota border, a kid with family in Neukirk.

These guys had no difficulty hearing the rages the young soprano threw from the top of the backyard stairs, including her specific concern. Not knowing Norm, you can imagine how they roared.

Right or wrong, that story drifted south across the state line and became part of the legend of Norm Visser.

Once Norm graduated and put the short and unfortunate marriage behind him, he did take a teaching job. In Chicago. And, rumor has it, he was successful—very successful.

But he, like Emily, longed to come back to Neukirk, although he didn't really recognize it himself until one day, in the administrator's office, as he was sitting there with his boss and a particularly difficult student. The administrator was black, as was the student, and the language he heard thrown between them was something not of Norm's world—not, at least, of the world of Neukirk. He sat there in silence, knowing somehow that he could never speak to the kid the way that Horace Anderson, the administrator, could, being black. And at that moment he felt himself an alien. He told himself that if he was going to stay in teaching, he would go back home to Iowa. So he did.

Now I need to clarify very quickly that Neukirk men tend to think of all teachers, good or bad, as something odd, because for generations the boys who became teachers did so by default—they simply lacked the strength or machismo to do farm work. So male teachers, even the good ones like Norm Visser, are not highly regarded—witness their pay.

What's worse is a man who stays in the profession after, say, the age of thirty-something. Youthful idealism is just fine in Neukirk. That some big, strong young fellow wants to teach and coach basketball, for instance, is quite noble. But if after a few years that fellow stays in the profession and doesn't move into administration or at least become an athletic director, Neukirk men start to see him as, well, deficient in some crucial chemical.

Norm Visser's been at the local grade school for seventeen years, after putting in five at Chicago's Roosevelt High. He teaches sixth grade. He'd already taught seventh and eighth and compartmentalized language arts, when the school went toward a junior high structure. But he's happiest with sixth, because, as he says, it's just a shade before adolescence rears its ugly snoot.

He's a forty-four-year-old grade school teacher with no visions of administration, and he's single. As you can guess, the story of his short and failed marriage is widely known, not only for its own uniqueness but for what that story lends to a definition of what would otherwise be the completely puzzling character of Norm Visser.

In this very Protestant town, you might think of Norm Visser as a kind of low-key Calvinist priest: someone thought of as having done something exemplary, even noble, but, at the same time, somewhat naive, even stupid, with his life—given it to teaching. His musical ability only adds to that characterization.

He sings often, and beautifully, in churches throughout the area, and is always available for funerals and weddings.

With all the discussion of AIDS, most Neukirk men who've thought it through have reasoned that if the surveys taken are correct and one in ten, overall, are in fact gay, then certainly Norm Visser is one Neukirk name they can put on the short list. At the same time, they know he's not about to head for some San Francisco bath house. But then, he's never set foot in a sale barn or played slow-pitch softball either. He's not particularly effeminate. He's simply different.

You can tell, I'm sure, that some of my sympathies lie with this man, if for no other reason than the fact that he finds himself on the outs with what some would call the Philistine culture of Neukirk. That alone commends him.

But there's more. He has on him the mark of suffering. After all he's been through—Margaret's death in his car, a failed marriage—the man has compassion in spades. Why beat around the bush? Norm Visser is, hands down, the finest real Christian in Neukirk. There, I said it.

That's one of the reasons he was there helping Emily, in the background, that day. I have the time to help her move in, he thought. In many ways, I owe her a great deal. She knows very few people. She can use the help. Besides, Marty Kamphoff is an ass.

How can you help but like him?

It took Emily five days to move in and feel somewhat comfortable. During that time, she never made a meal. Marty brought over pizza the second night, took out the whole family the third, had his wife cook up a hamburger hot dish on Thursday, and had them all over for a barbecue on Friday.

Every day about nine, Jason, his youngest, about twelve, would show up on his moped and somehow corral the kids. On Thursday, unexpectedly, the Servicemaster truck showed up and the guy told her that he'd been sent by the company to clean her carpeting, a gift from some anonymous donor.

But Marty was not the only one spilling sweetness all over Main Street. By Friday, Emily's freezer was stuffed with cakes, raisin bars, Rice Krispie treats, and at least six different varieties of brownies, not to mention four fruit pies and a half-dozen casseroles. Five days passed and all she'd bought was milk, butter, cereal, and bread.

So when Emily went to visit her mother, which she did daily, she overflowed with the virtues of the hometown, even though her mother sat unmoving in the chair in front of her, her eyes clear and mute as glass.

The doctors had long ago explained that it was altogether possible that Vivian Doorn understood everything she was told; she simply seemed unable to respond. But after three days or so Emily began reading her mother's eyes. I suppose no one will ever know whether or not Vivian comprehended anything her daughter said, but Emily was sure her mother was listening.

Now the hospital wing is a really fine place for people like Vivian Doorn. Several of the residents, in fact, are people who've come home to Neukirk from places like California or Oregon because they, or their families, are sure they will receive the compassionate full-time attention they require. And they do.

Vivian had been a resident of the wing for about three years by the time Emily returned home, and in all that time she'd had few visitors. There were plenty at first, of course, but it's a fact of life in Neukirk, as elsewhere, that as tragedies age they lose their attraction in the fresh wake of more recent others. Vivian, should she have spoken, would have been the first to say that in the last twelve months the only human being to register any interest in her was Nancy Greiman.

So while it may not have been right for Nancy to listen in to Emily's discussions with her mother, it was at least understandable. In Neukirk, there's an often indistinguishable line between gossip and heartfelt concern.

Nancy's eavesdropping was nothing so furtive as hovering

around outside the door with an ear pealed. She simply found things to do in Mrs. Doorn's room during Emily's visits, and Emily soon took her presence for granted. What's more, she trusted Nancy after their first meeting, as she should have, Nancy being not only a fine nurse but a wonderful human being.

"I've got things pretty much together now," Emily told her mother one day, maybe a week after moving in. "There's still some boxes in the upstairs closets, and I really haven't spent much time in the basement, but otherwise the kids seem to know where everything is now, and so do I."

Her mother sat in her rocker, dressed in a flower print dress with snaps up the front, her long gray hair back in a bun held tight by a long gold barrette.

"I don't think I want to change anything," she said. "Sometimes I stand in the middle of the dining room and look around and I know that I could really make that place special, but it's already special to me, Mom." Emily sat, knees together, on the only other chair in the room, no more than a few feet from her mother, close enough to touch her arm or hand occasionally.

"Sometimes I think that it's exactly why I came back. I don't know if I can explain it, but it just seems as if the whole place is a home. Maybe it's not mine yet, you know?—I mean, I haven't done much to it to make it mine, other than move in my furniture—but it's the home I wanted to come back to. I'm not sure I can explain that very well."

Nancy Greiman often thought she saw a play of emotions pass over Vivian Doorn's eyes, even though little on the woman's face ever changed, aside from her lips, which pulled in and out slightly, as if she were constantly cleaning her front teeth with her tongue and lips. After the stroke, a contented look had settled permanently on her face, a softness in her pale eyes.

"It's so different not to worry, Mom. I just can't explain what it's like to be away from Ben. I can breathe here—I know that sounds strange, but it's true. I go to bed at night, and I lie there asking myself to list the things I've got to be worried about—that's the way I've lived for years, it seems. It's a ritual I can't really shake. I lie there at the end of the day and try to list my worries, just like I've always done. But here, Mom—it's so freeing.

"All day the kids play outside, and half the time I'm not even sure where they are. Sometimes I'm startled when I think of them not being right there under my nose, and I get this panic. But then I remember where I am."

With her fingers, with the back of her hand, she rubbed her mother's arm where it crossed over the other in her lap.

"I don't know why I ever left," she said. "No, I guess I do too—I left because I really wanted something, and I suppose if I had it to do all over again, I'd leave again, wouldn't I?"

She sat back in her chair, glanced up at the wall over the bed.

"You must have hated to see me go. It's amazing to me that I could leave the way I did and not really think about what it must have done to you and Dad—what with Meg gone and everything. Maybe I did, too. I mean, I remember thinking that you were going to be alone, but it never registered that it might be hard on you."

She stood and walked to the window, looked out for a moment or two, then faced her mother again.

"Sometimes I think of you and Dad as almost the perfect parents," she said. "You know, we saw our share of marriage counselors, Benjamin and I. And one of them told me my problem was that I had perfect parents." Her voice dropped, lower and softer. "'You expect too much of your marriage perhaps because you had perfect parents yourself'—that's exactly what he told me."

Her mother's eyes fell to her hands.

"I know you think I'm wrong about that, Mom. I know you think you weren't perfect, but you were really wonderful. I've thought often that he was right—and I'm not trying to blame you for it. I mean, what you wanted to do was to be the best you could, and that's what you were."

Emily came back and stood behind her chair.

"Oh, don't deny it. Besides, what could you have done?

Could you have brought your little fights out into the open just for me? That wouldn't have been like you. Did you and Dad ever have big fights?"

Her mother chewed her lips lightly.

"You must have—everybody does. Money and sex, money and sex, money and sex. Every last counselor we ever saw wanted to draw everything into money and sex. I just can't see you and Dad quarreling about anything like that. But there must have been something. You two were just as human as anybody else. Me, I bet. Maybe you fought about how to raise me after Margaret's death—"

She stopped, looked closely at her mother's face, then sat again and took both her mother's arms in her hands. "Oh, Mom, was that it—how to raise this little girl on the farm? Whether to let her drive the tractor or feed the hogs? That was it, I bet, wasn't it? You must have had some disagreements, some little fights."

Emily anticipated that someday, during one of her daily visits, her mother would simply open her mouth and speak, probably right in the middle of her daughter's running monologue. It wasn't something Emily prayed for actually, but that kind of miracle was an impossibility she simply couldn't put out of her mind, and didn't want to.

"I miss him—Benjamin—though. I would never go back, but there's so much of me I left with him. And there's our kids. I look at them and sometimes I feel as if Benjamin is just out in the other room or something, even though toward the last I hated him. I'm not proud to say that either, because I know what you and Dad would say, but I did. I just hated him. But I miss him. Does that sound possible? With so much behind me now, and all the relief I feel here, I still think sometimes that he's going to come walking into the kitchen with the *LA Times* in his hand as if he's just come back from work, as if nothing ever happened. Do you think that's normal, Mom?"

She looked for something in her mother's eyes, then raised her left hand slowly, crossing the plane of her mother's stare, as if to see if anything were registering. She reached farther and touched her mother's cheek with the back of her fingers, looked for any sign of sensibility, any note of her touch.

"It's okay for me to say all of this, isn't it, Mom? I mean, I'm not hurting you by saying how I'm feeling—I mean, because you can't speak back, am I?" she said. "I want you to know that so often when I talk to you like this, when I tell you how I feel, I really believe that I know exactly what you'd say. You were always so good. If I can be half the mother you were—and after losing Margaret and everything. Sometimes I look at Rebecca and I can't imagine what it must have been like for you." She dropped her hand.

"I'm sorry," she said. "I was talking about Benjamin, wasn't I, and that I missed him? But I wonder maybe if it's not so much him I miss as just someone real, someone who doesn't come over and just give me things." She laid a hand, palm up, on her mother's arms. "I don't know, now that I'm here, maybe I miss the man I fell in love with. I guess I get a little lonely sometimes. I mean, it's not awful of me to want to be with someone, is it? Not that there's no one around. We still get meals, Mom. People are still bringing in meals, even though we're in the house. Actually, I'm getting a little sick of it."

Almost involuntarily, her mother started into a slow and gentle rock.

"I'm not saying I need a husband, even though that's probably what you're thinking. I know what the odds are, second time around, and I know pain. It's different than yours, but anybody who's been through what I have has to be wary. Sometimes I want to talk to someone who's not helping me, just to talk, you know?"

She unfolded her mother's arms and took a hand in each of hers.

"I don't want you to worry about me either. Remember what I said—sometimes I just stand in the middle of the house and I tell myself I don't want to change anything. It's so safe. I'm in a fortress, and all of that pain that's back there a thousand miles away can't touch me at all. But then I think to myself sometimes that it's not a real life here either. Do you know what I mean? I feel sometimes as if I'm the one in the nursing home, I'm the one getting all the care.

"And then I remind myself that it's not going to last, this honeymoon. There's going to be something. I got that from you too, didn't I?—this sense that something bad has to happen. Every last road in Neukirk is straight as an arrow, but I've got this sense that I'm on something much more curvy, where you can't see much, but you know that something could be just ahead—fallen rock or something."

Her mother rocked slightly in the chair and began to hum an oddly disjointed set of notes, her eyes moving around the room, over her daughter's face, then up to the ceiling, then back down to her hands in a pattern that seemed entirely random. She swept her lips into a tightened smile, as if she'd just heard a secret that confirmed her suspicions.

Emily read the smile as something confirming, and she sat there holding her mother's hand and listening to her humming, trying to distinguish a melody. Still, her mother's eyes kept moving around the room, unfocused.

She read the little song and the steady movement of her mother's eyes as a statement of her mother's peace, and for some reason she thought of the first question of the catechism: "What is your only comfort in life and in death?" And its answer: "That I belong, in life and in death, to my faithful Savior, Jesus Christ."

"She hums that one a lot." Nancy Greiman's voice startled Emily. "It took me a long time to realize it because it wasn't at all familiar to me. It's not in our hymnbook; it's an old one."

"What is it?" Emily asked.

"You don't know it?" Nancy said. "I always thought it was some old favorite she used to sing all the time."

Emily tried to place it, but the notes weren't always clear. She tried to hum along, just to follow the tune, but she couldn't.

"It's called 'Some Day the Silver Cord Will Break.'"

"It doesn't ring a bell," Emily said.

"Once when the preacher was here, he told me he thought

that was what it was, so I looked all over until I found it. I've played it on my piano at home, and it's really quite pretty."

Her mother kept humming.

"Emily," Nancy said, "please don't take this wrong, but I've come to believe that she sings it when she wants to be alone."

Far from being offended, Emily thought it wonderful that Nancy had been able to read her mother's slight reactions that carefully. "You think so?" she said.

"Sometimes when I read to her—even when I read your letters—when I finish, she'll start humming. If you watch her eyes—I don't know, maybe it's only wishful thinking—but sometimes when I watch her eyes when she hums that song, they look more open—"

"They do?" Emily said.

"Really. Of course, when you spend time with her you look for the little things. You do it, too—I can see it. And I know that your coming here means a lot to her. It's not something you can put your finger on—I mean, it's not that she sleeps better or anything, but I just know it—"

"Maybe because you know her so well."

"Maybe," Nancy said. "Maybe it's just that I've come to think I do." She stood directly behind the rocker, her hands on the back, and began to hum along.

"How does it go?"

"I can't remember the words," Nancy said. "Like I said, the preacher recognized it, and when I finally got the music, he was right. I could show you the hymn—"

"Just hum it," Emily said.

When she did, the tune was more distinguishable.

"I know it," Emily said. "Of course, I know it. 'Some Day the Silver Cord Will Break.' I remember the tune."

"I'll copy it for you."

"I may have it," Emily said. "I took some of her old hymnbooks. I probably have it at home already. I'll check."

Nancy reached over the back of the chair and took Vivian Doorn's arms in her hands. "You know, I've worked here on the wing for almost twelve years—often with patients like your mother. It's always been interesting to me what these people say and sing—you know, what stays in their minds."

"Mostly it's hymns, I suppose," Emily said.

"Often it's hymns, but not all the time. Way back when I started, there was an old man here—Mr. Sytsma—he'd lived in California for years, even though he was born here. For a long time, whenever I'd come into his room, he'd look up at the window and he'd say, 'We don't need no more rain, Florence.' Can you believe it? That's what he'd say. I created the whole story of his life in my mind just from that one line—'We don't need no more rain, Florence.'"

"He lost a farm, I bet," Emily said.

"See how easy it is? That's exactly what I thought. He lost a farm and went to California. Nobody ever visited him here that I can remember, and I got to thinking that maybe he regretted having to move that one year when there were no crops because there was too much rain. I could spend half my life trying to figure out the stories of all these people," she said. "Like your mother—when the preacher said he knew the title, it was a joy to find the music, to put it together somehow. That song is the only thing she can say."

"She's not troubled, is she?" Emily said.

"You find that music sometime, and you read the words. It'll bless your heart."

Emily did not go directly home to look for the music, but what she had seen and heard that morning was in itself a blessing, since this was the first thing she had heard from her mother, aside from occasional deep breaths. It was only an old hymn whose sentiments she could likely guess, but the tune stuck with her into the afternoon, when she waited tables at the bowling alley, a job she'd picked up once she'd read the ad in the *Shopper.*

Unemployment is almost unheard of in Neukirk, because the

place is overrun with industry, which is not to say there are dozens of employers or hundreds of jobs waiting to be filled. People work hard here, and they often do it at less than a fair wage. Industriousness, like cleanliness, is right up there with godliness.

It is not uncommon for people from outside the region to talk about a "Midwestern work ethic," as if it is a way of life in the rural heartland. Actually, it is. Just exactly what that characterization implies about us is sometimes questionable, however. Some think it admirable, I'm sure; others think it quaint, as though the whole region were peopled by quasi-Hutterites. And if the truth be known, some here dislike the image, as if the heartland were a prairie anthill, with each of us mindlessly hell-bent for leather about our menial tasks.

The job Emily Doorn took was, quite frankly, at the bottom of the employment ladder. And her stumbling onto the bowling alley job was much less providential than she thought, since Tony's Bowling Alley runs a "Help Wanted" ad at least forty weeks of the year, the wages they offer being (even at Neukirk's minimum standards) barely worth the effort. Those who work there rely on tips, and men in farm caps with steaming cups of coffee in front of them know very little about gratuities.

But a pretty face will get you a long ways in Neukirk, as it will anywhere. Plumbers, construction workers, retired farmers, and roofers all respond warmly to beauty, especially when they're away from their wives. And they love the hot roast beef, mashed potatoes and gravy, plus vegetable—the good, square meal the bowling alley serves up on the daily special. And while Emily knew very well that the money she was taking home was nowhere near what she could have made in any ordinary California restaurant, she was pleased with what she made; and it was, even though she didn't know it, considerably more than most of the bowling alley's previous part-time help made. Besides, money wasn't a crucial matter for her, since the child support she received was generous and punctual.

Beauty is only skin-deep, of course, but Emily has wonderful skin. So she was well-loved in the bowling alley, a place just about as male in the middle of the day as the town council board room. What didn't hurt her either was her attitude, thrilled as she was to be back home. It should come as no surprise that someone with her stage presence and her love of performance should enjoy the bowling alley. She was a kind of showgirl actually, at least as close as one can come to being a showgirl in Neukirk.

And that's what angered—maybe miffed is a better word— Marty Kamphoff. It was a simple case of jealousy. Not that he would ever have admitted it to anyone, not even himself, lust being the kind of sin, as Jimmy Carter knows and Christ clearly claimed, that grows from the inside out. He didn't want to share her, even visually, with the men he came to resent in Tony's.

Neukirk is not a commune. There are social levels here, and anyone who's been here for a few years knows it. Marty Kamphoff, local businessman, always dines at Mr. P's, where the noon specials are gourmet hamburgers and beer, even Heineken. So when Marty heard that Emily was prancing around the formica tables at the bowling alley, his temperature rose considerably.

"Who got you that job?" he asked her when he brought over a pair of fresh muskmelons one night.

"I saw the ad," she told him.

They were standing in the kitchen, Marty having driven up, as was his habit, to the back of the house, where the place still had what Neukirk calls a "town barn."

"They don't pay anything, do they?" he said, laying the melons down on the table, holding them in place until they were still. "They got a horrible reputation."

"I'm not in it for the money," she said. "It's part-time—just at a time when I can leave the kids fairly easily—and I like it. I meet all kinds of people."

If Marty were more stupid than he is, he would have said, "Men," right then, but he knew he shouldn't. "I told you," he said, "I could have got you a good job."

"I like it, Marty," she said, putting her hand on the table. "I really do. There were times in LA when I thought that maybe what I'd like to do more than anything was own my own restaurant—I'm not kidding. Except I don't like to cook."

"It's just that there are better places," he said. "I mean, there are places people eat here that have more class."

"I didn't come here for class," she told him. She said it without a tinge of sarcasm, but Marty took it as a personal affront.

He looked down at the table, then pointed at the melons. "These are firstfruits," he said, laughing almost angrily at his own little biblical joke. "I think they're ready. It's always a problem with muskmelons. You got to smell them."

"I don't know what to say, Marty," she said. "I'm already so indebted to you for everything—and to think that it's all out of the kindness of your heart. I just don't know how to thank you."

He looked directly at her, as if to tell her what he couldn't even mention to himself.

"Don't worry about me," she told him. "I've been through a lot already, you know. I can take it."

He reached in his pocket for a peppermint, stuck it in his mouth, and rolled it around. "You're better than that," he said finally. "I think you're better than Tony's."

"Thank you," she said. "But right now I like it very much. It gets me out. The guys are real. It's safe. It's pleasant."

"Well, just don't listen to them," he told her. "You know how men are." And he turned around and reached for the door.

She had sensed it already the first day, when she didn't take him up on his offer to find her a job, but right then Emily Doorn knew for sure that she could beat him, that she was stronger than he was, that it was all a show of some type—something meant to win her, in his own way.

"I don't know how to say this politely, Marty," she told him, "but you strike me as being strong enough, maybe, to take it the right way—the way it's meant." She smiled. "I don't need a father anymore. I don't want to hurt you, and the Lord knows I'm thankful for all that you've done, but I've already been through a great deal in my life, and I've done it myself. I don't need a big brother."

Emily knew Marty Kamphoff well enough to understand him, but not well enough to gauge his weakness. He took what she told him as a slap in the face, because from the moment he saw her he had never envisioned himself as anything but her peer—certainly never as her father.

In Neukirk repression of what's real is as much a way of life as hard work. Marty Kamphoff had never even admitted to himself that he wanted her; no, let's just say it biblically, that he lusted after her. So he couldn't tell her the truth: that he didn't want to be her father. But neither could he tell her what he wanted to be. Nor did he recognize what it was that prompted him to take up her cause, since some forms of lust, it seems, are little more than thirst for power.

There was nothing to say. She'd read him all wrong, he thought. All he was doing was practicing compassion—faith, hope, and love, as the apostle says, and the greatest of these is love. What he was doing was washing her feet, as Christ himself would have done, trying to be God's hands in the world.

So when he walked out the door without replying, without saying a thing, Emily felt what she'd done was wrong. She'd wanted an end to his patronizing, but she wondered if she perhaps hadn't broken him in the process, and she wanted no part of having done that. That night she stared at the bathroom mirror and watched tears emerge slowly from her eyes, her first good cry in Iowa.

After supper the next day Norm Visser drove into her driveway and found her in shorts, a cut-off sweatshirt, a bandanna on her head, and gloves on her hands, toting junk.

Most Neukirk women would have primped the moment they saw a car come up the driveway, would have muttered that they weren't ready for guests, and would have begun to create an elaborate apology for their appearance. But Emily just put her hands on her hips and smiled as she watched him get out of the car.

She'd recognized Norm the moment she'd seen him on the front porch the day she'd returned, but there'd been no rush of bad memories. She never had held any malice toward him. She'd been very young when her sister was killed, and her parents had never harbored bad feelings toward him, or so it seemed, through those years that followed her sister's death, the years in which Emily had grown up in Neukirk. Norm Visser had always been "the man Meg was with that night," but Emily, her own emotions directed by her forgiving parents, had grown up seeing him as simply another victim of that night no one in her home ever wanted to remember.

"I could round up six guys in a quarter of an hour to get that work done," he said as he slapped the car door shut quietly.

"I haven't been this pampered since I don't know when," she told him. "Don't tell a soul I'm sweating."

"People crowding you?" he said, walking over to her. He was wearing a henley shirt and a pair of canvas shorts, black tennis shoes, no socks.

"I don't want to complain. It's all well-meant and everything, and in some ways it's what I would have expected. Comes with the territory." She pulled the gloves off her wrists.

"Don't stop," he said. "I'm not going to take up any time. I just thought I'd come by and put a bug in your ear."

"You mean you aren't bringing chocolate cake?"

"My dog won't eat my chocolate cake."

"Honestly," she said, "I can't cook as well as we've been eating. I'm serious. Once all this charity stops, I won't be able to live with my kids." She folded her gloves in her hand. "But I don't think I'll want lasagna again for thirty years."

Behind her stood three old aluminum doors leaned up sideways against the garage, four kitchen chairs in assorted vinyl covers, a chunk of wall cabinet, a flattened baby buggy, three homemade chests stained dull gray, and chunks of lumber—all of it dusty enough to show the prints where she'd carried it.

"Barn cleaning?" Norm said.

"I called the garbage people and they said to haul it all out in front and they'd pick it up—for a fee." She pointed behind her with her thumb. "I've only begun to fight. I may have to take out a loan to get it hauled out of here." She shook her head. "So tell me, why do people save this junk?"

"Because you never know when something might come in handy." He flipped a piece of plywood over with his foot and found an old painted-on target with little indentations where some kid had flung BBs from his first air rifle. "Emily, you're serious?" he said. "You're throwing this out?"

"You really want it?" she said.

"Put a mat around it, some decent molding, and you got art here," he said.

She didn't say anything, just rolled her eyes.

"I know a guy who did a self-portrait on a Xerox— scrunched his whole face, rolled it from side to side on the glass of a copier—then put it in a frame and showed it at an exhibition . . . I'm serious."

"You really want it?" she said.

He picked up the target and laughed. "How much are the scavengers asking to haul this away?"

"I told you I don't know."

"Listen, I'll take this piece off your hands for what—thirty bucks?"

"Twenty-five."

"You picked up bartering in Mexico, I bet," he said. "Twenty-eight bucks. Last bid."

"What? And you get the old target for free? I know what you're after here. You think I'm just another one of those helpless dames, and you're going to con me, aren't you?" she said. She pointed a finger at him. "Listen, buddy, you're not dealing with just another dumb blonde here."

"You passed," he said.

She laughed. "What'd I pass?"

"Screen test. That's what I'm up to. Had to see if you could still act. I need somebody for community theater. 'Uncle Norm wants you'—think of it that way."

"What's community theater?"

"Strange people who don't bowl."

"Geeks?" she said.

"You got it."

"What do you do?"

"Try to find material that'll play at about a third-grade level. That way we can call it family entertainment and capitalize on all the couples who want their children to be exposed to the arts."

"Dinner theater," she said.

"Make 'em weep and wail. They love it," he said.

"Lot of laughs?"

"A dozen pratfalls or we won't even consider a script."

"Let them have their money's worth."

"Keep them happy—every entertainer's nightmare."

She pulled the scarf off her hair and wiped her forehead with it. "You sound like you hate it," she said.

"Hate what?"

"It," she said, "this place."

"Listen, lady," Norm told her, pointing, "if you want to live here, you've got to learn to be less direct."

Emily winced.

"It'll be interesting to see how it goes here for you. I know people in this town who hate it so bad that they live on their own bile. People who despise Neukirk but can't really leave—"

"Why not?"

"Because hate's their daily bread, and without it they'd starve."

"You're overstating," she told him.

"Maybe I am," he said.

"And you?"

He shrugged his shoulders. "This is home, for better or for worse."

"People leave home all the time," she said.

"Not at my age."

Norm Visser is tall and thin and balding. In a few months he's going to be on the fifty side of forty-five, but he dresses as if he were thirty, buys all his clothes from Land's End catalogs. With his musical abilities and his talents in design—he designed and built his own house—he is, in some ways, the arts in Neukirk.

"I'm a teacher, and I'm a good one," he said. "But I've got twenty-some years' experience, a master's degree, and on most any school's pay scale I'd bring home the big bucks. You tell me who's going to hire me to teach sixth grade?"

"Get out of it," she said.

"Why?"

"You're trapped."

He looked away. "Hey, I came to invite you to—"

"Don't change the subject, Norm," she said. "Why don't you get out of it? There must be something else you can do?"

"I like it—and I like living here, Em." Not for a moment did he take his eyes from her.

"Really?" she asked.

"There's a part of me that hates it, but there ain't no heaven on this earth," he said, moving into another voice. "'God grant me the patience to know what to change and the strength to change it' . . . how does that prayer go? You can find it on about every other wall of this town, decoupaged or cross-stitched."

"'Serenity'? Doesn't it have the word serenity in it somewhere?"

"Bingo."

She looked at him closely. "Do you have time for tea?" she said.

"I'd love it."

She grabbed his arm. "Come on. I'm not letting you go." She pulled him along up to the house. "I'm great on tea. It's the only thing I've made for the last ten days."

"Aggressive women don't do well in Neukirk," he said. "The men love it, but the women'll hang you in no time. Demure's the word. Repeat after me: demure."

"We're all actors, Norman," she said. "You know that much."

Despite her LA sophistication, at that moment Emily Doorn acted with incredible naivete. Walking arm in arm up to her own back door with a single man was something she should not have done. Maybe late at night it would have been all right, but then the darkness would have created different suspicions.

Norm Visser knew the peril, but for two reasons he didn't remove Emily's hand from his arm. First, he was too kind. To pull it away would have meant rejecting a gesture that was pure and loving. Second, he liked it. Besides, estrangement, alienation, has its benefits, and one of them, undoubtedly, is the strength that accrues to those, like Norm, who see themselves as individuals, especially in a place like Neukirk.

The house next to Emily's has no garage, few shrubs bordering the sidewalk on the south side, and no town barn. So the people who were just then leaving the mid-week prayer meeting at Grace Church, if they looked across the street toward Emily's house (as many of them did), saw Norm Visser and Emily Doorn, arm in arm, going up to her back door in semi-darkness.

Now puritanism is, in part, that kind of sneaking suspicion that someone, somewhere is having a good time, as H. L. Mencken once said; but it's fair to say that not all of the Neukirk puritans who saw Norm and Emily together immediately heard the sinful shriek of bedsprings. If the truth be known, the passersby who saw and immediately thought the worst were overwhelmingly male. I'll let you guess why. Most of the women did not react critically because the man on her arm was, after all, Norm Visser, about whom there was some question.

What made them such a spectacle was more than these two just being man and woman. The death of Emily's sister had become front-page news in town again, and those who didn't remember soon heard about it. After all, the couple looking so much at ease in the semi-circle of cement around the Van Voorst barn had a long history.

Now you might wonder exactly what Emily knew at that moment about the man who drove the car in which her only sister died. She was six when it happened, so she remembers Margaret, of course. And she remembers the way Norm Visser, then a college freshman, stood at their front door and wept when he came in. She remembers the way her parents took him in their arms and led him to the captain's chair at the dining room table, the table they used only on special occasions. She remembers the way she cried. As she's thought about it through the years, she's come to believe that even then, at that moment, the tears on her cheeks were as much a result of her parents' grief as the loss of her sister—something she didn't fully understand. She's thought—and she's had therapists tell her—that perhaps the greatest grief for her at that time, not understanding death itself, was the realization of her parents' strength having vanished and her own sense of desolation as her mother spent long afternoons in the bedroom, crying. All of that she remembers well.

Emily Doorn has no family, really, in Neukirk, her father buried, her mother still alive but unable to speak. So she took Norm's arm that night because a moment of conversation in her backyard made her feel that if anyone knew her in this town, this man did, this man whose voice had broken as he tried so hard to apologize to her family.

And she knows more. By the time Norm Visser returned to Neukirk, Emily was in her late teens, a time when the legend of Norm's failed marriage was just the kind of thing to make the rounds in high school. She remembers hearing it, in fact; remembers wondering about that same Norm Visser, a man who couldn't do it—as kids said—and about how or why that could happen.

She felt immediately what most Neukirk women feel in Norm's presence—trust. When she took his arm, then, it wasn't only because he was the man who had played such an awful part in her family's tragedy, or because she thought he, of all Neukirk people, male or female, would understand her. She took his arm because she could trust him.

Barely two weeks had passed since she'd moved in to the Van Voorst house, so boxes still stood on the counter, some of them opened, some empty. There was a certain pattern to her kitchen counter, however—the dirty dishes in one spot, the pans, washed and cleaned, across from the sink. The place, obviously, had been used.

Norm stood beside the kitchen table, something imported she'd bought on special at a fashionable store in Laguna Beach—a glass table with a white, thick plastic border and matching chairs.

"No one ever just 'comes over' in California," she told him. "I have so much food—can I get you something?"

Both his hands were on the chair in front of him. "You know, I'll have to call this in to the News," he said. "'Local Man Visits Former Celebrity.'"

"Quit it," she said.

"If I were to go to the bowling alley tomorrow—"

"Be careful," she told him. "I work there."

"You do?"

"Didn't you know that? I thought everybody knew it."

"You work at the bowling alley, Emily? My goodness."

"You sound just like Marty Kamphoff," she told him. She turned around and reached for tea bags and the teapot, a monstrosity sculpted into the shape of a pig.

"You work at Tony's?" he said again.

"Cut it out," she said. "You know what's worse? I like it."

"You get pinched?"

"It's none of your business."

"What I was going to say—before you brought up your slumming—is that if people at the bowling alley knew I was at your place for coffee, they'd have thousands of questions about what's inside here."

"Men?"

"You work at Tony's—you know."

"What do they care?" she said. She ran tap water into the tea-kettle. "Don't tell me they'd care about my remodeling—"

"They care about you," he told her. He pulled out the chair slowly, then sat, swung one leg over the other.

She shut the faucet, stood there with her back to him, and set the kettle on the divider between the sinks. "I know this sounds silly," she said, "but I really find that very sweet." She turned around to look at him.

Norm raised his eyebrows.

"Am I naive?"

"Terminally," he said.

"I don't care. I'll be naive then. But I really do—I like it. And no," she said, "I don't get pinched. I really do get the feeling I'm appreciated—for who I am."

"And for how you look," he told her.

"No," she said, scoldingly.

He shrugged his shoulders.

She searched for the right dial on her new stove. "I keep expecting I'm going to be hurt by all this somehow, that something's going to happen to break this little honeymoon I'm spending back here, but it hasn't happened. Talking to Mom has been wonderful," she told him, finally turning the right dial. She waited for the flame to ignite. "I need it, all right?" She put down the teakettle. "Is that selfish?"

Norm laughed. "Sinful," he said.

"I'm not naive," she told him. "I mean, I know everything's going wonderfully because I've just arrived. Something will happen to break it. But right now," she crossed her arms over her chest, "it feels just great."

"I'm happy for you," he said.

"No you're not," she told him. "You think I'm crazy."

"That's not true," he said. "Listen, if you want to have a wonderful, month-long beauty bath, you deserve it. You've probably been through a lot."

"I have," she said.

"I don't doubt it."

She pulled herself away from the edge of the counter and sat down across from him.

He reached for the salt shaker, a tiny mountain chalet. "The bowling alley, huh?"

"I like it," she said.

He shook his head. "I heard Tony was having trouble making it go. You're good for him, I'm sure."

She turned her face slightly. "Don't say it that way," she said.

He nodded. "I'm sorry," he told her.

It wasn't long and the teakettle began to tremble.

"Really, Norm, how long do you think I'll be able to live here?"

He looked directly at her. "What is this? The only reason you came back is to loll around in all the compassion?"

She pulled her arms back from the table top, sat back in the chair. "It's not why I came here, but—I have to laugh about it so often—it's amazing. Like all the stuff I get. Look at that teapot. It's a gift. Do these people know how rich I am?"

"I think they do."

"Why do they keep giving me things? I have so many desserts in my refrigerator, I could have the whole town over and still have more calories than I need."

Norm tipped the shaker and salt accidentally fell on the table. "Tell me," she said.

With the side of his hand he scraped what he'd spilled into his other hand, off the side of the table, then walked behind her to drop it in the sink. "I don't know what you're asking, but I think the real question is something else. Something like, what makes these people act the way they do?"

"And?"

"And I'm surprised that you don't know—"

"Why?"

He clapped his hands twice, quickly, like a magician. "Because I had you pegged for someone with brains."

She looked around, swept her hair behind her ear. "California girl, blonde ditz. Nothing up here but perfect cheekbones."

"You're right about that."

"So it's wrong for a woman to trade on her looks?"

"It's wrong for anybody as beautiful as you are to work in the bowling alley—"

"Why?"

"Delusions of grandeur. I can just imagine you waiting on a table of muttonheads, bringing them their ketchup for fries. They got you waiting on them?—they're in hog heaven."

"Is that so bad?"

"Their wives'll strangle you."

"It'll just be for a while," she said. "I know that."

"And then what?"

"If you knew the hours I spent auditioning, the hours I spent preparing for auditioning—shoot, the hours I spent waiting in line for jobs, worrying about jobs, even praying about jobs—"

"You prayed?" he said, coming back to his chair.

"Sometimes. Sometimes not. Most of the time not." She stood and poured the hot water into the teapot. "I'm happy just waiting on tables."

He gave her a big, cartoon-cat grin. "You love that," he said, "and just think of the adulation you'll get on the stage here. People won't even care how you act. They'll love the opportunity simply to stare at you."

"I'd think you'd be overrun with actresses, Norm," she told him. She took two cups out of the cupboard, two cups matching the pot.

"We don't need women, Em, we need you."

"Why?"

He looked at her slyly. "You're a marquee," he said. "You're walking publicity. People don't even dare to look at you—that's how intimidating you are. Shoot, all their largesse, honey—that's just oblation. You're a goddess."

"Come on," she said.

"Truthfully?"

"I've had enough of the other in the last week—"

"Truthfully, you'd pack the house. I could pick some inane

sit-com family drama, and I'd still have all of Neukirk wanting tickets."

"Really?"

"No," he said. "The truth is, I want you for myself."

She laughed, poured the tea, and set the cups, on saucers, on the table. "So tell me, Norm, how is it that you stayed here?"

"We were talking about your being in a play—"

"Okay, okay, I'll talk to my kids about it. But now tell me, really, what's in Neukirk for you?"

He held up one hand in front of him and started counting off. "I get to run community theater. I get to teach sixth grade. I get to sing a lot. I get to visit my mother. I sometimes visit my brother in Denver—"

"You know what I'm talking about," she told him.

"Why shouldn't I live here?" he said.

"What do you mean?"

"Why shouldn't I live here? This is my home."

"Don't be defensive," she said.

"I'm not. I'm just telling you the truth. Why should I not live here, you tell me that."

"Norm," she said, "you're single."

"So in California do they round up singles and put them on a reservation?"

"Don't get angry," she said. "Now drink your tea."

He smiled at her, and she knew, in an instant, that he resented something.

He put his hand over the cup and held it there for a moment, then took it away and rubbed the moisture between his palms. "What you're really asking is why I'm single, aren't you?" he said.

"No."

"Yes, you are too—I know you are. What I wish I knew is why you want to know." He took the cup in his hand, then looked at it closely. "This is the ugliest cup I've ever seen."

"I told you, it was a gift."

He took a sip.

"Peppermint," she said.

"I have a nose."

"Pardon me."

"You know what galls me? When people who grew up in Neukirk go away for a while, they come back and think that nothing has changed—that the only kind of tea in town is Lipton Flo-thrus—"

"There's more?" she said, jokingly.

"Emily," he said stiffly, "you give me fifteen minutes—five probably—and I'll find you some grunge-boy still in the throes of suicidal mourning for Kurt Cobain—"

She sat back quickly. "I don't believe it."

"Oh, ye of little faith. Know ye not that sin resideth here too, yea even in Neukirk?"

"I won't believe it—"

"Then prepare to be overwhelmed, Anne of Green Gables, because you're about to get a short course in that bowling alley of yours."

"Come on," she teased.

"Yea, we have here all varieties of sins. Be ye not deceived. We just cover our tracks but good."

She put her hand up to cover a smile. "Norm," she said, "I can't tell you how good it is to talk to you. It seems as if I don't talk to people anymore, I get talked to—as if I were some thing—"

He looked into her eyes, then scowled. "It's no easy thing, having to be the prophetic voice here, my dear," he told her, winking. "You think I enjoy this?" He turned his head. "And thus saith the moral arbiter, 'What kind of mother are you anyway? One of dem single mutters, huh? Don't know how to take care of dem kids. Dey could use some ditzipline is whad I t'ink.'" He dropped the face and voice. "So how are they doing?"

"Really good. I don't think they even imagined a place like this existed. The only time I worry is when they've been gone all day and I don't even know where—and then my only worry is that I shouldn't just let them run."

"You can say what you want," Norm said, "but a place like this is really a great place to bring up kids." He took her hand. "I want you to know, Emily—ach, maybe this is stupid of me to say. I mean, I don't even have any idea—"

"Say it, please. I treasure your honesty. I really do."

"What I want you to know is that the night your sister died has been with me for all of my years. I'll never forget it," he said. "Sounds stupid to even assume that I might, I suppose, but I want you to know that. I'll be forever sorry about it, about what happened, and there's really nothing you can do to change it—the way I'll feel it there forever." He reached with his other hand so that he had both of hers in his. "But I want you to understand, Emily, that I didn't come here because of guilt—really, it's not that."

She pulled her hands out of his, then surrounded his with hers and squeezed them, just once, before sliding them away and picking up her cup.

"I'm not here to score points, you know," he said. "I mean, like so many others, bringing desserts because it's the Christian thing to do." He looked down at his hands, then back at her. "You understand what I'm saying? I've got guilt up to the earlobes—you don't know the half of it. But I'm not using you—"

"Using me?" she said.

"I'm not using you to dump it. I'm not here because you're Meg's sister," he said.

"You feel like a brother, Norm," she told him.

"That's good," he said. "I don't want you to think that I've got reasons other than you to be here—you understand that? But I appreciate that—when you tell me I'm like a brother." He leaned back, stretched his arms, then brought his hands back down to the edge of the table. "It's mixed up. I know it is. It's all mixed up, even after all these years, because the fact is, I probably wouldn't be here right now if you weren't her sister." He shook his head. "Am I making any sense?"

"No," she said, smiling. "But I don't want to understand everything with only one cup of tea."

She meant it. Even when she'd enjoyed joking with the guys at Tony's or listened to the hundredth offer to help over the phone, she'd missed someone who talked to her for what she was, not what she looked like or what she'd been through or what she could be.

"Look, baby," he said, taking the voice of a movie mogul, "I know talent, an' you got it, and we need it. I can make you a star, toots."

"Will you be heartbroken if I say no?"

"My feelings have nothing to do with this," he told her. "What will be irreparably harmed is our production."

"You'll do just fine without me," she said.

"I'm after the bowling alley crowd," he said, "and only you can bring them in, toots. Think of it—more seed caps in that theater than there's been since the grade school musical. Theater finally makes it in Neukirk."

She shoved herself away from the table, threw her shoulders back, raised her chin. "You think so?" she said.

"Know so."

"I told you—I'll ask my kids."

"So who are they, the Supreme Court?"

"It'll mean a baby-sitter," she told him. "I'm already gone a couple hours every day."

"Tell you what," he said. "I know every kid in town. I'll line you up with sitters so perfect you'd swear they're wearing halos."

"Jason Kamphoff baby-sits," she said.

He pulled a face.

"You know him?"

He nodded. "I know every kid in town—remember, I'm a teacher. But I can get you quality."

"It's a disease, you know," she told him. "You get on stage and it can ruin you for life. Look at me, for example—"

"It leads to all kinds of unsavory employment."

"Like the bowling alley."

"Precisely," he said.

Her eyes moved to the corner of the kitchen behind him and followed the line to the ceiling where they suddenly seemed to lose focus, her eyebrows falling just a bit.

"Norm," she said, "do you think I'll be able to stay here?"

"In Neukirk?"

"Yes."

He leaned back, pulled a knee up and crossed his legs. "If I were a gambling man," he said, then paused. "The truth? Cross my heart and hope to die?"

She nodded.

"No."

She stood quickly, stepped back, and straightened some papers on the bar behind her.

"It won't be your fault," he said. "But I'm not sure there's room for you here. I'm just not sure."

"Room for me?"

"Looks, for one thing. Money. Lack of family. You got a log of years in California."

"That counts?"

"I've been to Europe a half dozen times," he said. "You probably know that the Dutch over there are famous for tolerance, for accepting people, different views." He lifted both hands, palms up. "Not these Dutch."

"Why not?"

"It's a tribe, Emily—a big family. There's not a lot of room for differences."

"Should I be worried?"

"Look," he said, "I've been wrong about things tons of times. I may be way off here. Maybe you'll just keep swimming in the bath of all this adulation. Maybe it'll all be just fine. Maybe you'll be just one of the folks here—get yourself porked up a little, get that hair cropped, and learn to make a tuna hot dish—"

"And what about you?" she said.

He shook his head. "Sometimes I'm not so sure about me."

"Then why do you stay?"

He rapped his fingers on the table as if he were typing out a sentence. "Gimme a week or so to answer that one, Miss Emily. I'm not sure I can say right now. I'm going to have to study up."

"I'm going to ask you again," she said.

"Then I'm not coming back," he told her.

"Oh yes, you will," she said, winking.

"Aaahhhooo," he moaned. "Arrogant! I've never seen such arrogance."

"Please," she said.

With his index finger he snapped her lightly on the hand.

Once Norm was gone, Emily felt his absence. It had been something of a tease to have him there, one quick swill of cold water on a dusty afternoon. Her loneliness hurt a bit, hurt again, because once more the big friendly house seemed vacant. She thought of Benjamin sitting in the easy chair in the living room, but it was dark in there, the only light a soft blue flicker from the television screen in the family room beyond, where the kids sat, lights out, the way they liked to watch TV.

It was late at night, close to ten, for kids as young as Emily's to be up watching some video she had checked out for them that afternoon, but it was July, when the late afternoon sun seems to take all day to clear the wide horizon west, and even when it's gone the sky glows with such remarkable brilliance that the whole region stays lit for what seems hours. During those long summer nights it's hard for anyone to get kids to bed.

Sometimes she thought that if she were really industrious, those evening hours wouldn't seem so lonely. She thought of herself as lazy. Neukirk women wouldn't let boxes stand around forever the way she did. She could work late and not feel herself alone if she'd only stay with the job of moving in. It had been ten days now, maybe more, and she even felt a little guilty when some well-meaning neighbor brought over a salad; she didn't want them seeing what she hadn't finished.

Emily recognized this for what it was: the kind of guilt she would feel only here, not having done what should have been accomplished long ago, at least according to the laws and the prophets of Neukirk. But she was tired. She'd worked four hours in the bowling alley and spent much of the day in Rebecca's room, arranging the drawers in her bedroom, hanging clothes in the walk-in closet that someday her daughter would love—how many homes in California had huge, walk-in closets?—and re-arranging furniture a half-dozen times because she wanted to get it just right.

Just off the dining room, in a little nook the Van Voorsts must have created out of what once was a spacious front hall, stood the piano, an upright so old the prior owners, with her consent, had simply left it behind. Once she noticed it there, Emily remembered her curiosity about the tune her mother had been humming.

She snapped on the light, opened the bench, and picked out an old maroon hymnal, her mother's, the same one that used to stand on the piano when she was a child. She let down the bench quietly, then sat, facing the keys, the hymnal in her hand.

She should start the kids at piano lessons, she thought. That idea had never entered her mind in LA. Here, it was in the air. It must be written somewhere: every Neukirk kid should take at least some piano. It was remarkable how things like this came back to her—like instincts buried somewhere away from the warm and dingy air of Southern Cal.

She paged to the Index of First Lines and looked for "Someday the Silver Cord Will Break," but didn't find it. She was about to put the hymnal on the rack when, for no good reason really, she opened to the first page, the blank page before the title page of the book, and found a short list written there, in a hand she recognized as her mother's plain but careful style: "Ben's favorite, 'Beautiful Savior,' Mom's favorite, 'Out of the Ivory Palaces,'" and then "Margaret's favorite, 'Some Day the Silver Cord Will Break.'"

She read through each entry again. The first two were in blue ink and the third, her sister's, in black. "Margaret's favorite, 'Some Day the Silver Cord Will Break,'" with "1962" written above the first word.

And, of course, she wondered why her own favorite wasn't there, why it wasn't added sometime, just as Margaret's was, why the listing ended the way it did, as if her favorite wasn't important, wasn't worth remembering.

What would her favorite have been anyway? If her mother had come to her some night and asked, "Emily, I'm listing favorite hymns in the old book, and I wonder what I should put down for you. Tell me—what's your favorite hymn?" What would she have said? "Oh, for a Thousand Tongues to Sing"? "Blessed Assurance"? "When Peace Like a River"? "My Jesus, I Love Thee"?

There was a pencil on the rack beside a little drawing Rebecca had made one day since they'd come to Neukirk. Emily took it in her hand, dropped the hymnal to her lap, and stretched the binding a little to give herself room to write.

What she wants, she understands, is to be listed, to be a part of this family record, to finish what her mother began, even though it strikes her as silly, even childish, that she should feel compelled to scribble something in.

"Emily's favorite," she writes anyway, trying to copy her mother's hand. The pencil looks out of place, but then so does Margaret's black ink. Besides, if someone were to read this someday, they'd simply think hers had been added at a later date, just as her sister's was.

When? she wondered. Maybe after Margaret died. Did Mom scratch in something that she remembered of her daughter—her daughter who was gone? Was that why her own name was missing? Because her mother needed some kind of tribute to Margaret?

She remembered the way Norm, so much younger, had stood at the door, crying. She remembered neighbors all over the house. She remembered the way her mother wouldn't come out of the bedroom for hours. She remembered the grim face her father wore and the way he'd cried—only once, only that first day, when the three of them had been in the sanctuary of the bedroom together, the rest of the house full of people. She remembered the way he'd held her and cried, and the way he'd stopped, with a prayer, with a long prayer, an out-loud prayer. She remembered opening her eyes and seeing that prayer come from his lips, his face raised, the only prayer she remembered her father ever praying with his eyes wide open, staring up at the ceiling—and all of it so loud, as if God on high were hard of hearing. She remembered her embarrassment, knowing the people were just outside in the front room.

She remembered the strange feeling of emptiness, not unlike the way she felt now, along with an almost touchable expectation, a sense that Margaret might suddenly walk out of her bedroom or the bathroom or come in from outdoors just as she always had.

That emptiness became a member of the family. Even though Margaret was gone, the space she'd left seemed drawn in by a cartoonist; it sat there physically at the table when they ate, it kept a place in the silence upstairs before anyone fell asleep. She was so young—it took them years to realize that Meg wasn't coming back. Every time they caught themselves forgetting her death and expecting her there at the supper table or in the back seat of the car on the way to church, wherever she should have been, they wept again, at least internally. Emily had sat alone in the back seat until one Sunday morning—she remembered now, for the first time—her parents had her get in front with them. After that, she always sat between them in the front seat.

She'd been so young, too. Other than those memories, what did she really know about Margaret's death? She knew Norm Visser had driven the car; she would never forget the way that boy, that handsome boy, had stood there in the hallway crying, unable to speak. She also knew where it happened: three miles south, two west, at an otherwise indistinguishable corner where two gravel roads came together at perfect right angles, cornfields on both sides, what her mother called "corn corners." Margaret had been killed by the blindness created by tall corn running right up to the edge of the gravel and leaning over the sight lines down the road. After that she couldn't drive down a country road without thinking of the way her sister had been killed: a corn corner, two cars completely oblivious to each other, dusk, no lights on, coming in at right angles.

But what did she really know of her sister? She remembered it was 1968, and Margaret had just graduated from high school. She was going to the university, to Iowa City.

My word, she thought, the wealth of memories that were there, left in her mind like a drawer full of photographs: Margaret leaning up to the mirror in the bathroom and putting on make-up; Margaret tightening her lips to smooth her lipstick; Margaret in her jeans, leaning over the kitchen sink, her long straight hair falling back over her shoulders. Margaret with her head in her hands in front of the television. Margaret sleeping with her during a thunderstorm. Margaret at the piano. Margaret's room full of stuffed animals.

Images. Still pictures. But there was little else. No long conversations, no words at all really, other than music, at the piano.

She was too young, she thought. Only six. And so much of Margaret simply wasn't there. She remembered the way adults had talked over her, above her, when Meg died—talked to her father and her mother as if she weren't even there.

She looked again at her mother's list of hymns, at the handwriting she'd put down beneath it—"Emily's favorite." Then she erased it, took the book with her, and went back into the kitchen for a pen. A pencil wasn't adequate.

She sat down at the table where she'd just been sitting with Norm and, imitating her mother's hand as perfectly as she could, wrote "Emily's favorite" in slender characters. And once it was in, she waited again to put in a title because she didn't know what would have been her favorite. There were so many. "Onward Christian Soldiers" for years, she thought, but it wouldn't be appropriate. It wouldn't be something she wanted someone to read—not all that war, not for a little girl.

"Amazing Grace," she thought. No, they hadn't sung that much when she was a child. It was a favorite today, but back then, in the church of her childhood, it had been too Baptist. She needed a hymn that would say something about her, like her father's solemnity in "Beautiful Savior" and her mother's emotion in "Out of the Ivory Palaces."

She paged to the index again and looked up the first line of her mother's favorite, but, like her sister's, it wasn't there. She knew it though, just as she knew Margaret's "Silver Cord." Out of the well of hymns and songs in her memory she could still draw both of them, in bits and pieces at least.

Strange, she thought. All those separate snapshots in her mind didn't include any of those last days, none really. Meg leaving the house, Meg, so pretty, so grown-up, Meg sitting at the table eating supper in silence. In silence.

In silence she thought. Margaret at the table in their home, eating supper around the table, no one speaking. Why? What she remembered came back to her as a silent movie. There was no memory of Meg singing "Some Day the Silver Cord Will Break." Why had her mother chosen it? And why now did her mother's strangely muddled mind keep bringing it to the surface?

"I've come to believe that she sings it when she wants to be alone," Nancy had said.

What brought her nearly to tears as she sat there in the Van Voorst home, what made her mind jump like some wound-up toy out of control, was a thought that had never once occurred to her before: the simple sense that she really hadn't known her parents—or at least her parents' suffering. That she really hadn't known what effect the loss of her sister had had on them.

She had been too young at the time of the accident to know whether, or how, it had changed them from the people they had been before. What did my sister's accidental death do to them? she wondered now. What in them did it kill? One thing she did know: her parents had chosen, for whatever reasons, not to speak of Meg's death. Within a few weeks they'd cleaned out her room, she remembered; and then the death, just like Meg's body, was buried.

Emily found Margaret's song in a box of old hymnals and other songbooks. She thought she remembered such a box in the stuff she'd inherited from her mother, and she rummaged around till she found it. "Fanny Crosby, 1893," it said beneath the title when she found it in another book. "George Stebbins"—same year, on the other side. Four verses. She scanned them quickly.

"You find that music sometime, and you read the words," Nancy had said. "It'll bless your heart."

> *Some day my earthly house will fall,*
> *I cannot tell how soon 'twill be;*
> *But this I know: my Lord, my All,*
> *Has now a place in heaven for me.*

Meg's favorite song, she thought. Supposedly these were Meg's favorite words. She looked back at the hymnal and noticed "1962" penciled in above the title, as if something had happened that year, something that made recording the date important.

She was eighteen when she died in 1968, Emily thought. So, six years earlier—that would have made her twelve years old in 1962.

She called Norm Visser.

"I'm sorry to bother you, but I just stumbled on something here. I thought you might be able to help me. Did you ever hear Meg sing a hymn titled 'Some Day the Silver Cord Will Break'? Do you know it?"

There was no immediate answer. She wondered whether she'd pulled him out of bed. She looked down at her watch.

"Yes," he said.

"Yes—what? Yes, I know it, or yes, I've heard it?'"

"Yes, I've heard it."

"Did you ever hear her sing it?"

There was another silence. Then, "You okay?" he said.

"Of course, I'm all right. I just found some stuff here and I'm trying to figure something out. Did you ever hear Meg sing it?"

"Emily," he said, then waited again. "Emily, we were eighteen years old and it was 1968. We didn't do much hymn singing."

"How about 1962?" she said. "You know anything about that year—I mean in Meg's life?"

"Let's see." He paused. "She would have been in sixth grade."

"Did she change?"

"From what?"

"From the time she was in sixth grade until the time she died, did she change?"

She heard him breathe deeply.

"Meg happened to go through adolescence—it's a rare disease," he told her. "Maybe you haven't heard of it." When she didn't respond, he added, "What did you find?"

"An old hymnal of my mother's, and in the front she wrote that Meg's favorite hymn was 'Some Day the Silver Cord Will Break.'"

"So what's 1962?" he asked.

"It's scratched in above the title."

Her mind was already wandering the streets of Neukirk, trying to locate someone in whom she could confide, someone who knew more about her sister than Norm Visser.

"It's a perfectly normal thing to do, I suppose. Your mother probably wrote down her daughter's favorite hymn so she could remember it. I don't understand—"

"Mine's not here," she said.

"Your what?"

"My favorite hymn," she said.

"So you feel excluded, is that it? So you figure that now you understand everything there is to know about a score of neuroses you've suffered for lo, these many years."

"Why are you angry?" she asked.

"I'm sorry," he told her.

"I don't understand anything," she said. "I'm trying to figure some things out."

"What?" he said.

"Why my mother would write down a hymn I barely knew, a hymn about finding heaven at last, a hymn I don't remember my own sister singing ever—and why I'm not on this list at all."

"Did you check some other hymnals? If I know your mother, she had plenty of others. Maybe there's another with a whole list." He paused for a moment, and she heard him swing around slightly. "For heaven's sake, Emily, your parents loved you—is that what you're after?"

She waited. She didn't know how to respond because the questions weren't even in her mind yet.

"Are you there?" he said. "Listen, I haven't had a cup of tea in at least a half hour. You want company?"

"Norm, how did my sister's death affect my mom and dad?" she asked.

When he didn't reply, she repeated his name.

"I'm here," he said.

"Did you hear what I asked?"

"I'm coming over," he told her. "Wait up."

While she waited, she did exactly what he'd recommended. She searched every last book in the box from her mother but found no other listing. And in the minutes that passed before Norm arrived, she kept reaching for the darkness, kept working at visualizing the outlines of something that seemed so indistinct as to not have been there at all. She kept the hymnal in her hands, kept looking at the handwriting as if something definable might still be there.

And why was this hymn the only one that ever came to her mother's mind now? Why not her father's favorite, "Beautiful Savior," or her mother's own "Ivory Palaces"? Why only Margaret's hymn?

The answer seemed obvious: Because her mother's mind, robbed by the stroke of so much of its functioning, had the ability to cling to only one hymn, one memory, one event that defined her life, Emily thought—the death of her daughter. It made perfect sense. Nothing in her life was ever so horrifying as that night.

My word, Emily thought, it's all that's there in her mind now, even when I visit. That's all that goes on in her head—my sister's death.

Suddenly she listened for the sound of the VCR in the family room, heard it, thought quickly how the two kids would be lying there on the floor, fast asleep by now, the darkness surrounding them. They'd stay asleep. Norm would come over and they'd sleep right through. She tried very hard to think, even though the pain she felt for her mother, for her mother's dilemma, nearly overwhelmed her. What did she need to know? What was it she wanted to know from Norm?

He came in without knocking. He was dressed in a running suit, sweat forming on his temples and sharpening the clumped tips of hair at the back of his head.

"You caught me just out of the shower," he said.

He stood at the doorway to the kitchen, his hands propped against the door jamb. "Where do you want to talk?" he asked.

She pointed to an old oak rocker beside the rolltop desk, then walked around the dining room table to a padded chair not far away.

"I wish I could come up with questions that make sense, but I don't even know what I want to know," she told him. "I just have this odd feeling that I've stumbled into something I need to understand, even though I don't know what it is or why I should." She brought her hand up to her face. "I'm sorry. I think I'm almost incoherent—" She tried to laugh. "Maybe I'm silly—"

"You're not silly," he said. "You were a kid." He paused, tightened his lips. "I'll never forget the way you looked that night I came to talk to your parents. I don't know what it was you were feeling because it seemed to me you were so young that you didn't understand." He took a long breath. "What I remember is that you sat alone, on the couch, while I explained to your parents."

"Just keep talking," Emily said. "Tell me everything."

"I remember feeling strange about you being there. I had this odd sense that you shouldn't be hearing all of it—that you were too young."

"What did I hear?"

"I suppose mostly crying."

"What did you explain?"

"The way she'd died."

"You mean the accident?"

"That's right."

"It wasn't your fault—"

"The guys in the other car were drinking—" He looked away. "They got a ticket. If they'd really smacked us broadside, there would have been a half dozen fatalities, Emily. We'd have all been dead."

She closed her eyes. "Some of that I remember."

"I wish I remembered only some," he told her, looking down at his hands, which had tightened on the arms of the chair.

She stood up and walked toward the family room. "I want to check the kids," she said, but she really wanted time, time to let some things soak. There they were, just as she had imagined, the television blaring away, the two of them sprawled on the floor, Rebecca half wrapped in a blanket from the sofa, Sam, as usual, uncovered. She let the television play but closed the door.

"What I want to know, Norm," she said, "is what I asked you before—did something happen to my parents when Meg died?"

"Of course something happened to them—"

"But I mean, did they become something they weren't before?"

She walked past the chair where she'd been sitting and pulled out a chair from the table, sat beside him.

"A year after it happened I came back to your house. Maybe you were in bed, I don't remember. You still were only a little toot. I came back and I told them again I was sorry." He tightened his lips, then raised his hands toward his face. "You had remarkably loving parents, Emily—"

"What happened?"

"I suppose it's kind of a cliché, isn't it, but they said there were blessings in Meg's death, too, real blessings for them. They'd learned to take one day at a time and all of that—you've heard that before. They'd learned to be parents—"

"They weren't before?"

"I don't think Meg hated them."

It was an almost stunning thing to say. "Should she have?"

"No," he said.

"Norm," she said, "this is all new. I want you to understand. I don't know a thing. I was a kid and so much of it is gone. I was just thinking to myself a moment ago that I don't even remember what Meg was like when she was . . . before she died. I have all these memories like little snapshots in my mind, but they're all silent. Like a still life. They're good memories, all of them—on a beach during vacation, Meg reading to me—good memories."

From the look on his face she could tell he was uncomfortable.

"Anything you can tell me, Norm—anything," she said. "Did you love her?"

He looked straight out in front of him, toward nothing at all, laughed. "Do you know what love is?" he said. "Really, Em—do you know?"

"Were you thinking about marriage?"

He waited for what seemed several minutes, then swung his eyes to her. "No," he said, with an odd kind of strength. "It was 1968, and I have no doubt in the world that had Meg ever made it to Iowa City, we might have lived together. But marriage, no."

"My parents—"

"Would have died," he said. "I knew that—so did Meg. Didn't matter. We were young."

"Did they know?"

He stuck his hands in the pouch of his sweatshirt. "I've been teaching for so many years I can't really keep track of the numbers anymore," he told her. "What I've learned in all that time— not only from teaching, I guess, but from myself too—is that we have, all of us, this capacity to deny things when it's in our best interest." He looked at her. "I don't know what they knew. But we were political back then—I was a year older than she was— you may not even remember that. I was already at the university, and I had friends who were political—radical, we used to say. Sometimes I think it was simply a means by which to have fun— talk politics a while, share some dope, and party." He shrugged his shoulders. "I'm sorry."

"What did they know?"

"I don't know what they knew," he said, "but I know that they feared what they felt happening in her—and they knew something was happening, even if they didn't know what." He turned away from her. "She tried not to hurt them. I couldn't believe it myself because most of us looked for confrontation. That's the way it was with my parents—we used to have big fights, Em. But not Meg."

"What are you saying?"

"You can't believe how hard it was for me to go over there that night and apologize. I mean, I knew it was their daughter's death, and that's the only reason I could do it—because no matter how much I hated to be there, I knew that my own discomfort at that moment meant nothing." His hands, clasped, were out in front of him now. "I didn't want to be there, Emily. I told you— I remember you sitting there alone on the couch. I remember thinking that you shouldn't even have to hear all of our bawling. But Meg was dead, and I felt—even the guilt I felt—didn't mean anything." He pulled himself up straighter in the chair. "It changed me too, Em. It changed them, and it changed me. You don't kill somebody without it changing you."

"You didn't kill her," she said.

"I wish my mind worked as cleanly as the law," he said.

"But they got a ticket."

"She flew out of my car."

"But they were drinking."

"It was a blind corner—a corn corner."

"It wasn't your fault."

"Sure."

"You still feel guilty—"

"That'll never change."

"Why?"

He stood up. "I need a drink," he said. "Don't sweat it, Emily. I'm no lush, but I really do."

"I haven't got a thing—"

"Not even a beer?"

"This is Neukirk," she said.

"You're so naive," he told her.

"Tea?" she said.

"Maybe it's just something to hold onto."

"You can use me," she said, reaching out a hand.

He smiled. "Tea too," he said.

She led him into the kitchen where he sat in the chair he'd taken only a few hours before. She filled the teakettle and turned on the stove.

"It's all new," she told him. "I'm sure you find this hard to believe, but it's all new to me. I don't remember a thing about problems. I don't."

"Meg had this thing in her, like a switch almost. She could be radical as heck, but I don't think she really showed much of that to your folks. When they had a fight, it was about getting in on time, normal things—like everybody else in Neukirk. I really believe Meg respected your parents, Emily, even though she was a continent away in the way she was thinking by then. She was a smart girl. My word, she was bright."

"How could she act that way?" she asked.

"I don't know. I never did understand her. In some ways she was as pure as they were, but her soul was moving in another direction."

"Her soul?" Emily said.

"I don't mean it that way. I mean, the world she was into at that time was so different that there were no bridges. And she tried to stay away from hurting them—she really did. Like I said, I think she respected them, even though they didn't agree polit- ically. They just didn't talk much."

"How could family be enemies?"

"You know that scene in *Easy Rider*? You know, the movie *Easy Rider*? You ever see it?"

"No," she said.

"There's a scene at the end. These two freaks—these two hippie types—are riding down a highway on a Harley, when all of a sudden a couple of rednecks in a pickup come along and blow them away."

She looked at him as if it made no sense.

"That movie really worked at that time. I mean, we all really believed we were in real trouble because at any time somebody from the other side—from your parents' side—might simply blow us away."

"Us?"

"As opposed to them."

"I don't understand," she said.

"I suppose you don't. We were us. Your folks were them. But your sister chose, out of respect, I think, and maybe more, maybe fear—she never showed them much of us."

"My parents?"

"And my parents."

"You're trying to tell me that people in Neukirk were like murderers?"

"To us, in a way, yes."

"How?"

"Because we were about to begin this whole new life thing. Because it was about freedom. No matter how I try, I suppose I can't help you understand. It was about a whole new start, even a revolution. It sounds stupid now, but your sister and I were in at the very beginning, and there wasn't anybody else in Neukirk who even had a clue as to what was going on. Certainly not your parents. They had their disagreements, but she could have been much harder on them, much harder than she was."

"Why you?"

"Good question. I've thought about that for a long time. If we hadn't been in it, Meg would be alive." He laid both hands down on the table in front of him. "Partially, I think, it was Neukirk. We were both ashamed of a place where the whole war business—we're talking Vietnam now—wasn't even much of an item. Neukirk didn't lose any boys to Vietnam, but it lost one girl—it lost Meg."

He was positioned firmly there at the table, stayed exactly where he was, arms out, eyes piercing—all of him, she thought, open completely to her.

"We were high when it happened, Em," he told her, "both of us. It was the night of Humphrey's speech at the Democratic Convention in Chicago, and the big story was what was happening in the streets. McCarthy was beat, and it looked like the old machines were going to move on as if everything people had worked for was just so much nothing.

"We were sitting in this guy's apartment in Sioux City, watching it—watching the convention—watching all the rioting in the streets, and there was lots of dope there, lots of stuff—and everybody was up because the whole world was watching.

"And Meg says she's not going home anymore. She's sitting right beside me on the couch, and she says she's not going back to Neukirk because there's too much going on in the world and she can't get lost in some place where people could care less about what's really going on. She says she can't live a lie with her folks anymore anyway."

Emily placed their mugs of tea on the table and sat beside him.

"I told her it was stupid. In a month or so she'd be going to Iowa City anyway, and she'd be out of there.

"'Don't you just hate not being there, Norm?' she says to me, and she points at the screen, at everything breaking loose in Chicago. 'I can't stand it. I feel as if the whole world is passing me by. I feel as if everything that's real is in a world I never see.'

"I told her that in a month, at the U, we'd be out every day if we wanted to. We had to go home.

"I knew I was high—so was she—so I took the river road, the one that runs west, you know, where there wasn't any traffic. And once I got closer to home, I took the gravel. We went slow. Then she hauls out a baggie—I don't know where she scored the dope, but she did—somebody at the apartment must have scraped together something for her, and we were smoking. When we hit that other car, Emily, we were smoking."

"It was your fault?" Emily said.

"No, it was his. I was going so slow nobody would have ever said I was out of control. The cops knew it. What they didn't know was weed. They had no idea we'd been smoking anything." He looked at her tentatively.

"The whole Vietnam thing hadn't hit here yet—I'm not so sure it ever did. But nobody, not even cops, knew much about marijuana then. I dumped what was left in the bag into the ditch."

"And you never told my parents?" she said.

"I didn't tell them any of that. What for, Em? I lied to them just like she had for so long. I told them what everybody thought."

"How could you do that?"

"Easy. I knew perfectly well they wouldn't begin to understand anything, just like Meg knew. It's not that they weren't bright people, but it was early days in that whole messy, ugly time, and they wouldn't have begun to understand their own daughter," he said. "How could I tell them we were smoking dope?"

"You made up a story?" she said.

"For a guy who was always screaming about telling the truth, all I coughed up was a lie."

"And no one knew—"

"Nobody, ever. I've never told anyone." He shut his eyes, leaned back. "I've often thought that if I'd tell someone—" He looked at her again. "You know how it is, you're raised thinking that somehow confession is good for the soul. I've always thought if it would come out, like it just did, that some cloud would be lifted, something heavy would pass and the whole world would be sunshine."

"You're telling me that's not happened?"

"I feel awful, Em. Maybe Neukirk is right about every-thing—about hiding secrets, about playing games, wearing smiles, and just lying low for your whole life long."

"You're wrong," she told him.

"I know it, but it's something you hold to. When you're in deep trouble, Emily—when you don't know where to turn—" He rubbed his forehead. "You think that if you can dump it all somewhere—'bring it all to Jesus'—you think the whole mess'll go away."

"You're expecting a miracle," she said.

"Yes," he said. "It's what I've been told since I was a kid— and so have you."

"In time," she said.

"I never saw those guys—I swear. Not until they hit us. She was thrown from the car—you know that. I mean, she was dead right away. I found her in the grass, and I knew she was dead. And the worst part, the really awful part, was just waiting there at the side of the road, waiting for someone to come and tell me clearly that it was no dream at all."

"You remember that?"

"I remember it was horrible, but a lot of that night is gone.

66

I mean, the minute-by-minute stuff. The mind can do miracles. Some things it just tucks away. I remember standing over her. I put my jacket over her and cried my eyes out. I knew she was dead, but I put my jacket over her because— Why? Because I suppose I thought I could cover something up. There wasn't any blood, really. She broke her neck. The guys in the other car were all injured and there was blood all over, but with your sister—" he paused, looked up again, "it was like a switch. One moment alive, the next gone—just like that. I was standing there."

There they sat in her kitchen, two cups of tea untouched on the table between them, and Emily didn't know how to go on— whether she should let him talk, now that the whole story was falling out of some place where it had been locked away all these years, or whether for tonight enough had been said.

She leaned toward him, held out her arms, and he came to her crying, as he had so many years before. Slowly, they stood, together, as if simply interlocking arms were not enough, as if more of them had to touch and give and take.

He spoke over her shoulder. "Your father took you away, I remember," he said, "and your mother just talked and talked and talked about Meg—I don't even remember what she said, but in a time like that nothing really makes sense, and what comes out is spun from so much that has to be said anyway, even if it's flung from pain and horror. She talked and talked, as if the silence was full of ghosts. And she said she'd always remember the first song Meg had played on the organ, in church—'Some Day the Silver Cord Will Break,' and then she started to sing it, right there, so I told her—I told your mother that I thought it was always her favorite."

"A lie," she said.

"I didn't know her favorite hymn. All I knew was that to Meg—and to me—the whole church business was part of 'them.'"

"You told them what they wanted to hear?"

"Your mother needed that comfort—I know she did. I know

they knew Meg was moving away from something. She tried not to hurt them, but I know she couldn't hide it all. But it's what she would have wanted—I really feel that way—and I have for all these years—"

"For you to lie?"

"For me not to break them. Your parents were fragile. I didn't want to break them—you understand that?"

"Of course," Emily said.

"So when you called tonight and asked what you did, I knew the time had come to tell you all of this. In fact, I knew the day I heard you were moving back to Neukirk you'd have to know. I knew you'd been through some horrors of your own, that you were different than they were, that you could take the truth—and I knew I would tell you sometime. I just didn't know when."

He pulled himself away. "Now sit down," he said. "All we need is some righteous couple taking an evening walk past your place spotting us together."

"Who cares?" she said.

He took her arms in his hands gently, pulled her away as if it was something that hurt. "You aren't going to last until next week with that kind of attitude," he said. "You'll never get out of the boxes."

She stood beside him, then sat back in her chair just as he did, as if they needed to mimic each other. "I'll never get out of the boxes anyway," she said.

They sat in an uncomfortable silence, each of them brimming with more, but neither ready to go back farther.

"It's so long ago," she said. "There's been so much since then—a whole lifetime almost. And here we are, the two of us, right back in this town."

"I can say this," he told her. "After twenty-five years, I think about it now, finally, less than I did. I don't remember it less often, but I think about it less."

"I would think that coming back here—" She stopped intentionally.

"What were you going to say?"

"No matter."

"Yes, it is," he said. "Don't protect me."

She tried to turn the words around to make them sound less bitter.

"Don't take this wrong, Norm, but I was thinking that your being here, your actually being in Neukirk, would be more painful than your being somewhere else."

"That's another story, I guess, isn't it?" he said.

"That's another story for another time," she told him, her hand back on his.

There comes a time in such conversations when silence isn't awkward at all, but relief, lying heavily as it does over what has been said. The two of them sat there at the table, the VCR still turning out some blurred cartoon dialogue through the closed door. Perhaps it was the years, perhaps simply the strength of the earthen wall Norm had long ago constructed in his mind to hold back the force of those memories, but there were no more tears.

"I won't let you go," she told him. "You're staying here tonight."

"I'm not a child, Em," he said. "You don't have to protect me."

"I'm not thinking about you," she told him.

He turned his hands on hers, like a childhood game of one-upmanship. "What about my car?" he said.

"I don't care."

"You heard what I said—you'll never get the boxes empty."

"Maybe it'll save me some work," she said.

"Well, don't worry, I ran over," he told her. "That business about the shower—that was another lie. I ran over because I didn't want my car standing here in your driveway."

She took her hands quickly out of his. "I can't do this," she told him. "I can't learn to live like that. I'm not asking you to—"

"I know you're not."

"What difference does it make if you sleep over?"

"The Neukirk way is to think the worst. They always do.

They always figure if a man and a woman—you and me—are alone together, there's an animal loose."

"It is a fishbowl, isn't it?" she said.

"If they think you're eccentric, like they think of me," he said, "and they likely do."

Emily didn't ask any more of Norm, since she thought he'd said enough that night, and that what he'd said after all those years—and for the first time—meant he had to have some time himself for things to reorganize inside his mind. Instead, as they talked late into the night, she told him the story of her divorce, play by play.

After he helped her carry the kids up to bed, Norm lay on the floor in the living room, with Emily stretched out on the couch nearby. He told her that every year he took his classes to Chicago to have them experience the city and that for two nights, to save money in good Neukirk fashion, they'd stay in a church, sleep on a floor covered with the thinnest nap rug he'd ever felt, but that he never woke up with a backache. Tired, yes, he said, but no backache. "I can sleep on the floor."

In a way it was like summer camp, both of them staying awake as if neither could abide being the first to check out. Finally, when both of them almost unwillingly fell asleep, it was close to five, the light of a slowly brightening sky making the long branches of the elms outside the old house appear out of the darkness.

So Norm Visser spent the night at Emily Doorn's, ten days after she returned from LA, and very little happened—at least if, like many in Neukirk, you are thinking sexually. And yet much did occur, really, because as you know, there is no peace quite so comforting as that attained when two people who care deeply hold each other in the kind of unhurried silence that often follows hard on the heels of truth—hard, fast, sometimes painful truth—and itself brings peace.

What began to haunt Emily already the next day, however, was a deep desire to know exactly what her mother knew about Meg. If the story Norm had told her the night before was true—and she had no reason to believe it wasn't—then some things about her mother had to be called into question. Perhaps even her faith, constructed as it must have been on a view of her daughter's heart and soul that was skewed by Meg's own reluctance to hurt her parents, and by Norm's compassionate lying.

Can lying be compassionate? That's what she asked herself. Was it right for Norm not to tell them about a daughter they didn't know?

In early afternoon, Emily went out to the barn, pulled on her gloves, and tackled more of the junk she'd found in the corners of the place. But what stayed with her was a sadness that grew from a new and darkened view of things. For the first time in her life, she felt pity for her parents—not simply because of what the stroke had done to her mother, but pity that everything they believed about heaven and earth was built upon little more than fancy. And what made her bawl, tracking her face with tears which she wiped away with dusty gloves, was a painful feeling that what she'd always believed about them, about the strength of their faith, was plain wrong, fashioned as it was on a lie.

While she was gratified to have heard the whole story, while she was even proud to feel that Norm respected her enough to tell her everything, she knew that what she'd heard had the power to cloud every vision she'd ever seen or wished to see. She began to see her own return to faith in California as a fake, little more than wish fulfillment, and her homecoming as something childish, at best.

And while the barn swallows who'd set a nest on a rafter above her car stall swooped indignantly at her—and at the kitten her kids had been given by a neighbor—she couldn't help but see herself a victim of the truth that may well have made her free, but left her cold and fearful. Emily, like Meg, was no dummy. She saw a lot of lies.

There was a loft in the old barn, what might have been a hay loft at one time, when Neukirk was smaller and the Van Voorst home stood at the edge of the long, flat fields east of town. There was no hay up there anymore—no trace of it, in fact, even though the manger of the carriage stall still held some graying, flattened straw. The sun was out that afternoon. It was hot. Upstairs in the barn, with only the cracks in the siding allowing any ventilation, the air was almost unbreathable.

A stack of screens—maybe twenty or thirty, she didn't count—stood up against the south wall, all of them green, even though the trim on the windows of the house was black. They hadn't been used for years, not since someone—maybe Van Voorst himself—had installed central air and made the annual window-changing ritual unnecessary. The storms on the house were painted in. She wouldn't use the screens again, even if she wanted to. Like the big porch around the front, the screens were really of another time, when summer heat could be fought only by breezes.

She stood there, sweating, listening to the scolding those swallows were giving the kitten, and wondered why on earth anyone would keep old screens, even though at one time they likely cost a fortune, each of them built specifically for the old house. She looked at the door in the east wall, the only way to get them down and out to the dump, and she realized, of course, she couldn't do it herself. Her mission had been to make this barn into something clean and their own, but all this weight up here—a whole set of old screens and even some old windows, an old storm door or two—would stay in the barn, despite her best intentions. Some things were simply too much work to get rid of.

It's both a blessing and a curse to grow up, as Emily did, in a world whose boundaries are clearly drawn by what Neukirk people consider "the word of God." When biblical stories are repeated over and over and over, not simply for their plot lines but for their meanings, it's not hard for men and women blessed with intelligence to look at something as lifeless as unmovable, obsolete screens in a gray quilt of thick dust and realize that what they're seeing is more than junk. Just then, maybe, it was a blessing to be able to think in parables, as Emily did when she saw those old screens: that there are some things simply too heavy to get rid of. What would have happened to her parents if Norm had told them the truth that night: that Meg had been smoking dope at the time she died, angry at them, wanting to move out?

People who passed her house that afternoon and saw the junk out in front of the barn likely thought it was wonderful to see the way that woman, who'd suffered so badly in California, was back on top of things and getting her house in order in Neukirk. In a world where stacks of old screens often have some moral to them, it's helpful to remember that people can still be wrong sometimes.

Emily thought about missing her meeting with her mother that day. Every day since she'd returned she'd visited her, telling her what had happened since her last visit, as if her mother were waiting for her to come home from school, anxious—as she always had been—to know everything. From now on, she knew, visiting meant the kind of deceit that Norm had thought righteous.

But she knew that if she avoided the wing that afternoon, it would be more difficult for her to go the next day, or the next, or the next. Emily had fought hard for the custody of her children—and she fought alone. Painful as it had been to experience, the divorce and the custody battles had made her into someone who was not afraid of facing fears, even though she felt them deeply as fears.

She leaned up against her car, which she'd taken out of the barn to better clean up the trash inside. She loosened the knot on her scarf and wiped her face with the inside, wiped it hard, scoured it in fact.

The swallows sat together on the basketball hoop nailed to the front of the barn, twitching their heads, their Batmanlike capes, as they watched her leave.

II

Emily didn't shower. She went back in the house, climbed the stairs, removed her blouse, and washed her face and arms with a washcloth that grew very dingy. The water left a heavy ring around the sides of the sink, a ring she splashed away. She looked closely at her face to scrub out the dirt in her hairline. As her skin dried, her face felt stiff and rigid, as if she'd only smoothed out the dirt, leaving it in a thin paste.

She didn't shower because she thought of getting primped as the Neukirk thing to do: you have to be clean or someone will suspect sin—or worse, laziness. The kids had left their towels on the floor, so she picked one up from the heap, still damp from that morning, and buried her face in it.

She didn't shower because she didn't want to be at her best for her mother today, not because she was angry with her, but because somehow it would feel wrong to be fresh as a daisy.

She changed, but only to an old T-shirt with a high collar, her most comfortable plaid shorts, and a pair of old tennies— friendly clothes, nothing for show.

Back outside, she looked at the car shining in the sun, and for the first time she was conscious of what it was—a BMW, the kind of car that drew stares all over town. She decided to take a bike, even though she could have walked the four blocks to the hospital. The idea of walking Main Street right now seemed garish.

Outside the hospital, the groundskeeper was sitting on his

haunches trying to adjust the flow of water going into the shadowbox flowers at the side of the building. She tried to place him when he looked up and smiled, but his name was gone, even though his face, thinner than she remembered, was there in her memory.

"Welcome back, Em," he said, getting to his feet. He even tipped his cap, not in an old-fashioned way, but as if to mock old-time country manners.

"I'm sorry," she said, "the face is familiar, but names—"

"Ed Reinders," he said. "My daughter went to school with you. Lives in St. Paul now—three lovely grandchildren, too. Of course, they're a long ways away."

"Mary, of course," she said.

"Landersmith. Quite a mouthful. Married a boy out of Sioux Falls. Met him in a hospital as a matter of fact. She's a nurse. Not right now, though. She's got all she can handle with the kids."

The man's smile seemed to rise from his soul; it made her want to believe again that people here could be really human, really loving.

He took off his cap and rubbed his hand over his bald scalp, then looked at it, as if there might be dirt on his fingers.

"How's your mother coming along?" he said.

Surprisingly, it was a question hardly anyone asked, perhaps because they sensed that there was no easy way to answer it. Was she fine? Was she suffering? Was she happy?

"I sometimes stop in to see her when it rains—when I'm not busy out here. Just look in. I'm no preacher."

"I'm sure that she doesn't have much pain," Emily told him.

"Looks right with it," he said. "I told her once what kind of man her husband was."

He pulled back his sleeve and showed a long tapering scar that ran from his wrist up into his shirt.

"Nearly lost a wing to a power take-off years ago already," he said. "Maybe you remember. I think you were living here then because it was twenty years ago now, and Mary was still at home—she's the one that found me—" He left his arm out there, as if to confirm the pain.

"Oh, yes," she said. "Mary's dad." It was a lie.

"Your father used to visit me a lot in those days, not because he had to either, not even because we were best of friends. He said it wasn't nothing really, just to stop in for five minutes once in awhile."

"Sounds like Dad."

"Lost the farm," he said. "My wife shut it down while I was in the hospital." He laughed. "She told me, 'no more,' just like that. 'I'm not losing you.'"

"That hurt I imagine," she said.

"That was twenty years ago," he told her. "There ain't much twenty years can't heal." He looked at her closely. "Mary was in a play with you, I remember. She had a little part, and you were the star. Golly, I'll never forget how you could sing. You still do that?"

"Not much," she told him. "Not so much to sing about." She surprised herself saying that.

"Sure," he said, "I understand that. Anyway, it's good to have you back. You're good people." He raised a hand, one finger slightly raised, almost like a salute, and turned back to the shadowbox.

She walked through a door that opened for her, and as she passed through the hallways toward her mother's room, she wanted to cry, even though she didn't know why. "Frequent and uncontrolled crying," the TV commercial said, an ad put on by a big Sioux Falls hospital, "is a sign of depression. Call us, day or night."

She wasn't depressed.

But things seemed different when she made it to the room. Her mother's name, in a thick italic print, beautifully drawn in heavy black, was taped to the door, along with a Bible verse cut out from somewhere, a little square of white paper, the verse in fancy script. "Blessed are the meek, for they shall inherit the earth," it said. She'd read it before, every day she'd seen it, but it meant something different today. She couldn't help wondering whether meekness, the Sermon-on-the-Mount variety, was really another word for childishness.

Her mother was sitting in a wheelchair, facing the window, a position Nancy insisted was best for her because it gave her access to life. Nancy believed that if her mother would ever communicate in any way again it would be because someone found the right key to trigger her will.

"It's really all will," Nancy had told her. "I've read a lot about cases like this one—your mother's is far from the first around here—and what researchers seem to say is that it's a kind of sleep for some of them, a sleep that can be overcome if they want to."

Nancy thought her mother wanted to. "She likes being by the window. Sometimes I bring her to the sunroom, but she's not always comfortable with other people."

Emily had asked her how she knew.

"You just know. You wait, Em," she said. "You can see it in the eyes."

She stood there behind her mother now, as if she could look through the back of her head and see something, even though Nancy had always said that life was in the eyes.

"I could show you patients," she'd told Emily once, "where the lights are on, you know, but nobody's home. I can tell the difference. Anyone can. You want me to show you?" But Emily had no desire to witness anyone else's suffering.

"Your mother's selective about things," Nancy told her, "but I know—I'm sure—that things go in. Not everything either, but what she wants. It's the will," she said again. "It's the will to live."

Emily looked around at the shelves and the pictures of herself and her children, very recent pictures; she'd always tried to keep her mother up-to-date with pictures because she knew it wasn't easy to have grandchildren so far away. And Meg—high school graduation, a picture Em herself knew so well because it was the last, and the most beautiful: Meg's long straight hair falling perfectly over her shoulders, a single, small daisy pinned beside her temple.

She felt an impulse she hadn't felt before, a desire to go through every inch of this room, even though she was sure, having been in Neukirk at the time her mother was admitted to the wing, that there were no secrets, no unseen diaries, no letters. It didn't matter. There were things now that she wanted to know. Not to damage her sister's sainthood, for that's what Meg's life seemed to have been when Emily was growing up in the shadow of a big sister who'd died unexpectedly; and not to make her mother face the truth, for the truth really wasn't worth it—not when the accident happened, and certainly not today when whatever was alive in her mother's mind was undoubtedly less focused on this world than the next. No, what she wanted from her mother was some kind of explanation of faith, of how it was supposed to work when what you knew simply didn't harmonize with what you were supposed to believe.

"I was wondering if you were coming," Nancy said, coming up behind her. "She had an uncomfortable night. I don't think she's any worse off physically or anything, but the night nurse said that she could tell her usual sleep was stirred. And this morning I can see it." She pointed at her mother's back. "You'll be able to see it. She's tired."

Emily turned to Nancy. "You should be paid twice as much," she said. "I can't tell you how much I appreciate the kind of attention you've given her. I don't even understand it—how you can care for her so much. You didn't even know her."

Like many Neukirk people, Nancy Greiman did not take compliments well. "When you see them everyday, you get to understand that they're really still human. Not everybody thinks that way, but it's not our ability to talk that makes us human, is it?"

"I don't know," Em said.

"I know she feels."

"And that's what makes us human?"

"That we feel? I don't know," Nancy said. "But it's easy to love your mother, Em. She's such a loving person."

"Isn't everyone in her condition?" Emily said.

Nancy giggled, almost mischievously. "Of course not. They aren't all sweet. People in apraxis like this are really little more than what they were before." She pointed up the corridor. "There've been people here who . . . well, let me put it this way: I've seen nurses pick straws to determine who had to go in—just to check them."

"Come on—"

"Seriously." She nodded her head. "Your mother's a gem. I'm so glad you came home." She stopped talking, bit her lip slightly. "Do you mind if I tell you the truth?"

Emily shook her head.

"It's not very hard for a nurse to start hating kids who don't come," she said, looking away. "I'm not saying I hated you, living in California the way you did—and especially once I heard about your problems and everything. But you started with the compliments, Em, so let me give you one. I think your coming home is the greatest gift you could ever give your mother—ever. It's the very best gift."

Had Emily tried very hard, it might have been possible to stanch the tears that came just then. It might have been possible not to have hugged Nancy Greiman. But she lacked the strength to try as hard as she would have had to. And when the tears finally came, she edged very close to what Neukirk people would call "breaking down." She fell into Nancy's arms.

"I know it's hard," Nancy said. "I think that's why some kids won't even come—because it's so terribly hard to have to face their parents in this kind of condition." She wrapped her arms around Em, held her, without moving a bit. "You knew her when she was so much more, but no more alive."

They stood there together, a step into the doorway, a step out of the corridor. "It's so great—what you're doing," Nancy said.

"I give you all the credit in the world. You are a Christian."

She pulled herself gently away, left Emily standing before her, embarrassed by her tears.

"Go talk to her," she said. "There's nothing better for your mother than to hear your voice, to listen to what you're doing and thinking. The best therapy in the world is what you're doing. When people get old, all they care about is what their kids are doing—because that's all they've got left in the world. It just astounds me sometimes that some people don't recognize that." She shook her head.

Then she kissed Emily and left the room, left her standing there, her back to her mother.

And all Emily could think of was how Norm did find comfort in the lie, how he must have looked at her parents and fallen into a kind of love himself, telling them a story that never happened, realizing what a gift it was to tell them no more than what they wanted or needed to hear.

The squeak of Nancy's shoes on the hallway tile meant she'd left, only that faint sound and Emily's perfectly clear sense that her presence was gone. She took the wooden chair from behind the desk across from the bed and placed it beside her mother's wheelchair, facing the window.

Hundreds, even thousands of Neukirk's residents strive throughout their lifetimes to be righteous, make work of trying to be angelic; but pity Emily Doorn, who, according to Nancy Greiman, had just attained it, at a time when she couldn't have felt less deserving.

What was there to talk about? Weather? The kids playing happily in the neighborhood? Church last Sunday? All of it seemed cheap, an invitation to avoid the truth, a lie she had no desire to construct—the very thing that had irritated, even angered her about Neukirk.

It seemed to her that there was nothing she could say, nothing at all. The choices were so stark: either the deep plunges of the kind of truth that would bring pain, or more lying, saying things so insubstantial they would make being here a lie.

It was early afternoon, and Main Street, just outside the windows, was hardly busy. Some cars, a few vans, and now and then a cattle truck easing up with a backward roar as it slowed for the red light on the south end of town. So little of life from this window, so lean a portion of what was happening to people, even here in Neukirk—that was all her mother saw. Nancy was right. All her mother had was her daughter and a fragmented view of Main Street traffic.

When her father died, she and Benjamin had come back for the funeral. Before that, she'd been here maybe once a month in the last half year of his life, the time it took for the cancer to destroy him. And she remembered how her parents' minister had told her once in those last months that her father really didn't care much anymore about what was happening to anyone. He'd said it was natural. He'd said that just like anybody going on a trip, her father was already creating his own sense of his destination—preparing himself for that new place with whatever senses and thoughts and feelings he had left.

She'd thought about that often: the leave-taking, the way in which his mind had begun to depart even before his body relented in the war against cancer; how part of him was gone already—maybe the most important part—even as he lay there.

Now, she wondered, what of her mother was already gone? How many of her things were already packed?

And wasn't the answer there in the hymn? Maybe it *was* Meg's favorite hymn in 1962, she thought, but maybe there's more to it. Maybe it's something she wants to remember to put the best face on the loss of a daughter that could otherwise be obliterated by the most awful vision her mother could ever experience—Meg's not being among the saved. But maybe that's not all. Maybe she hums that melody because she's packing, or because she's already packed and ready to go. Maybe that was it. Maybe it was her mother's own doxology, that last hymn at the end of worship.

The thought came to her almost as relief, almost as a blessing. If that hymn had nothing to do with Meg whatsoever, then everything that she'd been anxious about—what really happened, what her parents knew, how they might have raised her with a kind of lie—was meaningless anyway. If it wasn't a problem for her mother, why should it have to be a problem for her?

She reached over and took her mother's hand. Her hair was long and perfectly silver, her face more wrinkled than it might have been—she really wasn't as old as she looked, but her inability to move had made her waste away. Was there something visible even in the face, in her slightly crooked mouth, exaggerated now by the stroke? In the high cheekbones, like her own? In the eyes so blue that Benjamin had told her once long ago, when they were in love, he couldn't imagine any man not falling into them when her mother was young.

Maybe it didn't matter, she told herself. Maybe all this shaking in her fingers and chest was really unnecessary. If her mother had peace, why should she worry?

"I wish I had known Meg better, Mom," she said finally. "I've got lots of memories, you know, tons of them—they could fill a scrapbook. I remember one time when Dad rented that little trailer and we tried to camp, and it was late at night and she told me to sleep with her. I don't know if she was scared or what— it was raining. I think she just knew that I was. I'll never forget that."

She wished her mother would actually address her with those eyes. She knew what Nancy meant because her eyes did seem to have the life to focus—they seemed understanding. But she wished so much that they would sweep over from whatever it was they were looking at, that they would rise to hers and put a seal on something.

"She was too young to die," she said, and immediately thought it a foolish thing to say, so obvious, something her mother must have thought of so often that it came to her as natural as breathing.

"I mean for me," she said. "I know for her, and for you too, she was too young, but for *me*—I never really knew her. I know I was proud of her. I think the biggest thrill of my life when I was little was that I got to be that miniature cheerleader. You remember that, Mom? When Meg was in high school, they asked you if I could be a miniature cheerleader, and I got a sweater and a skirt. You made it, didn't you? You made that skirt. And then I learned some of those cheers. I'd go out on the floor with them, in front of all those people. It's a wonder I wasn't more nervous about it, but I suppose when you're that young you don't really think about it all that much. I guess that's what I resent most about her dying—"

Her mother's lips quivered slightly.

She'd never talked about Meg's death with her mother before. Not because she never thought about it, but because— why? she wondered. Because for the most part her parents had never talked about it. It wasn't an obsession with them. There weren't warnings when a boy came to pick her up for a date— nothing was ever said in that regard.

Death was never comfortable to talk about, and accidental death, like her sister's—it was something that was always there, she thought, something like the ghost that's *not* seen, a presence that's there even though it's gone. You don't need to talk about something you never forget.

"May I just say one thing, Mother?" she said. "I wish I'd known her better. I wish she hadn't died." She squeezed her mother's hand. "That's two things, isn't it?"

For a long time she sat there in silence, not only because she had so much to say, but because she had the sense that even to mention Meg's death was enough for one afternoon.

Fifteen minutes passed. Business picked up a bit on Main Street. More cars, even some pedestrians. From down the hall voices floated out of other rooms. A soft yet almost unearthly moan rose at such regular intervals, it seemed someone was watching the second hand of the clock. A few muffled laughs, the low tone of conversation one expects in a place where twenty-some people are doing little more than waiting for death.

What she wanted to ask was whether her mother worried about Meg, even today, long after the accident, when there was nothing she could do. Mormons pray for the dead, so do Zuni Indians—so do lots of people, she thought. But her mother's faith drew more rigid lines.

And how is it that you can believe? That's what she wanted to know. She wanted more lessons from her only surviving parent, wanted questions answered, like a child, her mother's only child.

Maybe next time, she thought. Maybe it was enough for now simply to nudge Meg's life—and death—into the conversation.

When she stood, her mother showed no reaction. Neither was there any humming. She leaned over and kissed a cheek whose texture she didn't remember at all, and the act seemed somehow insubstantial, almost grandmotherly.

Nancy met her at the door. She took Emily's elbow and raised one hand as if to say to wait. Then she went into her mother's room and came back with the old Bible.

"Sometimes people like your mom—really devout people—mark up their Bibles, see?" she said. She flipped through the pages slowly to show the underlining, the little notes in the margins. "Your mom—maybe this is your dad's writing too, I don't know—"

"Let me see," Emily said, and she took the Bible in her own hands. She didn't recognize it; it wasn't the one they'd read from at almost every meal when she was growing up.

She opened up to Isaiah and saw her father's sticklike printing above a chapter: "Rev. Wondergem, 'The Glory of the Immanuel,'" it said. Must have been a sermon topic.

But her mother's familiar handwriting—its characteristic long tails even in a cramped hand in the margins—was there too, in quiet affirmations. Here and there a "yes," some places, "wonderful," others, "how comforting."

"When your mom first came, I took this out because sometimes you can just tell what passages of Scripture are most important to them—their favorites—the Bible almost opens up to them. You know what I mean?" Nancy pointed to the open pages. "The ones they go back to time and time again," she said. "Here, let me show you."

She took the Bible back and opened it. "Look," she said, "look how dirty this page is. There's whole books in the Old Testament that are hardly opened, but you turn to some passages and—"

"What is that?" Emily said.

"Matthew 11—'Come unto me all ye who are weary and heavy-laden'—you know."

"Must be a favorite."

"Once a week I read it. I can see that she loves it." She rolled her eyes. "Maybe you think I'm crazy."

"I don't think there's a person in this world that I'd rather have taking care of my mother," Emily said.

Nancy flinched slightly, nodded a kind of thanks. "I wanted to show you this. I found it inside."

She opened the Bible's back cover, where long ago someone had glued in a small envelope, and she took out a half-sheet of paper, yellowed, dog-eared, a grease stain of some sort in the upper left-hand corner, folded precisely.

"This is Matthew 11 too," Nancy said. "Look."

The words on the note were typewritten, full of errors, done on a typewriter so old that it couldn't keep its letters on the same line: "Come unto me all ye that labour and are heavy laden, and I will give you rest. Take my yoke upon you, and learn of me: for I am meek and lowly in heart: and ye shall find rest unto your souls. For my yoke is easy and my burden is light. — Matthew 11:28–30."

And then beneath it, written in pencil, in the unmistakable hand of her mother: "Profession of faith, 1962." There was no name after it.

Nancy said, "You might resent my poking around—"

"No, really."

She looked almost sheepish. "I've thought about this a lot.

Meg was confirmed when she was twelve, right? I mean, I went to high school with Meg—she was a year older than I was. And in 1962 she was in sixth or seventh grade, that's all. Am I wrong? That's really young in your church, isn't it?"

"I was only a year old then," Emily reminded her.

"Your mother loved this piece of paper—what it represented, that's for sure. Here it is in this special little envelope." Nancy flipped to the back cover again.

"Was there anything else in it?" Emily said.

Nancy shut the Bible and took it back into the room without answering the question. When she returned to the hallway, she shut the door behind her.

"I heard you say to her you wished you knew her better," Nancy said. "I overheard it—I'm sorry."

"That's okay," Emily said. "I do. You can't believe how much I do."

"Look," Nancy said, "there's a little sitting room down the hall. It's the middle of the day and there's probably nobody around. I'm on duty, so I can't take long, but I'd like to tell you some things."

On a little table stood a thermos coffee pot and a half dozen cups, upside down, on a clean napkin. Beside them was a plate full of oatmeal cookies covered with Saran Wrap. Without asking, Nancy poured both of them a cup and put one in Emily's hand.

"There's this," she said then, and she slipped another perfectly folded note out of the pocket of her uniform. "It was also in the Bible, but I didn't want to bring it up in front of your mother."

"Dear Ben and Vivian," it said. "It's hard for me to try to minister to two people whose faith I've so grown to respect. Without going on and on as preachers can, let me just say this. Meg's soul, at this point, is something God only knows. You know His promises. You remember her faith as a child. As you've always done with every other burden you've faced, bring it to the Lord and then leave it there. He will shoulder our burdens. You know that. Peace to both of you. You're in my prayers." It was signed "Mike Stellinga."

"I don't know this man," Emily told her. "I don't recognize the name at all." She looked back down at the note—a small piece of stationery stamped with the imprint of the University of Illinois.

"He was a student pastor at your church a year before Meg died, an intern," said Nancy. "He worked with kids."

"And this?" Emily said, pointing to the imprint.

Nancy shrugged her shoulders. She pointed at the letterhead. "Maybe he went back to school."

Maybe she had been wrong, Emily thought. Just exactly what her mother knew about Meg, or thought about her daughter's soul, was still a question, but that her mother had known Meg wasn't all she pretended to be seemed very clear—or else why the letter? Her parents had grieved Meg's death all right, but they'd also grieved for her soul.

"Why are you showing me this?" she asked Nancy.

"I heard you tell your mother that you wished you'd known your sister." She sat on the soft chair, her knees tightly together, arms at her sides, cup clasped in two hands. "I was afraid you were thinking exactly what your mother used to think—about Meg. And I wanted you to read the letter they never threw away."

Emily sat there, paralyzed. Her mother had known more than she thought she had. So had her father. Obviously they had written this man—this young pastor—asking for assurance. They knew much more than Norm ever thought they did, maybe even more than Meg herself thought they did.

"When your mother sings that song—did you look it up?" Nancy said.

She lacked the strength to explain the whole story, even though right then she trusted this woman more than anyone. "Yes," Emily told her. "I found it in an old hymnbook."

"When your mom sings, I think it's a testimony to how deep her faith must be," Nancy said. "I went to school with Meg. I remember her."

"Sometime," Emily said, "sometime when you're not at work and we have a little more time, would you tell me some things about Meg, about what you remember?"

Nancy waited a moment before she said, "How old were you when she died?"

"Just six," Emily told her.

Nancy looked away, took a deliberate sip on her coffee.

"I know it's not all great," Emily said. "I know that. I know things, probably, that you don't know—and they're probably worse. I have to know the truth."

"It's all so long ago—"

"I want to know," she said again.

Nancy put her cup back on the table, even though she hadn't had more than a couple sips.

"Of course," she said. "I'll tell you everything I remember about Meg—and it isn't really so bad either. Maybe I'm making this out to be something it isn't. But she was different, Em. She was much different, and in some ways she was only kind of ahead of her time." She reached for Emily's hand, then leaned toward her in an awkward hug.

What Nancy told her that day didn't change anything, but it did continue to fill in the shadows of her sister's life with information that wasn't as much startling as it was revealing.

Cheerleading. Meg had been, in many ways, as talented as Emily, and probably, according to Nancy, more athletic. She'd been a high school cheerleader, a good one. What Nancy remembered most, though, was how Meg had simply dropped cheering completely at the beginning of basketball season her senior year.

At the end of the previous year she'd been chosen to be the '67–'68 season's captain. But, Nancy said, Meg had started to miss summer practices rather frequently, and when she'd return she'd seemed in no mood to apologize for not being there. Meg cheered all through the football season—sometimes, however, as if she didn't care anymore. Nancy knew all this because she had been junior varsity herself that year.

Then, in late October, Meg announced to the other girls that she was quitting the squad. She didn't make a big splash of it, but the story was that she said the whole business seemed to be something she'd grown out of. She'd made the announcement at a meeting of the varsity squad so Nancy wasn't there, but she'd heard that's what Meg had said.

Of course, none of them understood in the least, all of them simply assuming that some kind of announcement about her being pregnant would occur soon after. Why else would anyone quit?

They were wrong. And although she'd tried to make her feelings clear, without hurting or humiliating the others, Meg's motivations were never understood.

"I mean, we talked about what was happening around the country in civics classes and things, but, I mean, nobody really thought of Neukirk as even being in that world." Nancy seemed almost repentant when she remembered. "Your sister got a head start on everybody. Then again, there's some people, even today, if they'd remember that far back, wouldn't understand what so many of us felt at that time. I don't know where Meg got her head from, but she just didn't think like the rest of us—at least not right then."

"Nobody else?" Emily said.

"I think Norm Visser was the first kid to really let his hair grow, and of course everybody knew she was seeing him. But he was a good kid, too—no trouble-maker. Maybe she got it from him."

The importance of Meg's quitting right before basketball season was that it was a public act, even if the explanation was offered in confidence. The captain of the cheerleading squad didn't simply resign, mid-season, without being noticed. People talked. You can bet they talked, Nancy told her.

But when it came to nothing—when it turned out Meg

wasn't pregnant—her decision seemed only strange. Some kids were afraid of her, Nancy said.

And then there was Memorial Day. "You know how it is in Neukirk," Nancy said. "It's still the same today. Nothing's changed. People gather at the cemetery, rain or shine, to commemorate the men who died in the great wars of the twentieth century."

That year, Memorial Day came the day after graduation, Nancy said. Maybe that was why Meg did what she did. She played the French horn and marched in the band. But when she showed up for the parade downtown, she wore a black armband over her uniform sleeve. Everybody saw it as she marched down Main, and everybody noticed it when the band stood at attention in the village cemetery and played the national anthem.

"People hated her for it?" Emily asked.

"People hated the music teacher for letting her get away with it. They thought he should have ripped it off or sent her home. In fact," Nancy said, "he *was* fired." But she said you couldn't really make a federal case out of it because you know how hard high school kids can be on music teachers, and the guy—she remembered him well for having this thing about high school girls—was just out of the army and hadn't really got himself together.

"Maybe he influenced her somehow," Emily said.

"I was in band and chorus," Nancy told her. "The guy was strange. Sometimes we could go for a week without singing at all. He just didn't have much control, and I wouldn't be at all surprised—I would have been shocked then, but not now—if today you'd ask somebody who was on the school board at that time and he'd say the man was a drunk. I don't know."

"Did he go out with Meg?"

"I don't know this for sure," Nancy said, "but I'd bet any money that Meg wouldn't have given him the time of day. He was one of those guys who didn't seem to get it. I felt sorry for him in a way, and in another way I didn't. Sometimes he'd just scream at us—for no reason—"

"So she didn't date him or anything?"

"Meg was something else, Em," Nancy told her. "She had a mind of her own—she really did. But she wasn't arrogant about it. I mean, even when she quit cheerleading—and I understand why she did. I went to the U too, you know; I got my share of what was happening in 1970. But this was '68, and in some ways it made all the difference in the world."

She stopped, tried to locate some way of explaining.

"I know she found cheerleading silly. I didn't know it then, but I knew it myself a couple years later. But the point is, when she told the other girls, she didn't try to make them feel like airheads. It was just her decision. That's what made Meg's quitting so hard to take, so hard for the others to understand—that she could hold such strong views and not be condemning.

"You were born in another time, Emily, a whole different era completely," Nancy said. "Even in Neukirk, eventually, people went to war—and I don't mean over there, in Vietnam."

She told Emily how Meg would talk about issues in class, how the views she held were so "different" that the rest of the kids would react either angrily or in a kind of shocked silence, as if what she'd said shouldn't be repeated outside the classroom.

"There are ways—now that I think about it—there are ways in which you might say that people were scared of Meg Doorn," Nancy told her. "Her ideas. What she stood for."

Emily waited for a moment. "What about this thing with Norm?" she asked.

"We all thought they were doing it. Everybody did. We all thought they were smoking up, too. If you had asked anybody at Neukirk High in 1968, 'Which kid is likely to smoke marijuana?' everybody would have said Meg Doorn."

"Do you know whether she did?"

"Nobody does, I suppose, because at the end of her senior year she didn't hang around anybody. She was always with Norm, always with kids we called 'freaks.'"

"Freaks?"

"Odd isn't it?" she said.

"I've heard it before," Emily said. "It just sounds so harsh."

"That's what they called themselves," Nancy said. "Really."

If people in Neukirk knew what Emily had learned about her sister's life and death, and if they understood how that news had affected her, I'm sure many of them would have thought her hurrying off to work at Tony's to be the kind of blessed diversion that only the Lord, in his wisdom, could have planned. But I'm not so certain.

And regarding what happened that day in the bowling alley, let me just say this in defense of the men who gather there, mid-afternoon, for coffee: No community on earth has learned how to deal perfectly with its real eccentrics. I won't try to excuse the bowling alley crowd, nor blame their behavior on human nature, as if what they did to Will Kruse was something they were destined to by Adam's curse or God's negligence. Andy Vellinga and the others who designed this little trick knew very well what they were doing. But occasionally events that look absolutely brutal to those who don't understand the people involved are less ugly than they appear. So it was with Willard's birthday cake.

Willard Kruse. It may surprise you to know that Neukirk has its drug victims. Willard is one, perhaps the most notable: the son of a preacher, who got himself so mired in drugs in the seventies that something flattened in his mind and left him, if not retarded, certainly slow, incapable of holding a job.

No one disputes this or blames him for laziness. And it doesn't mean that Willard Kruse does nothing all year long. He does. In fact, there are times when Andy Vellinga has work for him—an old farm house to bring down, for instance, or a barn to move. On those days, Andy will pick up Will from the hotel where he lives and take him to the site, put him to work, pay him a good wage, and bring him back home, spending half the day himself trying to keep Will at the tasks he's brought him out to accomplish. It's an act of mercy.

And such mercies are not uncommon. Will Kruse is shielded from vagrancy by the consideration of good old boys in seed caps, and that point cannot be emphasized enough.

Of course, all of that was unknown to Emily Doorn, who had no particular sympathies for Will Kruse herself. Actually, the man scared her, staring at her the way he did while slowly sipping the medium Coke he ordered every day at a bit after two, just about the time men started coming in for afternoon coffee. He'd never yet spoken to her, except to order. He just sat there in silence, often nodding his head and shifting his eyes about, at the end of the curving countertop. He'd read the comics from the *Register*, which still lay there, in pieces, left over from the breakfast crowd. When he found something funny, he laughed out loud, as if wishing he could read the whole piece to everyone there.

Emily was not a woman who found preying eyes all that bothersome. If she did, she wouldn't have been working at Tony's. But Will's leering chilled her. She feared him because she felt his eyes on her constantly, and his eyes seemed dangerous, a perception and a fear only another woman could understand fully.

The men know that Will Kruse is harmless, and they seem to feel he has a place right there at the end of the counter. Besides, people say, he's a better ad than the finest TV warnings about drug use. He's a walking case-in-point for all the righteous concern people have for their kids and the drugs they sometimes wish were only in cities far away. In fact, some good people of Neukirk long ago assumed that Will's reason for being is exactly that: his disability has proved a blessing. Wouldn't it be wonderful if righteous theories translated into righteousness?

It was early—quarter to two—when Andy Vellinga brought in the cake, but already there were a dozen guys sitting around the front table, an unusual number so early in the afternoon.

Andy couldn't keep the joke to himself; he'd told others that it was coming and nobody wanted to miss the fun.

He had the cake in an aluminum pan, the kind familiar to anyone who's ever been to a church social. In the pouch of his sweatshirt he had candles, a dozen. He didn't think to count out an exact number; besides, it would have taken him half the day to find out how old Will was.

He set the cake down, to a lot of fanfare, on the front table and poked the candles into the thick chocolate frosting (and yes, it did say "Happy Birthday," so Tres, his wife, had a hand in this as well).

Emily saw it all happening from the back, where she was helping clean up from lunch. Birthday celebrations are not rare at Tony's, so a cake was not unusual. And it didn't strike her as strange that Andy should come back through the swinging doors and lay that cake on the counter in front of her.

"This here's for Will," he said. "We thought he'd like it best if you gave it to him when he comes in."

Emily's no one's dupe. She understood why Andy wanted her to present the cake. If this were a Shriner's convention, he'd want her to jump out of it naked.

Now some of the things that had been said to her by this time could be considered transgressions of the new codes of sexual harassment. But she'd kept a stiff upper lip, so the men considered her a good sport. And to be honest, she'd really not felt herself humiliated—embarrassed occasionally, yes, but she'd enjoyed most of the banter. She looked on working at Tony's as a kind of game anyway, realizing that it was the best stage in town. She knew she was being used, and she went into it fully aware of her own complicity. She'd used her looks in the past; after all, she made good money in soap commercials.

"It's his birthday?" she asked.

"He ain't got no family anymore around here, you know," Andy said, tugging at her heartstrings.

She thought this a nice gesture, something that would happen only in a place like Neukirk. So she told Andy she'd bring the cake to Will and went back to slicing hamburger buns for the supper hour.

When Will came in and took his end-of-the-counter stool, she heard things quiet down a little, although she noticed that no one went out of his way to say "Happy birthday." It would have been unusual for that to happen, though, for while the men employed Will if and when they could, they never gave him a spot around the front table. Andy Vellinga might well say it this way: "I can be nice to the guy, but I wouldn't want to go fishing with him."

So Will took the spot at the end of the counter, opened the paper, snapped it half-folded, laid it down beside him, and started reading the funnies.

Andy looked at Emily and shrugged his shoulders, as if to say *when* was now up to her.

"Coke, Will?" she said.

He looked up with his heavy eyes and nodded. "Easy on the ice," he said.

She scooped out a few ice cubes, placed the glass on the grate, hit the button on the machine, and watched him as it filled. Nothing in his demeanor suggested anything different about this day.

The cap cocked over the back of his head was his favorite, the black one that said "POLICE" in tall white letters. She'd seen his T-shirt before too, a black one with a drawing or a monogram of something weird and wild that had been made almost unidentifiable by a thousand washings, probably advertising a heavy metal group that bit the dust a decade ago. His hair was disheveled, as usual, and his face seemed puffy, almost as if he'd just come from bed—which was possible.

She looked over at Andy, who looked around at the front table to check if everyone was there. Then he shrugged his shoulders once again, as if to indicate that she could do it whenever she had the time.

So she went back to the kitchen, took the cake from the counter, and almost left through the swinging doors without lighting the candles. Quickly, she put it down, drew a match from the box of "light anywheres" in the catch-all drawer, and finished the job. They were dripless, in fact.

She smoothed back her hair, straightened her apron a bit, even looked in the mirror hung from the wall beside the swinging doors. Then she remembered she'd forgotten his Coke.

Once more she put the cake down, banged through the swinging door, grabbed the glass off the grate beneath the machine, and brought it quickly—too quickly, because it spilled over the edge—to where he sat.

"Oh, I'm sorry," she said, and pulled a rag out to dry off the bottom. "I forgot all about it. I filled the glass and just left it there."

Will looked up as if she were speaking in a foreign tongue.

She wiped off the counter where the glass had left a ring, then stood there in front of him.

"We got a policy, Will. If we forget an order, it's on the house." And, without thinking, she winked at him.

Something tripped in Will, and the minute she'd done it, a hungry grin fastened each corner of his lips to his ears.

She glanced at Andy Vellinga. The men, at full attention, sat there around the front table like the burghers on a box of Dutch Masters cigars.

"By the way," she said. "We've got a little surprise for you."

"What?" he said. The eagerness in his face seemed threatening.

"Let me get it."

She stepped back through the swinging doors and brought out the cake, held it out in front of her in both arms, and just as she got to the counter the boys at the front table started singing "Happy Birthday."

In Neukirk, there are a dozen estimates of poor Will's real mental age. It's not simply intelligence that's gone either; it's a whole volley of other tools we use to live. But at that moment, with Emily carrying an aluminum cake pan out from the back of Tony's, then placing it before him on the counter, a dozen candles glowing, the chorus of "Happy Birthday" in deep bass behind him, the look on Will Kruse's face was unmistakably childlike. And whatever fear Emily'd had of him was gone. His eyes seemed vacant, his lips parted and his bottom lip curved slightly in astonishment.

The men from the front table came up slowly and surrounded him like a choral group.

Will sat back on his stool, put both hands down on the counter as if to keep balance, and then laughed. Actually, he *harumphed*, deep in his chest—all told, a deep belch of astonished laughter repeated six times. (Ralph DeMeester videotaped the whole thing. The harumphs were counted later, like the tolling of a bell.) The poor boy was moved.

Now I don't want to overstate what happened next, but you must keep in mind that Emily had been profoundly shaken by what had happened to her in the last day or two. Revelations about a past she never knew had left her feeling as if the earth beneath Neukirk was ever shifting. So when this transformation—someone so scary suddenly given the eyes of a boy charmed completely by a birthday surprise—she thought the whole scene perfectly wonderful. She bit her lip, in fact—you can see it on the tape.

"Well, Will," Andy said, "let's have at it."

He took out a knife he must have hauled along from home and proceeded to cut out a huge piece, maybe two inches by two inches, that belonged to the honored. This was a flat cake, of course, not a round layered one.

"We'll keep the writing as long as we can," Andy said, and he lifted that gigantic piece out of the pan. "Got a dish somewhere, Em?"

Emily reached under the counter and pulled out a clean one, laid it down on the counter, and held it while Andy unloaded the first gargantuan piece, perfectly white with a heavy roof of chocolate frosting.

Will's eyes were a marvel. His mouth dropped open into a full-fledged gape as he watched the cake come up between his arms on the counter in front of him.

"Go on," Andy said, echoed by the others.

"Happy birthday," Emily said.

She should have noticed what was going on when he had trouble forking through the first bite, when he had to hold it in his hand to get off a chunk. But she didn't. She was high, you might say, enthralled. Had she had time to think it through, she would have said that acts of mercy and love like this were the very reason she'd come home to Neukirk.

Finally, he wore off a hunk by diligence alone, and when it didn't quite get perfectly on his fork, he did what men will do: picked it up in his fingers, still wearing that workmanlike grin, and shoved it into his mouth.

I don't think anyone expected that. Perfect silence reigned.

The shot of Will Kruse scarfing down that first bite does not bring laughs when people see it on the screen. Giggles, yes, but not laughs. Astonishment was what it bred right there at the end of counter. The men fell speechless.

The cake was styrofoam.

Emily looked quickly at what was left in the pan and found it ridiculously solid, perfectly white, little tiny bubbles of styrofoam chinked off where Andy had lifted out the first piece.

But Will was eating it!

There he was in a circle of men he'd been charmed into believing his buddies, chomping down styrofoam with the broadest smile Neukirk might have seen between homecoming coronations.

Remember, there was no laughing. The whole crowd was a powder keg of silence. They weren't shocked or full of guilt. They were just amazed at what was happening, like children full of pent-up giggles, M-80s with lit fuses.

Will choked down the first bite and looked up at the guys.

"Little dry," he said, and the whole place exploded.

Men fell, literally, in the aisle. Andy Vellinga and Rich Linderd held each other up like fully bagged town drunks. It's all on tape. There's already forty copies around. You can see it most anywhere.

But the footage stops before the real action because Ralph stopped shooting the minute he was commanded to put that camera down. And you won't be shocked to know who shouted.

"STOP IT!" Emily screamed. "This is awful."

Everyone turned to her, but she kept looking at Will Kruse, who was still struggling gamely to swallow a chunk of styrofoam the size of a Chunky chocolate bar—without, of course, dropping the smile.

When he went after another forkful, Emily snatched away the plate she'd put in front of him herself.

"Stop it," she said. "It's a terrible joke!"

Silence once again. The men weren't so afraid of *her*, as of her wrath.

Will's eyes shifted uncomfortably, even angrily, as he held the fork like a miniature pitchfork.

"It's not cake," she said.

Honestly, he licked his lips, thereby destroying whatever semblance of order her outburst had begun to build, and the men stood around—how can I say it any other way?—like barely stifled naughty boys.

"This is wretched," she screamed. "I don't know how on earth you guys can do this to him. Have you no souls?"

It wasn't a matter of soul with them, of course; it was a matter of entertainment. When she looked at their faces and saw no remorse, she threw what was left of the piece back into the pan and shoved it into the face of Andy Vellinga.

"I won't have people treating others like this—not while I work here," she said. "Now get out!"

Even Will looked mystified.

Only once in the history of the institution had anyone been thrown out of the bowling alley in the middle of the day (it happens at night frequently), and that time the job was accomplished by the police, who came in to end what was threatening to become a fistfight.

"Go on," she said, forcing Andy to take the pan into his hands. "This isn't even civilized," she said. "This isn't Christian."

I won't say she thought of it right then—her mind having almost gone into a blur—but it's possible to excuse her violent anger on the basis of Christ's clearing the temple of the money-changers. Unfortunately, she'd crossed a line when she told Andy to leave, for the men in Tony's had, long before this fallen starlet returned to Neukirk, made these linoleum floors their own. And none of them, Andy Vellinga included, took kindly to being asked to leave.

Had it been a command merely to sit down and be about their own business, what happened might not have occurred. But Emily drew a line in the sand by demanding that Andy leave. And she wasn't about to back down. But neither was Andy Vellinga.

"Why don't you get back into the kitchen and quit preaching about something you don't understand?" he said.

I doubt that many women in Neukirk would have taken that kind of reprimand and turned the other cheek. Emily certainly didn't.

I won't excuse what she screamed at him then, but neither will I write it. Just think the worst, because the words brought a heavy blush to the faces of Tony's crowd and stopped them, once again, dead in their tracks. No giggling, no back talk, even though there was close to a dozen of them and only one of her.

Will Kruse stood up in the middle of all that silence, still swishing his mouth out with his tongue. The battle lines were set, as they say, but he stopped the war by raising his arms, like Moses, and handing over the victory to the men.

"They didn't mean no harm," he told her. "Now give me back my cake."

There was no place for Emily to go but home, so that's where she went. She walked to the back, stripped off her apron, threw it on the counter where the cooks read the orders, and walked out—not out the back door, which would have been easier, but out the front door—down past the counter, past the cash register up front, and then, in something the men called a righteous strut, right down the forty-foot walkway that separates the lunch counter from the front door, chin raised, shoulders back.

Credit her with this: she waited until she got home to scream again. She walked right down Main Street in that same pose, with that same strut—people gawking from both sidewalks, cars nearly whacking each other at the stop light—marched four blocks south to the Van Voorst home, walked up the driveway to the back door, when she could have taken the front, climbed the back stairs, went in through the kitchen, turned into the dining room and passed the shelves of books she'd set there only the day before, then threw herself down on the couch in the living room and just plain screamed into the pillows.

I don't have to tell you what she thought about Neukirk.

Postscript. If Emily could have seen what happened at Tony's after she left, it might well have restored some of her faith in humanity, if not Neukirk. Andy Vellinga picked up the cake pan, looked around at his buddies, and walked out. Three guys went up to Will Kruse and slapped him on the back, as if what he'd done was something heroic. The fact is, the place cleared out in less than ten minutes, and none of them said much as they left. They wore the oval faces of children caught with their hands in the cookie jar.

Now it would take a good deal more than Emily Doorn turning the air blue at the bowling alley to beget a revival in Neukirk. But she would have been happy the way it turned out, because as she lay there on the couch—half embarrassed, half in rage—all she could see was those men dying of laughter, telling the story over and over, repeating the very words she'd screamed.

When finally she looked up, at least ten minutes later, she saw open boxes all over the place and told herself that her laziness was a blessing because she couldn't live there anymore, not in Neukirk. Norm Visser was right.

She stood slowly and wiped her eyes with the back of her hands, then went to the dining room and sat on the floor, her legs beneath her, and started to put the books she'd carted along from

LA, the books she'd already stacked on the shelves, back into the boxes.

When she heard the back door open, she ran upstairs to the bathroom because she didn't want her kids to see her face streaked the way it was. She stood there at the mirror, just as she had the night before, wetted a washcloth, and held it, warm, to her eyes, breathing in slowly to get her breath back.

"Rebecca," she said, assuming it was her daughter.

There was no answer.

She listened for some sound from the kitchen—the ring of refrigerator shelves when Rebecca would put back the pitcher of Kool-Aid, the scrape of a chair along the tile, the sound of water running in the sink—anything.

"Rebecca," she said again.

Still no answer.

She put down the washcloth and folded it neatly, questioning whether or not she'd even heard the back door. She might not have, given her state of mind. For the first time, she laughed a bit at the whole thing, at the way it had ripped her up. She looked back in the mirror, smoothed her hair, pulled loose strands behind her ears, took a deep breath to collect herself, blew it out hard, straightened her shoulders, reminded herself of what she'd already gone through in California. She told herself that small-town lunacy didn't amount to anything, that it was just proof of the idiocy of these men and she shouldn't let it get to her.

She walked out of the bathroom, confident that what she'd just experienced was an irritation at best, a mosquito bite in comparison to what she'd been through since Norm's revelations. She came down the steps and turned around the banister, looked at the piano sitting there with the old hymnal still on the rack. She stopped for a moment, as if to brace herself with the resolve of knowing that she had much greater problems than a malicious practical joke.

In the dining room, she saw the boxes where she'd already stuffed back some of the books she'd just last night put on the shelves, and when she looked up toward the kitchen, she saw, standing in front of her, none other than Will Kruse.

"I knocked," he said, nodding with each word, "but nobody came."

All she knew was that he was bigger than she was.

"I come to tell you that they didn't mean no harm," he said. "It was all in fun."

Twenty feet, at least, between them.

"They told me to come tell you," he said. "They told me I ought to say it was okay with me. It's my birthday," he said, giggling.

She didn't know whether to hate them more or not. Right now they'd be sitting back at Tony's laughing because this boy was here trying to apologize.

"They told you to come?" she said.

"Andy told me. He left just like you said, and then so did everybody else. And when I walked out, Andy picked me up in his truck, like he does." He smiled, obviously pleased. "He said to tell you they were sorry for what they did."

"To you?"

"No, not to me," he said. "To you?"

"To me?" she said, incredulous. "What about to you?"

"Me don't matter," he said, laughing.

It took every bit of Emily Doorn's best character to come closer to Will Kruse, a measure of strength that could rise only from sources other than herself. She held out her arm, as if to shake hands.

"Do you think they're really sorry," she said, taking his hand in both of hers. "Do you think they mean it?"

"I'm sure," he said, pleased.

"You think they hate me?"

"They're probably still laughing about the way you swore," he told her. "Where'd you ever learn words like that—a woman like you?"

"I shouldn't have said all of that," she told him.

"That was something," he said, not about to let her hands go.

"I'm sorry," she said. "I really am. But I think it was wrong to play that trick."

His jaw jutted out in a way that made his teeth uneven in his mouth, and his tongue rolled slowly from one corner of his lips to the other.

"I didn't get no other cake," he said.

Then she hugged him. But maybe she shouldn't have, she thought, when his hands drew her toward him like steel belts.

"Tell you what, Will," she said, over his shoulder. "I'll make you something myself. You come over later, and I'll have a little something. My kids'll be here, and we'll have a party."

He still didn't let go of her.

"Okay," she said, pulling away. "You come back pretty soon," she said. "You hear me. I got to bake something yet." She was speaking to him the way she talked to Rebecca, she thought. "I have to throw something together and we'll have a party—you and me and the kids."

"What time?" he said.

She looked through the hallway toward the kitchen clock.

"An hour or so," she said, "something like that." She wondered if he could tell time until he looked at his watch.

The look on his face turned boyish and innocent, a smile of joy and thanks.

"Sure," he said. "I'd like that."

"You just go now and you do whatever you do in the afternoons—"

"I never do too much," he said.

"Well, you just do it, you hear? Because I can't have people in my kitchen when I'm baking a cake, see? I can't have it."

"I make pancakes," he said.

"It's not the same as cake," she said. "Whenever I bake I've got to get my kids out of the kitchen. You know how that is, Will, you got to concentrate."

He looked at her emptily.

"Go on," she said, and she took his arms and spun him around in the doorway, then aimed him out the door of the kitchen and down the steps to the back door. "You can come back, okay?"

"Where'd you ever learn those words?" he said from the back door. "You work on an elevator once? I used to work on the elevator—when they were putting it up in town. You know, the big one. I worked on that."

"Did you?" she said.

"Sure, I did. It was hot." He raised his eyebrows as if she should be amazed.

"Will," she said, "listen. If you see Andy, you tell him for me, okay—you tell him, 'No hard feelings,' . . . 'no hard feelings'?"

"He ain't mad," Will said. "I seen him mad already, and he ain't mad."

"You're sure?" she said.

He nodded at least a half dozen times. "He ain't mad," he said again. "Everybody likes you down there. They don't want you to quit."

Maybe she could have hugged him again, but he was at the bottom of the stairs.

Emily had more than one reason to call Norm Visser. When he'd left that morning—out of the back door and looking both ways, like a child crossing a busy street—they hadn't taken much time to talk. Now she'd been to the hospital once again, learned about what her mother knew about Meg— things she thought Norm didn't know himself. She'd blown up at the men at Tony's, then stormed out, putting her job in jeopardy. Now Will Kruse was going to show up, walk in without knocking, and sit at her table waiting for attention. And she was still afraid of him, even though she wished she weren't.

What really scared her was the possibility of not being able to find Norm. Just because he was single didn't mean he would be home. He gave a few singing lessons, taught a little tennis, and played golf himself, he said, when he wasn't running around worrying about community theater.

She was lucky. She found him home and came right out and told him: Will Kruse was coming over, a result of a series of things she didn't want to explain over the phone, and she said she was somewhat afraid of him. "Do you call him a man or a boy?" she asked him.

"Good question," he said.

"I'll tell you about it," she said. "When you get here, I'll tell you. Poor guy. I feel sorry for him."

"What on earth happened?" he asked.

She sat on a stool in the kitchen, pulling *Betty Crocker* out of the kitchen cupboard.

"I grossed out the whole blessed place," she said.

"You what?"

"I cussed 'em—the whole bunch of 'em," she told him.

"You're kidding—"

"I'm not."

"I can't believe it. Cussed?"

"It was wonderful while it lasted," she said. "But now I'm sick about it."

"Em," he said, "put the cookbook away. I'll pick up something at the bakery. I'm coming right over."

"Don't wait so long," she said.

She flipped open the cover and picked the tab that said "Desserts," then fanned through the pages slowly to locate a recipe for a cake. Glancing at the pictures made her weary, less of a mom certainly for never baking up something that looked so perfect. She poked at the ingredients of one recipe with her finger, followed the list down, then realized that it was stupid to think of baking a cake from scratch when she likely had a mix right in the cupboard somewhere.

Mix? she thought. For heaven's sake, I've got extra desserts coming out of my ears.

She slapped the cover shut, jammed the cookbook back in the cupboard above the counter, and went downstairs to the freezer, where she'd stowed all the extras that had come out of nowhere during that first week.

The door wheezed open and her first thought was for the half dozen or so cake and pie pans that women in Neukirk had to be missing by this time, like picking up the family room for the first time in too long and discovering a wealth of overdue library books.

"I don't need guilt," she told herself. They should have realized all of their sweetness would turn her house into a dessert shop; and she couldn't feed this stuff night and day to her kids. Of course they'd know that. They'd understand. My goodness, they were mothers too.

She pulled out a cake pan with a transparent cover, revealing perfect white frosting. What did she care what flavor the cake was? What did Will care? He wasn't going to tell her that he wanted angel food, for pity's sake.

She lifted off the lid and touched the frosting carefully with her fingers, as if by some fluke the cake might not be frozen. She could put it out on the deck, she thought, let it sit in the sun for awhile—cover on—and by the time Will came back it would be edible.

Candles, she thought.

She ran back upstairs, the cake's iciness nearly numbing her fingers. Where on earth would she find candles? And why did she ever take that job anyway? She should have waited another two weeks and moved in completely—cleaned up all these yawning boxes all over, messes in every last room.

She filed through an inventory in her mind, but it was huge, having gone through almost everything she owned in the last week. Candles simply didn't register. They were in a cupboard above the grill in the old house, she thought, along with the silver serving dishes and the fancy napkins.

She put the cake down on the counter, looked out the patio door at the square picnic table, and wondered whether it would get too hot.

He won't care, she thought. Will's not going to be fussy—he's a man.

All she needed was candles. She had to have candles. She should have told Norm to pick some up somewhere on his way over. And then it hit her: NORM WAS BRINGING CAKE. "I'll stop at the bakery," he'd said.

Was she losing her mind?

She looked up at the clock, drew a breath, and picked up the cold cake pan, then swept open the patio door and set it outside anyway. Maybe she'd send it home with Will—his own birthday cake, something he could eat all by himself. Double the fun.

What about the pan? she thought. Could she trust Will to bring back the pan? After all, it belonged to someone else. She picked up the cake again and lifted it enough to see a piece of adhesive tape stuck to the bottom. "Please return to Alyce Bakker," it said.

Alyce Bakker, she thought. Heavyset woman with a beautiful face and lovely skin. She'd remembered her from years ago. Meg's age, maybe a little older. Homecoming queen. That's right—two years older, because Meg was a freshman attendant that year, and she'd been so proud because her sister was up there in front of the whole town at the coronation. Three years old, she thought. I must have been only three years old then. Were there other things she knew if she could just jog her memory?

Meg.

She looked at the clock again and realized that she didn't have to go crazy here. It wasn't that big a deal, and already there were two cakes where before there was only styrofoam.

Meg, she thought.

And how exactly could she tell Norm that he was wrong about her parents? That when he'd lied to them the night of the accident—when he protected them from the truth—they could well have guessed he wasn't telling them everything. They knew something or there wouldn't have been that letter. What was the name? Mike something. Mike Stellinga—that was it. A youth pastor, Nancy had said, somebody everyone liked.

Once more she looked up at the clock. She had a lot of time. Maybe she should clean up a little, she thought, looking around at her kitchen.

She needed to get the kids, of course. They'd be with Jason Kamphoff. He'd been helpful, baby-sitting the kids and leaving notes if he took them somewhere. She looked out the back toward the barn, turned open the window to see if she could hear voices. Maybe they were next door; they loved the sandbox there.

Benjamin would not believe how freely she let the kids come and go here. But then Benjamin never had understood Neukirk. He'd never seen a place like this—called it a kind of cult, without a single charismatic leader.

They'd been married in California, of course, because Emily knew very well that she couldn't expect Neukirk to throw open its heart to a Jewish guy from West Los Angeles. They'd been married in California because it was convenient: only a magistrate, the whole business of religion left on hold. But her parents had insisted on a celebration in Neukirk, something they set up themselves, having felt cheated out of not paying for the wedding of their only remaining daughter. They'd had it at the Wooden Shoe Restaurant, the best broasted chicken in town— nothing kosher within miles.

There were so many reasons for people not to talk to Benjamin, she thought: a city boy from California, educated at Stanford, rich, articulate, brimming with knowledge and anxious to discuss current affairs, dark-skinned, curly black hair, always well-dressed, handsome enough to make everyone in town nervous around him. And he was Jewish.

She stood at the back window and looked at the patio behind the house across the alley, where a young girl in a bikini lay in the sun, the edges of her bath towel draping over both sides of a lounge chair. Beside her sat one of those cylindrical drinking things fast-food places gave away and a Windex spray bottle full of water. Perched perfectly on her thin triangular bottom was the Walkman whose buds she had stuck in her ears.

Benjamin would have never believed it. If he were there just then, looking out the window with her, he'd shake his head. The only backyard fences in Neukirk were the ones the law made mandatory, the ones that surrounded swimming pools.

If he would have called right then and asked to speak to the kids, and if she'd have to tell him that she didn't really know where they were, he would explode. That's how little he understood. He was so much of what Neukirk never was and never would be. She wondered if maybe that was why she'd married him, or at least part of it.

She left the window open, went out the back door, and walked toward the barn. Even though a massive ash tree towered over the whole backyard, there was always enough sky in Iowa to read the weather. Huge billowy clouds seemed to linger up there longer than they usually did, but the long branches of the ash were barely moving.

There were times—and that moment was one of them—when Emily Doorn had to pinch herself to remember that she was back in a hometown that seemed at once so familiar that everyone was family and yet so different that she'd never felt, even in California, quite so alone. She stood out on the wide cement apron laid years ago in front of the barn door, now piled with a ton of trash she'd been hauling out. Another job left unfinished—so much to do.

She'd quit Tony's, she thought. It was silly of her to want to work right away. Tony would call any minute now, wondering whether she was coming back in. She'd tell him there was too much to do in her life right now, that maybe once everything had settled down she'd be back again. What had happened was proof she was trying to do too much.

She walked into the garage stall and listened. Voices seeped through the cracks of the ceiling, and she knew Rebecca and Sam were upstairs with Jason. They were talking quietly; she couldn't catch any words.

When the Van Voorst house had been described to her, when she remembered it standing where it did on Main Street, she remembered the barn specifically and thought of it as something appealing. A barn for her kids—in Neukirk.

"Guys," she called.

"Mom?" Sam said. "You home, Mom?"

"I came home early," she told them.

There was some movement above her as the kids scrambled to the hole where they climbed up into what once was a hayloft.

"I came to tell you that we're going to have some cake pretty soon," she said. "I'll call you."

She thought about telling Jason to go home, but she knew Norm was coming, that she had things to say to him she didn't want to say in front of the children.

"Right now?" Rebecca said, almost mournfully.

"No. You can keep playing. I'll call you," she told them. "I'll come out and get you pretty soon when it's ready."

She walked back outside and looked over the horribly dirty top of an old formica table, spotted with the marks her hands left on it when she'd dragged it out of the back. A coaster wagon, orange with rust, two decades beyond repair, she'd shoved beneath the table. An old hand cultivator—she didn't know what to call it really—one steel wheel and a pair of long handles above a set of prongs that curved forward like ram's horns. Maybe an antique, she'd thought.

"You never know when you might want something exactly like that," her father would say. "And then you ain't got it and you wish like anything that you had."

All stuff that had value to somebody, she thought. Stuff that someone, Mrs. Van Voorst or somebody else, just couldn't throw away.

And who knew what new old things were being discovered by her own kids right now, upstairs in the barn? Junk someone else would look at someday and wonder about the same way— why on earth would anyone keep this stuff?—not knowing that once upon a time three kids in the loft of that old barn thought it some kind of treasure.

"Kids?" she called, from the front of the barn, "you having fun?"

There was no answer. Maybe they were surprised she was still there.

"Sure, Mom," Sam said. "Of course."

Of course, she thought.

"Mom?" Rebecca said, "what kind of cake?"

She didn't know. "You'll have to wait," she said. It'll be a surprise."

"Chocolate?" Sam said.

"I told you," she said again. "It'll be a surprise."

How easy it is, she thought, to lie to kids.

Norm wanted to know every detail of what had happened at the bowling alley and what exactly she had said—the very words—and she couldn't remember them exactly.

"I'm not proud of it," she told him.

"I'll hear it anyway," he said. "Whether it comes from you or not, you can bet I'll hear it."

Neukirk's Main Street has no room for parking, so he'd driven up the driveway and left his pickup right in front of the junk outside of the barn.

"I'm already a fallen woman," she said, standing at the kitchen window. "And now this. Are you sure you want to be associated with me?"

"Reputation, my dear," he said from behind her, "'is an idle and most false imposition; oft got without merit, and lost without deserving.'"

"I'm supposed to know that, I take it—"

"*Othello*." He was standing at the table, beside the patio door. "The idea of you standing there in front of all those yokels, berating them in their own tongue—that's rich."

"I shouldn't have," she said.

"You're starting to think too much like one of us," he told her. "I thought in all that beach time the whole business of 'what you *should* have done' would have washed out of you."

"What do you mean?" she said.

"'Thus conscience does make cowards of us all; and thus the native hue of resolution is sicklied o'er with the pale cast of thought—'"

"Hamlet wasn't from Neukirk."

"Good," he said. "You're improving. And now, for a free trip to Sioux City, how about this? 'Tomorrow, and tomorrow, and tomorrow, creeps in this petty pace—'"

"*Macbeth*," she said. "Best female role in Shakespeare—"

"Kate's no dummy," he said.

"Kate?"

"*Taming of the Shrew*. You're eliminated, by the way. You missed what—two out of four?"

"Always the teacher, aren't you?"

He sat down; she could hear him. "No," he said, "I'm not always the teacher."

She turned around and looked at him, then glanced away, picked up a dishtowel and dried her hands, even though they weren't wet.

"It's something more, isn't it?" he said. "Must I come in the kitchen, or are you going to sit over here at the table?"

"Stay over there," she said. "It's more comfortable that way."

Oddly, she wanted to hurt him. She didn't know why exactly, but it wasn't right of him to think life should simply go on after what he'd told her last night, and after everything she'd learned about what he didn't even know.

"I'm being glib," he said. "I shouldn't be."

The cake he'd bought—with a bouquet of frosting flowers and "Happy Birthday" in a flowing hand—sat on the countertop between them. She'd found the candles in the dining room, in a box that held her formal silverware.

"Norm," she said, "who was Mike Stellinga?"

"Name is familiar," he said.

"A preacher or something?"

"A preacher, sure," he said. "He was a student preacher, an intern, they call them. Long ago already, long ago. My goodness a long time ago. Sure, I remember him. His hair was a bit too long—"

"After Meg died?" she said.

"No, before the accident."

"A young guy?" she asked.

"I can picture him because I remember his hair—you know, Beatles-ish." He brought his hand up to his head. "I just remember that he was a young guy, kind of cool."

"Did you know him?"

"He was kind of in-between," he said. "He was a preacher, and yet he wasn't, because he was still a student. But he spent some time here. Not a whole year, I don't think. Maybe half a year. Good guy. Kids liked him—I remember that."

She came up to the countertop and leaned over the cake.

"There was a note in my mother's Bible from him—from after the accident. I can read it to you." She went over to the refrigerator and picked it up from where she'd left it on the top.

"Where'd you get it?" he said.

"In my mother's Bible. There's a little envelope glued in the back cover, and there were these two notes—this one and another one with a Bible verse, something about Meg's profession of faith—"

He got up from the table and reached for it, but an odd fear arose in her, something that warned her that he shouldn't hold it in his hands.

"Let me read it," he said.

She pulled it back.

"Em," he said.

For a sharp, uneasy moment, she found him distant.

"Just let me read it, Emily," he said.

She gave it up. This was the man, after all, who Nancy

claimed had been the only other kid in town back then with the eyes of a rebel. He was the guy who'd been smoking dope with Meg the night she died. He was the guy who'd told a lie to her parents. This was the guy everybody thought got Meg pregnant.

"So what?" he said after he'd read it.

"He knew some things, Norm," she said. "This guy knew that Meg wasn't as straight as—"

"As what?"

"As you claim my parents thought she was."

He looked down at the note again. "University of Illinois," he said. "I remember. He became a campus pastor after he left here. That's right. I remember that."

"What else do you remember?" she said.

He looked up. "What do you mean?"

"You lied to my parents," she said. "How do I know you're telling me the truth? Maybe you don't want to hurt me."

He seemed stunned. "With what?"

"With everything—I don't know. With the whole story."

He tossed the note down on the countertop and sat back in the chair just a foot away from the counter.

"I don't know what I did to deserve that," he told her. "You believe I didn't tell you the truth?"

"What happened that night?" she said. "What really happened?"

"I swear, Emily—I'll swear on a Bible. It was just like I told you. My word," he said, "I've been sweating all day long wondering if you'd ever want to talk to me again. I mean, once it all sunk in, I thought you'd blame me—"

"I don't blame you," she told him.

"Then why am I getting attacked?" he said. "I don't understand what's going on—"

"*They* knew something about Meg. My parents knew she wasn't all square or something—I don't know. But that note makes it clear they had deep hurts. Not only because she was gone, Norm, but because they worried about her—"

"About her soul."

"That's right, about her soul."

He rubbed his fingers across his eyes, once, twice, three times, then kept them there.

"They had to know something," she said. "You don't snow parents that easily."

He dropped his hands. "Maybe it's what *I* wanted to believe," he said.

"Why?"

"I don't know. Maybe because I just assumed for all these years that if I'd lied to protect them, I was doing the right thing."

It made perfect sense. She took the cake in two hands and squared it on the counter.

"Nancy told me about cheerleading and about—"

"Nancy?" he said.

"The nurse—Nancy Greiman. She told me how Meg quit cheerleading and how she told the others—and what she told them. And she told me about Memorial Day—the black armband."

He tipped his head back. "Meg did some public stuff, I remember. I don't know what happened. I remember telling her some things. She was so smart, Em. Meg was about the smartest girl—the smartest *woman*—I ever knew. And after I told her some things—I mean, about the war and racism . . . shoot, you don't understand that, do you?" He turned away, put a hand over his mouth, then raised his eyebrows and started in again. "After we'd talk sometimes and I'd tell her what I was reading and hearing, she'd sit beside me with that strange silence in her, as if everything were going in and staying there."

"I don't understand," Emily said.

"I don't even know if *I* meant what I said back then," he said. "I don't know if the real reason I was telling her all that radical stuff was because I wanted her radical or just because I wanted her."

"What are you saying? Wanted to sleep with her?"

He stood quickly, took one step toward the patio door. "I don't think I'm up to this," he said.

117

"You're not leaving. I'm not letting you go, Norm. Don't think about walking out."

He stood at the door, but he wouldn't look at her.

"Tell me," she said. "You weren't lying, were you? I mean about the accident. But you're not telling me everything."

"I wasn't lying about the accident. We were high—both of us. Like I said, she'd scored some stuff at that place where we watched the convention on TV, and she had it on her. She was smoking—we were smoking—on those back roads."

He stood there with one hand up at his mouth.

"Norm," she said, "sit and tell me. I deserve the truth. We're talking about my sister. My mother can't tell me anything." She came around the counter and took his shoulders, brought him around the corner to a chair and pushed him down. "You aren't telling me everything. It didn't all happen as simply as you say, Norm. My parents knew."

"I don't know what," he said. "I'm as surprised about this as you are. I mean, there were some things that happened her last year in high school—some things that she only mentioned in passing. I suppose you're right. She couldn't snow your parents completely. I remember the armband."

"What happened, Norm?" she said.

He sat almost stiffly in the chair, hands down at his sides. "I can only tell you this much: that for all these years I've felt responsible for her death."

"I know that," Emily said. "We've been all through that."

"In other ways," he said. "In a way, I think, I used her."

"Someone to sleep with—"

"That too, but more. Something happened to Meg during that last year of high school. She was so young; but all the way though, Em, your sister was always aggressive—more aggressive than other girls. I don't know how to put it. She joined church when she was just a kid. Nobody else did that. Everyone else joined together, when we could hold each other's hands. Not Meg—"

"What is it?" she said when he paused.

"That last six months we were together, she went right beyond me," he said. "It's like when you teach really talented kids. You can feel it. You know that these kids have so much more than you ever had."

"Meg?"

"She like grew beyond me. She was maybe worse than I ever was. I mean, more radical. It sounds so dumb to say it that way now, so strange. But she was more angry about things than I ever was, Em. And in some ways, after she died, I blamed myself. Not just because she died in my car when I was driving and we were both high," he said. "It was like I made her what she became."

"You made her angry?"

"I killed your sister," he said.

She pulled out another chair and sat half-facing him. "You didn't tell her to wear the armband?" she said.

"I would have been too scared to do something like that myself," he said. "Em, if I was the big-time hippie radical I tried to be, why would I come home to Neukirk at all? Neukirk thought Vietnam was another Midway Island, only more gooks to be wiped out. Why would I come back here?"

"You couldn't control her?"

He tried to speak carefully, nodding with almost every word. "Something happened to her," he said.

"But the point is that my parents knew," she told him.

"I really don't know what they knew about Meg," he said stiffly. "I suppose I was happy thinking the best."

She put both hands on his knees, then ran her fingers up to his hands, took them in hers. "How can I find this guy?" she asked him. "How can I find this student preacher?"

Norm himself made the three calls it took to find Mike Stellinga. First to Mabel Frens who, he knew, kept scrapbooks of every last news article that had even the least bit to do with the church: marriages, funerals, building projects, preachers coming and going. Mabel was eighty-some, but she remembered Mike Stellinga, and somehow she knew that he had left the ministry. ("And he was so good with kids. Oh my, but everyone loved him. Except the Reverend Daniels, of course. But you must remember, Norman. That was about your time too, wasn't it? You went to school with my Henk?")

If anyone would know, Mabel said, it would be Herm and Carol Brink, because Mike Stellinga had lived with them for the six months he'd been in Neukirk. And she thought she'd heard Carol say one time at ladies' guild—years ago already, long before that group disbanded—that every year she got a card from Mike at Christmas.

Call two.

"Why yes, Norman, of course I remember Michael. He was such a fine boy, so serious and everything. Oh, we thought that hair of his was a little out-of-place, but then those were the times, weren't they?

"I have a whole pile of old cards I rarely look at, and I don't know why on earth I keep them. But then again, you never know, do you? Let me look once. Here they are. And what else here? Ach, stupid of me. All kinds of coupons in this drawer—from 1974. What good are they, Norman?

"Here, here. Michael. Married, you know. Yeah, when he was here he was single, but he married. I didn't know the girl, but I think Herm and I got invited. It was so far away though, and towards the last Herm hated to drive like anything in the world.

"Yeah, here, here. He left the ministry, you know that of course. When I wrote him and told him how bad we all need good preachers, then he told me that he felt called to try to help people who have special problems. Said that was a ministry too—and it is, don't you think?

"Yes, here. Omaha. I have it written on the card because I never save envelopes, thank goodness, or I wouldn't have any room in these drawers."

Call number three. Directory Assistance. Nebraska. Omaha.

"We have an office phone listed. But I'm sorry, sir, the residence has an unlisted number."

"Give me the office," Norm said, and as the number spilled out in the computerlike voice, Norm sketched it on the scratch pad Emily put in front of him.

Omaha. Three hours away.

"I've got to go," Emily said.

"You can call him," Norm told her. "You can sit right here in Neukirk and talk to him on the telephone."

"I've got this feeling," she said. "I've got this sense that I'm supposed to see him."

"What if he was in Fairbanks?"

"It's only Omaha," she said. "Thank goodness it's only Omaha."

She ripped the page with the number off the pad and picked up the note from her mother's Bible.

"I don't really want to step in your way, Em," Norm said. "Really, I don't. But I wonder what exactly you'll gain by all this? What do you think he can tell you?"

"I need to know what my mother knows—"

"Em, in the shape your mom's in, she's not troubled by all of this."

"How can you know?"

He realized immediately that he had misspoken. "I'm sorry."

"Meg was my only sister," she said. "Can you blame me?"

Will showed up a few minutes earlier than the hour Emily had given him. He knocked, didn't ring the bell, even though it worked. He knocked hard, in fact, almost angrily; but when she saw his smile she knew it was simply eagerness. What she noticed right away, even though she was distracted and wished now she hadn't asked him, was that he'd changed his shirt, had dressed up for his birthday party.

He'd come to the back door, and when he came up the steps and spotted Norm, his smile widened—more people at his party.

She walked out to the barn immediately and called the kids.

"What you guys doing?" she said when they tumbled down the ladder. She stood at the bottom and grabbed them both as they clung to the worn steps. "What you playing?"

Sammy's black T-shirt—he insisted on wearing it, his favorite, even though she told him it would be hot—was tinged with dust, his arms patchy with dirt that clung to a haze of sweat.

"We got a clubhouse," he said. "We're building this place upstairs."

She lifted him down, set him on the floor, and waited for Rebecca.

"Think we can eat up there?" he said. "Sometime we want to eat upstairs."

That they were filthy after playing in the loft didn't really surprise her. Nobody'd been up there for years. Besides, it didn't matter where they played, whatever she dressed them in ended up filthy at the end of the day. They'd found every sandbox in the neighborhood after two days in town, and sometimes Jason had them digging worms in any of a dozen places. He'd promised to take them fishing.

Rebecca was younger, a little less sure of herself on the steps. At first, her going up the steps nailed onto the wall inside the barn had worried Emily, but Rebecca had scrambled up, following her brother. It had been monkey-see, monkey-do with her, ever since she was old enough to play with her brother. When Sam got a new tricycle, one with a seat that lifted to reveal a little compartment, he was so proud of it that whenever someone would come around, he'd have to take the seat off and point at that cubbyhole beneath it. The moment he'd show it off, Rebecca would scramble after her little four-wheel walker, haul it out, and lift the seat in exactly the same way, even though there was no secret place.

She'd wanted the children together, she remembered—

didn't want either of them to grow up alone, like she had. And she had never second-guessed herself on one idea: that as far as her kids were concerned, coming back to Neukirk was the best move she could make.

She grabbed her daughter around the stomach, beneath the little shell of frills that buttoned up at the top of her back. Rebecca had begun picking out her clothes at least a year ago already, when she was four; this morning Emily had wondered whether the old frilly playsuit was the right choice, but Rebecca had insisted. Persistent, independent.

"What you guys doing?" she said again.

"What kind of cake?" Rebecca said.

She was wiry, like her brother—like their father, Emily thought. Sam was almost a clone. The only bit of his mother, it seemed, was a set of long fingers and toes. "Better for piano," Benjamin had said as they'd examined him, inch by inch, seven years ago in the hospital room. Both children had been born with a full head of hair—dark hair.

"Two cakes," she said. "One cake for Will—the man whose birthday it is—and one for us."

"Who's Will?" asked Sam.

Jason came down, and she stood beneath him, as if to be there should he slip. She watched his tight muscles flex as he reached for each step.

"You want to stay, Jason?" she said, backing away to give him room.

He made it to the bottom, slapped the dust off his fingers, then rubbed his hands on his pants.

"I'll be going," he said, almost as if embarrassed. He didn't seem to have his father's pushiness or his ready smile, but then he was a kid, an adolescent.

"You're welcome to stay," she told him. "We've got plenty of cake."

He walked toward the open barn door, not looking back. "I got to be going anyway," he said, looking down at his hands, then at Norm's car in the driveway.

"You want to wash up first?" she said. "How about a piece of cake to go?"

He kept his eyes averted, shook his head almost nervously.

"I'll call you, okay?" she said. "I'm not sure when I'll be working again, so I'll just call."

He wiped his forehead with the back of his hand, nodded, and was gone.

She caught the kids before they could get into the house, slapped the thick edges of dust off their clothes, and held their hands beneath the garden hose.

"Now don't wipe your hands on your clothes either," she told them. "I'll get you a towel when we get inside." She made them take off their shoes in the back hall.

"Whose birthday is it?" Sam said.

"A man you don't know," she said quietly, one finger up to her lips. "And he's here already. It's his cake."

Sam bent his head forward and mimicked his mother's hush. "How come we got a party for someone we don't know?" he said.

"It's not a party really. Just cake," she said. "He didn't have anybody to give him a cake."

"What kind of cake?" Rebecca said again.

"Mr. Visser brought it," she told them. "I don't even know."

They crowded against her once the three of them came up the back stairs and stood in the kitchen. Norm they'd met before, but Will was a stranger. Rebecca held on to her mother's shorts as Emily introduced them.

Will didn't care a whole lot who was going to be at his party; it was clear he wanted to get on with the cake.

The two kids sat on either side of their mother, across from Norm. Will sat at the head of the table in the captain's chair, grinning.

"When I was little we used to have hats," he said, not to anyone in particular. "I remember we had hats with tight little strings—" He pointed up towards the spot beneath his chin where they would have pulled tight.

Emily thought it was a mark of the way Neukirk had begun to work on her children that they didn't take long to warm to this stranger. They began to look up at her approvingly when he tried to say something funny or something aimed particularly at them. One difference between small towns and city life was that here kids learned to trust each other, a quality city people would call naivete—and maybe it was. But she considered it a good naivete, even though it was a kind of trust that would likely be broken someday. She'd always thought it was better for kids to trust first and then learn distrust, rather than simply picking up fear as a way of life.

It was a good birthday party, and Emily felt the grace that blesses those who offer graciousness to others. Will charged through a gigantic piece of bakery cake, then looked up as longingly as a hungry house dog who knows better than to bark.

"I'll bet you want more," Emily said, and he smiled hungrily.

The moment she laid that second piece on Will's plate, Emily knew what Sam was thinking. "And *you're* going to have to stop with that one," she told him, pointing with the spatula. "It won't be long until we eat." She turned her wristwatch toward him, and he scowled.

Will Kruse, despite his joy, was not a talker. Emily tried a volley of questions to get him to open up, but it seemed that what interested him more than anything was merely being in their house with them—that, and the cake. He seemed content just being part of the circle. "Are you working somewhere, Will?" "Are you having a good summer?" "Do you have a girlfriend?" Nothing really seemed to engage him.

Her fear lessened as he sat there in the kitchen with the kids and Norm, but his silence still made her uncomfortable. She sensed that whatever was going on in his mind was not being shared—and it wasn't going to be.

Norm didn't say much at all, although occasionally he'd poke his fork at Rebecca's cake and force her bottom lip to curl at him menacingly.

"What are you building upstairs in the barn?" Emily finally asked the kids, hoping to get some kind of conversation going.

"We got a store up there," Sam said. "We got a grocery store."

"A grocery store?"

"Not a real one," Rebecca said.

"Just empty boxes," Sam said. "Just play."

"You having fun?" she asked.

Rebecca shook her head yes. Her cake was in shambles, the frosting off to the side of the plate, the cake picked apart as if she were mining it, crumbs afloat in melted ice cream. She looked at Will, then at her mother. "Doesn't he get any presents?" she asked.

Emily hadn't thought of presents, of course, so she turned the question on Will. "Did you get any presents, Will?"

He nodded almost triumphantly.

"What'd you get?" Sam said.

Will looked around at each face, as if he were worried. Then, without saying a word, he reached down for the backpack he'd carried in, unbuttoned the flap, and pulled out a Walkman, the wires for the earphones still knotted. He held it in his hands in front of him, then looked around at each face again, as if reading each individual reaction.

"That's great," Norm said. "Who'd you get it from?"

Will slid the earphones over his head and adjusted them to his ears, keeping the Walkman right up close to his face. "You turn it on right here," he said, indicating the switch with his thumb. "I'm going to buy some tapes. I got some already, but they're eight-track."

"I bet it really plays well," Emily said.

"From your parents, I bet," Norm said.

He shook his head. "Naahh," he said, laughing. "They don't like me listening to music."

"Your sister then," Norm said.

Will fiddled with the dial, then bobbed his head in time with music he turned up so loud that they could hear it themselves.

"Got it from Andy Vellinga," he said. "He gave it to me in his truck."

Emily wasn't far wrong in creating the scenario in her mind: Andy had given Will this present as he told him to go to Emily and apologize.

"Rechargeable batteries," Will said, holding up the Walkman like an ad man. "You plug them into the wall and you don't have to buy new ones all the time." He shook his head as if he were really on top of this.

"More cake?" Emily asked him.

His eyes furrowed. "Maybe a little one," he said. "It's my cake, isn't it?"

"Sure is," she told him. "I've even got another one for you." She turned in her chair and pointed at the cake pan on the patio. "You have to promise to bring back the pan, but if you want it you can have it."

"Great," he said, plunging into a smaller piece.

She was surprised that she'd ever been afraid of him. Sitting here at the table, he seemed no more dangerous than a child, his dark hair combed neatly behind his ears, a smile set proudly on his face, sugary frosting stretching in a threadlike ridge at either corner of his lips.

"Does he like to play ball, Mom?" Sam asked.

"Ask him yourself," she said.

Sam turned rather uneasily toward Will, eyes averted.

"Go on, ask him," Emily said.

"I got a new glove," Sam said. "When we moved from California, my dad bought me a new glove."

Will nodded.

"Maybe he'll play catch with you," Emily said. "Why don't you ask him?" She pointed at Will as if he were deaf.

Sam's forehead fell. He looked back up at his mother.

"He won't bite," she told him.

All this time, Will just kept smiling, kept playing along.

She nodded her head towards Will. "Maybe you ought to just ask him once. Maybe he'll play ball."

Sam stopped eating completely and laid his fork at the side of the plate. "You want to play some catch?" He kept staring at Will, not moving a muscle, as if the wrong answer might break him completely.

"I don't like to play in games," Will said, as though laughing at himself, "but I can play catch."

Sam beamed up at his mother.

"Why don't you go play some catch right now?" she said, knowing very well that Rebecca would tag along. "Mr. Visser and I have some things that we'd like to talk about."

"What things?" Rebecca said.

"Just some things is all."

"Secrets?"

"They aren't secrets," Emily told her, reaching down and squeezing her shoulder. "We don't have any secrets." She looked up at Norm, whose face seemed stoic.

"You want to play catch right now?" Sam said, pushing himself back from the table.

"Got to finish the cake here," Will said. "I'll play catch all right. You ever play pickle?"

When her son looked up at her with an emptiness in his eyes, she knew Will had no sense of her Sammy's age.

"He wonders if you've ever played a game he knows called pickle, Sam," she said. "I don't think you have, have you?"

He shook his head sadly, as if it were a fault he'd have rectified in a minute if he knew how.

"Maybe Will'll teach you," she said. "It's a lot of fun. We used to play it all the time when we were kids."

"Pickle?" Sam scrunched up his face.

"He'll show you," Emily pointed at Will.

"What're you going to talk about?" Rebecca said again. Emily looked at her daughter and realized she wasn't going to get out of this easily.

"I'm going to go to Omaha," she said.

"To where?" Rebecca said.

"Omaha. It's not so far away."

"What for?"

"I don't have my glove along," Will announced.

"I got one in the car," Norm told him.

"Where's Omaha?" Sam said.

"It's about what, Norm? Three hours away or so? I'm going to take a ride down there and talk to a man," Emily told them slowly.

"What do you have to talk about?" Sam said. "Are we going too?"

She looked up at Norm, and the seriousness in his eyes made it even more impossible for her to make up some line they'd fall for, even though she knew she could.

"About my sister," she said. "And no, you aren't going."

Sam looked confused. "You don't have a sister," he told her. "You just got Grandma."

She'd opened something she knew she couldn't close now, at least not easily. "I had a sister once, but she got killed."

"Who killed her?" Rebecca asked.

"Well, nobody killed her exactly," Emily told them. "She died in a car accident."

Both looked confused. Will kept eating cake, spearing perfectly square little bites.

"I want to talk to a man about her, a man who knew her," she said. "He lives in Omaha. He's a doctor."

"Was he her doctor?" Rebecca said.

"No," Emily told her.

"Then why do you want to talk to him?"

Emily picked up her fork and tapped it on the edge of the plate. "I never knew my sister," she said. "Her name was Meg."

"That's funny," Rebecca said.

"Meg—really Margaret."

"Margaret's a pretty name."

"She was pretty—"

"'Prettiest girl in town,'" Will said, out of nowhere.

She looked at Norm who shook his head. Will couldn't have known her. He wasn't more than twenty-three or four.

"Who's going to stay with us?" Rebecca said.

Emily hadn't even thought about that. After all, the whole thing had just come up—the phone call, locating the man. She ran through a day in her mind: she could leave early, get there by noon, in time for lunch maybe, an hour with him, no more, then back again, maybe by five.

"I'll get Jason, and I'll give you some money so you can eat dinner at the bowling alley—"

"Not Jason," Rebecca said.

"I won't be gone long," she told them. "I'll be back for supper for sure."

"Why not Jason?" Norm asked.

"You can buy tapes at Kmart for less than two bucks," Will said, his new Walkman in his hand.

"Why not Jason?" Norm asked again.

"He's so heavy," Rebecca said.

Emily's first thought was how hard it might be to try to find somebody else, how it would be difficult even to know where exactly to start. Of course, Norm had said once that he knew baby-sitters.

"He's too heavy?" Norm said.

"You know, when he crawls on me," she said. "I don't like him to crawl on me."

Emily fell so far, so fast, that for a moment she didn't trust her own sense of balance. She looked up at Norm, who was staring at Rebecca.

"Why does he crawl on you?" he said, almost playfully.

"Is there another cake here, really?" Will said.

Emily got to her feet quickly and brought the pan, cold as ice in her hands, from the patio to the table.

"Here it is," she said to Will, pushing it gently towards him. "It's all yours."

He burst out laughing.

"Emily," Norm said, and when the question came out of his mouth it was in a whole different voice than she'd ever heard from him. "How would it be if I played with the kids for awhile? I got a glove in the car."

She didn't know how to read him.

"I can talk to them while I play," he said, his whole face lit brightly. Only she could see his eyes.

"Maybe I should play too?" she said. "You think that would be okay, kids, if Mom plays catch too?"

"I was thinking of pickle," Will said. "Pickle's a lot of fun."

"Maybe he can stay with us, Mom?" Sam said, pointing at Will.

"I'll stay with you," Norm told them. "Shoot, I can stay right here in the house and you guys can play—and I'll be here."

"Aren't you going to play catch?" Sam said.

"I'll play catch, all right," Norm told him. "You want to play catch, Sam—we'll play catch."

"This is a great party," Will said.

Emily tried to keep cool.

"We can have Jason over too," Norm told Sam. "We can ask Jason to come over and play catch with us."

Sam wrinkled his nose. "He's so rough," he said.

"How rough?" Emily said.

"Sometimes I got to wrestle him—"

"Why?" Norm said.

"To get him off Rebecca," Sam said.

Not once in her life had she ever felt such hate, not even for Benjamin, not even after he'd left her, not even during the fights, not even when she'd found out about Sandra. She felt something like sickness reaching up the back of her throat.

"Jason does that a lot?" Norm said. "Does he bother Rebecca a lot?"

"Just sometimes," Sam said.

"We going to play pickle?" Will said.

Norm pointed out through the window. "My glove's on the seat in the truck, in the duffle bag. Why don't you grab it, Will?"

As if it were a worth a fortune, Will took the Walkman off the table and laid it perfectly in the backpack, shut the zipper slowly, and stood. He shifted the pack over to his left hand so he could carry his cake down the steps to the backdoor.

"You guys coming?" he said.

Sam looked up for his mother's approval. Rebecca flipped the dishtowel her mother had wound around her up and over her head, then followed her brother down the stairs and out the backdoor.

There was no question about what both of them feared. Emily bit her lip and looked away, out the patio door.

"I don't know what to say," she said.

"You *should* be thinking what you're thinking, Em," he told her. "It's not wrong to think that way. It's not wrong at all. It's the right way."

She brought one hand up to her face, then the other. She tried to breathe three times, in and out, quickly.

"You have to think that way, Em," he said. "For me, it's a law. When things like that happen, I have to—I can be held responsible. Every teacher has to be responsible."

She closed her eyes, but saw nothing but Jason Kamphoff— in his shorts, in his cut-off T-shirt, on his dirt bike coming up the yard, his baseball cap on backwards.

"It doesn't necessarily mean what you think it does," he told her, "but you have to think that way. You must."

She put her elbows down on the table, hid her face in her hands.

"He doesn't come around here any more," Norm said. "That kid does not get on this property."

Her chair screeched as she backed it up from the table in order to lean harder into her hands. A part of her mind tried to offer her pictures of that kid, undressed, beside her daughter.

"I'm going to talk to Marty myself," Norm said. "That kid's been in trouble most of the last year of school—I'm not kidding, Em." He took her arms. "This is my fault. Right from the first, I should have said to you about him—I should have warned you—"

"You mean he's done this before?"

He shook his head. "I don't know that," Norm said. "But he's trouble, Em. I knew it too. I knew it from the moment that jerk said he'd get his kid over here to baby-sit. I was standing right there at the front door when he said it—Kamphoff, the royal jerk. I was standing there, and sirens were going off in my head, Em."

"Why didn't you tell me?" she said. "Why didn't you, Norm? They're my children!"

He shook his head.

"Norm," she said. "Why didn't you say anything?"

He looked at her sharply, as if he were holding himself together with the strength of his own clenched fists.

"Because I was scared."

"Of what?"

"Of Kamphoff."

"Of Marty Kamphoff?" she said, angrily. "You were scared of Marty Kamphoff?"

He stood up from the table, took a step behind his chair and held it in both hands, cracked it down on the floor.

"I was afraid it would get back to him that *I* said it. Afraid of him, Emily." Fiercely he shook his head. "That's it. I was scared of him."

She could feel herself turning inside out, feel everything inside whirl and spin. She put her hands flat down on the table, pushed herself up and back, tried to straighten herself.

"I didn't know—not for sure. Nothing for sure. Nothing except I didn't trust that kid—not once." He turned for the door. "I'm going to leave," he said. "It's my fault—"

"Don't you dare leave. Don't you dare go a step closer to that door," she told him. "You owe me, Norman Visser—for what you did to my sister, too. You owe me."

She came at him quickly. "I'm not letting you go," she said. "I'm not letting you go, because I'm not strong enough to do this alone. You hear me? And you owe me. I'm not letting you run away."

He half-turned and took a step back to the table.

"You're right," he said.

"Of course I'm right."

And when he saw her shoulders fall, he knew there was nothing left for him to say, so he went to her and held her, not because he thought she was more wounded than he was, but because he knew it was the only thing that would keep her up. Even as he held her, her hands stayed at her sides, her body motionless in his arms.

"What did that boy do to her?" she said, over his shoulder. "What's he already done?"

"I think—by the way they talk about it—I think it could be worse, Em. They don't seem afraid. Trust me."

She used every bit of her strength to hold back tears. "You're trying to make me feel better."

"I'm not going to lie, Em. Listen to me," he said, "I'm telling you you're right to be afraid of something, you're right to be suspicious—you have to be. But I think it could be worse."

Her whole body tensed as she pushed him away. "How do you count *worse*, Norm? What's really bad here? What's *not* really bad? How do you grade it, Mr. Visser?"

"By fear. Your kids aren't afraid."

"You heard them—"

"I heard them say they didn't want Jason anymore because he's too heavy and he's too strong," Norm said. "They're afraid of him, but not scared enough not to say it."

She backed away from him and leaned against the counter. "Why did I come here?" she said. "What ever possessed me?"

She turned, walked into the kitchen, and stood at the sink, her back to him. "If I ever see that kid again—"

He stood beside the table, watching her. She arched her neck and let her head fall back, then brought it forward again and pulled her hands to her face.

"You don't have a gun," he said.

"I'll buy one."

She reached in the cupboard for a glass, turned on the faucet and filled it, sipped once and tossed the rest, then put the glass down beside the sink.

"What I want to know is what he did to her," she said.

"It won't happen again."

"I have to know."

"Just keep that kid away, Em—that's all you can do."

She turned toward him. "We can make him confess—"

"To what? He'll lie anyway. He'll tell us what he thinks we'll take. You don't know kids, Em. He'll never tell the truth anyway," he said. "Look at them out there. Are they playing?"

She turned back to the window. Sam was twisting his glove shyly as the ball came hustling back from Will. She watched her daughter for a moment, saw her smile.

"Tell me, Em. Tell me what they're doing. Go ahead," he told her. "As if I were blind, tell me."

She took a breath, waited, then another. "Rebecca's running between them," she said. "She's kind of running between the two guys." She brought her hands up to the window. "They're throwing the ball and Rebecca's running. Sammy just tagged her out—"

"She bawling?"

Rebecca was flopped on the ground, laughing.

"Is she bawling? Tell me."

"No," she said.

"All we can do is keep that kid out of here," Norm told her. "That, and we got to tell his old man."

She looked at him.

"I can do that. I have to do that," he told her. "You're right. I owe you."

III

When Emily came back from California, most of Neukirk identified her beauty as more than skin deep, blessed as she is with such perfect features. But most people also recognized that her attractiveness was manicured by the kind of attention to detail that Neukirk women, for the most part, abandon sometime during their child-bearing years.

That afternoon, however, when Emily looked at herself in the bathroom mirror, while Will and the children were still playing catch in the backyard, she saw puffiness around her eyes, a colorless mouth, streaky cheeks. She looked a mess. And she saw sadness, the kind she'd already noted in the faces of some Neukirk women. In her case it came from the assault she'd suffered in the last twenty-four hours: shadowy secrets of her sister's life, and now the possibility that her kids had been fighting off this boy—something she never would have imagined might happen here. What she recognized in herself was exhaustion.

When she came out of the bathroom, saw Norm there seated at the table with a fresh cup of coffee he'd brewed himself, she told him, "I'm starting to look like Neukirk."

"I called," he said. "I told his secretary you were coming in tomorrow—an old friend, an old family friend—and that you'd like to have lunch."

"What are you talking about?"

"Stellinga—the psychologist, in Omaha. He knows you're coming."

"I am?"

"You are," he said. "It's all in the past, but we've got to pull something over it, something real—and I don't mean just cover it up. I mean bury it. It's the first thing you've got to do."

"Bury her?" she said.

"Maybe."

"What about the kids?" she said.

"They're mine. It won't take you long. Nothing's going to happen. I've been watching them. They're fine."

She sat down beside him at the table, reached for his hand. "Who did you tell him was coming?"

"Mrs. Benjamin Forcier," he told her. "You said you didn't want him to know."

She nodded.

He didn't stay for supper, although Emily asked him to. He had things to do, he said, and he wasn't lying.

On the wall above the table in his office, Marty Kamphoff has a wooden rack he built himself to hold his collection of golf balls. It's quite large, maybe two feet high and three feet wide, with ten or so separate rows about two inches apart, just wide enough to hold golf balls. He filled the rack within a year or so after he made it, and has slowly accumulated another six or seven dozen balls in a plastic bag he keeps in the bottom left side drawer of his desk. Each of those balls has a logo stamped into it: everything from the Burlington Railroad that comes through Neukirk, to a dozen feed companies, to printers, office supply companies, insurance agents, and more than a few country clubs he's played.

Marty started collecting logo golf balls about six years ago, and for a time it was his only passion. But then, almost unexplainably, his interest died. The rack serves as a good conversation piece in the office, and occasionally he still picks up a ball somewhere when somebody who's seen his collection sends him one out of the blue. But he long ago quit chasing them down himself.

Across the office another rack is built into the opposite wall at a height of about five feet, intended to show off Kamphoff's latest collection craze: Coke memorabilia. This rack is wide and runs along that whole side of the office, constructed of a dark-stained oak intended to match the paneled wainscoting that runs all the way around the office to a height of about three feet. That shelf's full too, with just about everything Coke's ever used for advertising: model Coke trucks, four or five different serving trays, an old cooler, church keys, a couple pairs of socks, a laundry bag, sunglasses, frisbees, sun visors, three different baseball caps, and a host of other things.

On his desk he has a Coke pen and pencil set, and three separate golf balls mounted on dark wood bases, each of them in cubes of plastic: one of them is marked with a Coke logo, one of them with Victor Soap—Kamphoff's own way to wealth—and one of them with Mickey Mouse.

Marty Kamphoff's mother never cut her hair. I suppose that's overstatement; somewhere along the line she must have snipped it some. But even when she died at eighty years of age, she was still wearing it up in the bun she'd always worn, out of conviction that women shouldn't cut their hair. I think it's in the Bible somewhere.

Conviction? Maybe that's overstated too. Sadie Kamphoff probably never sat down with that verse and decided, then and there, to apply it strictly to her hair. Whatever conviction there was in her came from hundreds of years of tradition in her own parents' families. Way back in the thirties, when she was young, she probably would have no more considered bobbing her hair, say, than she would have dreamed of something as evil as going dancing.

Marty's father was a farmer, but he had no more choice in the matter than Marty's mother did in choosing hair styles. Had you seen them together in their last decade, the seventies, you would have thought them the kind of portrait one connects with dust bowl tenant farmers from Oklahoma, even though by that time they weren't as poor as they were before the war—the Second World War, that is—and they weren't as backward. At least their home had toilets and running water.

It's likely you have little sympathy already for Marty Kamphoff, thinking him to be a species of the kind of small-town hypocrite one expects in every story about Midwestern prairie life. Unfortunately, that's what he is. I do want you to understand him a bit, though; not so much to sympathize with him, because he doesn't really merit a lot of sympathy, as to understand that his lust for accumulating things grows rather plainly out of his own parents' penury. And his desire for a high profile in Neukirk likely stems from the fact that throughout his childhood he rarely came to town at all—once a week at most, for groceries. And when he did, once he was old enough to see himself, he thought of his whole life as green, hickish.

Townspeople would say Marty Kamphoff is from Palsrock, a town that used to exist about six miles west of Neukirk, on a hill high enough to see over the Big Sioux River valley—not a town really, little more than a gas station, a grain elevator, and three homes. Many, many summer Saturday nights during his childhood, Marty—and his brothers and sisters—already Saturday-night clean, would go to the Palsrock station (Ben Verrips owned it, but he's long gone), where Marty and the other kids would play games outside, while Abe, his father, went in and sat in one of the chairs huddled around the black-and-white TV in the station's office with other Palsrock men. His mother would sit with the women on a homemade picnic table underneath the three or four cottonwoods just south of the pumps. That was their big weekend entertainment.

Marty's a man who came from that kind of background to make his fortune by himself, his fortune being considerable in a town like Neukirk, where there are very few very rich people. He's a man whose faith is much more a commitment to a way of life than it is a commitment to God. And although his own parents would not approve of his lifestyle today, including his frequent trips all over the upper Midwest, often on the Sabbath, he has inherited their characteristic rigidity.

About twenty years ago Marty's cousin in Ohio sold him into a pyramid sales operation, at a very low level, with Victor Soap, a company that started out selling vitamins and various kinds of degradable detergents at a time when few people were talking about environmentalism. Victor made it, and made it big, marketing itself as a truly American business run by a group of fervent Christians.

Marty's office is not large, but his salespeople are everywhere, although few families in Neukirk are on his payroll. He stockpiles the products his people need in the metal building he owns. His business, for the most part, is keeping them supplied with product to sell and the conviction they require to stay at it. For that he takes a requisite cut, modest in percentage but substantial in amount, proof of the extent to which his own pyramid has grown.

Norm Visser had been in Marty's office only three or four times, usually seeking donations for community theater or something at school, trips which were usually successful. In fact, the only real link between Marty Kamphoff and Norm Visser was the community theater, Marty even taking a turn or two on stage himself a few years back. Norm always thought of Marty as an ace donor, and Marty thought of community theater as another attraction of living in Neukirk and, therefore, something worthy of support. Most everyone would say that Marty is community-minded, and just about everybody respects his money. Few, on the other hand, respect him.

When Norm called and asked to speak to him someplace yet that night, Marty Kamphoff offered his office. He never once assumed that Norm's visit would be a request for money. Marty's a man with his ear to the ground, after all, and he knew—who didn't by that time?—that if any man was gaining ground on

Emily Doorn, it was Norm. Marty might not be wise, but he was skillful at turning things to his own benefit.

Norm parked on the gravel outside the front door of Marty's office, got out, slammed the door. The window air-conditioner was whirring. Just south, the lights of the softball diamonds a few blocks away glowed with enough intensity to brighten the sidewalk up to the front door. That was the only outside light, aside from the faint glow coming through the closed curtains.

As much as Norm hated fund-raising, as much as he despised ingratiating himself with people like Marty, he would much rather have been asking for a couple hundred bucks than taking on what he was about to. He saw himself as the sheep before the shearer, and the only drive that pushed him up that sidewalk was the clear sense that this job was *his* and not Emily's. After all, he'd not voiced any of his concerns about Jason Kamphoff the day Marty had announced to everyone that his son would take care of Emily's kids.

But Norm knew walking in that his going there would accomplish nothing, because he knew Marty Kamphoff—knew, absolutely, that the man was constitutionally incapable of accepting blame for anything, and that he would protect his children as if somewhere the Bible said that blood was eternally thicker than water. He knew all that because he'd been a teacher in Neukirk long enough to have seen all of Kamphoff's kids come through the system, all of them spoiled. And he'd heard enough horror stories about accusations Kamphoff had leveled at teachers when any of his kids misbehaved.

I won't run through the list of his older children's problems—Jason's the baby—because they're not relevant here. All you need to know is that no one in Neukirk thought it odd that Kamphoff would have so many headaches with his kids. As people here say, some birds come home to roost, after all.

To Norm, Marty's office always seemed like a "men only" dorm room, with dust everywhere. Marty doesn't employ a secretary or even a cleaning woman; he doesn't need one, he thinks. And his wife never goes there because she doesn't know much at all about his business. It's the way he's got his life nailed down, the way he was raised—Dad in the barn, Mom in the house.

Marty was seated behind the desk when Norm came in, both arms up over some order forms, a pencil in his hand, a pair of reading glasses perched on his nose.

"Come in," he said, once he heard Norm in the hallway. "I'm in here." The rest of the building was dark.

He pointed to a dusty chair, and Norm sat. Norm had put on long pants for this meeting, feeling he needed to be dressed up, not in shorts and a T-shirt.

"So how's it going?" Marty said. "You got a play coming up. Shoot, I wish I had time to get in it again, but things are busy right about now. I got orders to fill and a couple of meetings in the Twin Cities."

"Late July," Norm said.

"What play you doing?"

"*Father of the Bride.*"

"I saw that movie," Marty said. "Steve Martin, wasn't it? Dang, that's funny."

"Ought to be a scream," Norm said.

"Who you got to play the dad?"

"Nobody yet," Norm said.

"Think you could do it?" Marty said. "I mean, not having kids or anything?"

Norm felt his arms go rigid. He shrugged his shoulders.

"Ought to get Emily up there, you know that?" he said. "Chunk of woman like that'd have people lined up for blocks."

Norm wished he hadn't asked her. "I brought it up," he said. "She has a lot of talent."

"Woman like that don't need talent," Marty said. "She going to do it?"

"She's busy."

"Yeah. At the bowling alley," Marty said, shaking his head. "Bowling alley, Norm. You believe that? Of all places, the bowling alley."

"She likes it," Norm told him.

"Did until this afternoon," Marty said. "I hear she cursed the bedevil out of the whole lot of 'em. Nobody in this place's going to think the same of her after that. Shoot, I bet you go down there right now, there's still people saying those words—whispering—"

"Too bad it happened," Norm said.

"She didn't understand. It's unfortunate, really. I can see it—somebody like her coming here from California, not knowing nothing at all. I can see how it'd crank her off to see what Vellinga did." He leaned back, threw his hands up behind his head. "Funny though, eh? Guy, I'd have loved to been there myself."

Norm didn't say anything.

"Was funny, though, wasn't it?" Marty repeated. "Shoot, Vellinga didn't mean no harm."

"I don't know."

"Come on, Norman," he said. "Don't go getting soft on us here, for pete's sake. Vellinga didn't mean nothin' by it and you know it. He's just having a little fun. You're too tight, you know that? Loosen up."

"She didn't take it that way—"

"I know *she* didn't take it that way. Whole town knows by this time *she* didn't take it that way."

"You got to understand her too—"

"I said that, all right?" Marty said, his arms coming down. He leaned forward and slipped off his glasses. "I said that right away, okay? I said, 'I can understand how Emily'd take it the way she did, how she'd fly off the handle—'"

"You did," Norm said.

Marty swung his chair around and put his foot up on a bookshelf. "You hear what she said?"

"She told me herself."

"What'd she tell you?" Marty asked.

Norm shrugged his shoulders. "Doesn't make any difference," he said.

"What'd she say?"

"What difference does it make, Marty?"

"I'm just wondering what she said. Wondering if what I heard matches. What'd she say?"

"I'm not going to repeat it, Marty," Norm said. "She feels bad enough about it. She thinks she shouldn't have let loose like that, all right? She wishes it hadn't happened. So why do you care exactly what she said?"

Marty picked up a clip off his desk and squeezed it between his fingers. "I don't know," he said. "I guess I'm interested in her somehow—"

"What do you mean?"

"I don't mean what you're thinking," Marty said right away. "I mean, I think this woman's not just some poor little thing, you know? Here we're all falling all over her because of the divorce and the way her Ma is and everything. But you tell me this," he said, pointing. "What kind of woman, good-looking as she is, would take a job in the bowling alley? I told her I could get her a job—"

"She doesn't want to be indebted to anyone."

"Who's talking about being indebted?" he said. "I just said I could get her something good—better than getting whistled at in the bowling alley."

"It's what she wanted—"

"That's exactly what I'm saying," Marty said. "I wonder what kind of woman *wants* to work in a place like that. Shoot, Norman, you're enough of a man to know what those guys look at when she struts around—"

"It's her business," Norm told him.

"I can't believe it," Marty said. Then he looked up and stopped, sat back again, put both fists down on the table. "So you getting close to her or what?"

Norm was letting Marty control things, and he knew it, and it made him angry because that's the way it had been for far too long. He had been determined to tell Marty about Jason, then get out, but here he was letting Marty steer them through all this garbage.

"I came to tell you something," he said.

"Don't change the subject, Norman," Marty said.

"What subject?"

"I asked you, you getting close to this woman or what?"

Norm didn't know exactly where to look. "It's not any business of yours—"

"I figure it's because you're safe, isn't that right?" Marty said. "I figure it's because of what happened—I mean with Margaret. She figures she's got this history with you anyway, ain't that right? And she's not afraid of you."

"Why should she be afraid of me?"

"I'm saying that she's not afraid of you. You got no risk, you hear?"

"I have no risk?"

What burned Norm more than anything was the way Marty rolled his eyes, as if he were speaking to a third grader. "I mean," he said, "you don't scare her."

"*Some* people scare her, Marty—is that what you're saying?"

"Yes."

"Most everyone else scares her, Marty? Am I hearing you right?"

"Yes," he said again.

"*Men* scarc her, Marty—is that what we're edging up to here?"

"You're the one said it," Marty told him.

Norm pulled himself up on the chair. "Well, I'll tell you what scares her, Marty. You know what scares her? A kid who tries to jump on her little daughter—"

"What are you saying?"

"I'm saying what scares her, Marty, is a kid like your Jason who's got no sense—that's what I'm telling you. Your kid's been trying to do things to Rebecca—"

"You're talking nonsense here, brother," Marty said.

"I sat there and listened to her kids say it."

For a moment, Marty was quiet. He sat up, took his feet off

146

the shelf, put his elbows down, and raised a hand to his face. With his right hand he picked up the pencil, scratched something on the desk pad, then threw it down.

"This has got something to do with me," he said finally, covering his mouth with his hand. "This has got something to do with me somehow, doesn't it?" He threw up both hands. "What did I ever do to her? You tell me that, Norman. What did I ever do but try to give her everything she needed? Shoot, who was there in the street when that van come in—you tell me that."

"It's not you, it's Jason," Norm said.

"Baloney!" Marty said. "It's me, somehow, and I'm not going to let her slay my kid just because of something she's got against me. She's scared of me, isn't she? She's got this thing about me, and I never once tried anything on her."

"She doesn't have anything against you, Marty."

"She's got something against me all right, but I tell you what, I'm not going to let her turn this into something that makes a pig out of my kid. What'd they say?" he asked.

"Who?"

"Her kids?"

"They said he was so heavy—"

"That's it? 'That he was so heavy'? Kids wrestle, Norm—real boys do anyway. You ever think of that?"

"She doesn't want him around anymore," Norm said. "That's all I came to say. She won't have him with her kids."

"Who's going to find out about this?" Marty said, quickly, getting up from his chair. "I suppose she's going to tell everybody in the world about this, isn't she? She hates me, so she's taking it out on my kid. Norman, you tell me . . . you tell me—"

"This is not about you, it's about Jason."

"It's about me," he said. "She's scared of me somehow because she thinks I'm coming on to her. I'm a man, Norman—that's all. That's my only crime here. I'm a married man too. You aren't. I didn't come on to her either—never, not once. Didn't even think of it. I never did a thing. I never touched her." He turned toward the wall, stared up at the golf balls. Then he hit the wall with the heel of his fist. "I know why she's scared of me," he said.

Norm got to his feet. "I'm leaving," he said. "All I came to say is that Jason can't come over anymore, and let me say this too." Marty kept his back to him. "I think you ought to get Jason some help, Marty. I'm saying that as someone who used to have him in class."

"I know why she's doing this," Marty said again. "It's really clear, too. I should have thought about it long ago—I did, but I wouldn't believe it myself. She married a Jew to start with, running off to California, trying to be something she's not. Comes back here and expects the whole world to bow to her, but the fact is she's trash—just like she always was."

Norm felt himself go rigid.

"She's after my kid because she's after me, but she's worthless scum is what she is. I know what kind of woman she is—"

"You're a real jerk," Norm said.

Marty turned quickly. "Well, she sure don't want you. After what you done to her sister, it's kinky anyway—even if you were a man," he said. "You know, I been thinking about it." He looked at Norm in a way that made Norm think the man didn't even realize he was there. "Now when this kind of stuff comes out, it all makes sense, you know. Any woman puts that much time into looking beautiful . . . anybody primps like she does, she's got to be hungry. And what's she got over there anyway? Who's she got for her needs—you tell me that? Then she goes and prances around the bowling alley in front of all those men. You know? What kind of woman is that, Norman? You tell me—what kind of woman is that?"

"Sit down," Norm said.

"And you hang around over there all the time, people say, but she don't have to be afraid of you. Too much between you already, and you being the way you are—"

"Sit down," Norm said again, but nothing seemed to get through.

"What right's she got accusing my kid of something. She's

148

dreaming, you know that? That woman's dreaming, and I won't have my kid suffering for her being what she is. I won't say it either. I don't want to filthy my mouth with the word. But you know, don't you? You know better than any, 'cause you been over there."

"Sit down," Norm said again, and for the first time since he'd come, he felt Kamphoff's eyes locked on him.

"Don't tell me to sit down, you fag."

"What'd you say?"

"You heard me," Marty said.

Norm took a step or two over to front of the desk. He tried to reason with himself, keep himself from swinging, even though he didn't want to.

"You're a waste of my time, Marty," he said. "You're a big-mouthed waste of my time, because it doesn't make any difference what I'd do or say—what anybody does or says. Doesn't make a dime's worth of difference. You don't hear, Kamphoff. You're missing something. There's nothing in you but a black hole."

Kamphoff took a step toward him, no more than a arm's length away. "Gutsy, isn't it," he said. "You talking about something a man don't have?" He laughed in Norm's face. "Any man'd take me on for saying what I just did—"

"I don't have to," Norm told him. "Look at you. Just look at you, Marty. You're pathetic—"

"Shut up—"

"Now I told you—don't let that kid back in her yard," Norm said. "That's what I came here for."

"I wouldn't let my son close to that woman."

Norm picked up the cube enclosing the Mickey Mouse golf ball, looked at it just for a second, then flung it at Marty before walking out, down through the darkened corridor, and out the front door, a chorus of taunts filling the emptiness behind him.

He got into his truck and slammed the door, switched on the lights and turned on the ignition before he saw Marty out there after him, holding the front door, screaming.

149

Now some people might consider what he did the action of a man scared to take on somebody with his fists, but Norm is an athlete of sorts, a tennis champion, who, in his mid-forties, is still in fine shape. And if it had come down to a fight between them, I'd put my money on Norm Visser, especially with the rage he felt inside him.

But he didn't jump out of the truck and hit Marty. He didn't even scream back. He merely put his truck in gear, climbed the cement blocks that separated the gravel from the front lawn of Marty's warehouse, and gunned it up to the front door, stopping only when the glass shattered and he heard the sound of his fender shriek off the steel sides of the building.

He had Marty pinned inside the entrance to his own shop.

The screaming didn't stop, of course, even when Norm got out of his truck and leaned up against a fender he examined for damage.

"You're crazy, you know that?" Marty yelled. "You're paying for this—"

"No, I'm not," Norm told him.

"I'll sue—"

"No, you won't," Norm said.

Marty's tirade continued, Norm standing there and taking it all, watching him, but not moving an inch. The whole time Norm felt the fear in him pass almost noticeably in the silence he offered to Kamphoff, the silence and the smile he wore, leaning up against the side of the truck.

Marty kept screaming until he could think of nothing he hadn't said, and then Norm spoke, quietly. "You don't want to bring this up," Norm told him. "I think you'd just as soon keep this whole business under lock and key, Marty."

Then he got into his pickup and backed away, and as he turned his head to look behind him while he backed up over the blocks, Norm knew nothing would ever come of this whole encounter. It would cost him to get his truck fixed, but he knew if Marty ever tried anything against him, it would all come down to a simple case of his name against Marty Kamphoff's. And in

Neukirk, that would be no contest. It was something Marty himself was smart enough to understand.

But the trip up the road and back into town wasn't a total triumph. Someone as fine as Norm Visser doesn't walk away from confrontations, even when he's in the right, without a sense of shame—not just at what he'd done, but at what he'd seen and heard. And yet it was sweet, he thought—very, very sweet.

He walked into his empty house, the sound of the shrieking metal still there in his memory. He sat in his living room with three educational journals he'd not read, pretending he could lose himself in a series of articles on accountability. He knew he had to talk to Emily; she had to hear that Jason wouldn't be coming back. But he didn't want to go over there until his nerves were settled, until he'd had time to put away his own anger;

So he went over later, when dusk was only a few shades from night and the streets of Neukirk were dark. He didn't take the truck, and he left his bike at home. He walked. He knew he'd probably be needed again, and Neukirk didn't need to know his whereabouts.

He told Emily that he'd let Marty Kamphoff know about his son, that Marty hadn't taken it very well—didn't believe him entirely, in fact—but how that was characteristic of Kamphoff, and how it was settled now and she didn't have to worry tomorrow when she left. He didn't tell her what he'd done with the truck.

"I'm still going to Omaha?" Emily said.

"You're going," he told her. "I'll watch the kids. Everything'll be fine."

He'd found her in the dining room, sitting on a chair, three boxes of plates and cups and serving trays around her, each of them only half-emptied into the gaping doors of the oak buffet.

She looked around at the boxes. "I'll never use this stuff," she said. "I really won't—not here."

He pulled up a chair and sat on it backwards, facing her, near the door to the kitchen. "Just put it away," he said. "Who cares?"

She rolled a coffee cup out of the wrapping paper and stuck it on the top shelf inside. "I don't know if I can take it."

"What?" he said.

"Omaha," she told him. "Everybody's got a point in them somewhere, don't they?" She took another cup from the box. "We all have something that measures what's inside—how much pressure." She held the wrapped cup with both hands. "Mine says 'no more.'"

"Don't quit," he said.

"After the divorce," she said, "home—here—looked like a place I could sit still."

"You know what happens to people without a pulse?"

"You know what I mean."

"I know what you mean," he told her.

"I'm halfway through unpacking," she said. "Maybe a little more than half. But it would be so easy just to throw it all back in the boxes—"

"You're kidding yourself," he said.

"Why?"

He swung his chair around and stuck his hand in the box. "There's things that have to get straightened out here," he said.

"It would be so easy to run away."

"No, it wouldn't."

"How do you know?"

"I know—believe me," he told her. "Your mother's here. Remember?"

"My mother wouldn't even know."

"You're lying, Em."

"She can't talk, can't eat, can't do anything. She wouldn't know if I was here or in Kalamazoo."

He unwrapped a plate and laid it on top of the buffet. "You don't believe that for a minute," he told her. "You've never said anything like that to me before."

"I can't go to Omaha," she said.

He looked into the open box closest to him. "There isn't all that much left in here," he said.

"I'm overdrawn or something," she told him. "I feel as if I can't put anything into my head anymore. I didn't expect any of this, and look at me—I feel as if I could cry all the time if I just let myself. I don't even know why." She began unwrapping the cup. "I don't want to know more. I want to live like Mom, without knowing anything." She rolled the packing paper up angrily. "I envy her."

It was close to ten according to the clock in the dining room.

"You got an appointment—" he said.

"I didn't get it. You did."

"I don't care," he told her. "On some desk pad in Omaha, some secretary's got your name down, and you're not backing out—"

"Why?" she said.

He reached into the box and took a stack of saucers out in a bundle.

"You tell me, Norm. Why do I have to know about what happened so long ago? I mean *now*, with everything else? My kids, for goodness sake. Why should I go? I don't care."

"I told you," he said. "Jason's not coming back. Besides, I'll be here." In a minute he had all the saucers out. "Give me that box," he told her. "I'm going to get this done." He pointed at the larger one beside her. "We get a bad rap sometimes for intolerance. But in a place like Neukirk you're stuck with people. You can lose 'em in LA. You can choose where you want to live and who you have to see. But here you can't."

"And what about you?" she said.

"What about me?"

"Why do you hole up here?"

"I said to push that box over here—"

"Please answer me," she said. "I've asked you before—why do you stay here?"

He sat back on the chair, stretched his arms up, then rested his hands on his head. "I could give you six reasons, maybe seven, maybe eight. But I once had a principal in Chicago who said if you can list six reasons for doing something silly, you don't have a really good one."

"Give me one," she said.

"I love kids."

"You can find them anywhere."

"Good school."

"I suppose there isn't a better one in the country—is that what you want me to believe?"

"Home is where the heart is."

"Don't give me that."

"My parents need me."

She stopped, pointed. "Okay, that's one. That one I'll write down."

"Maybe I don't even know myself," he said. "It's a lie we've been taught, Em—all of us. You start to think that you have to be able to understand every last motivation you have? Shoot, who knows? Sometimes I wish I was just somebody who never gives a dime's worth of attention to why this, why that. Somebody who just lives, sticks all life's horrors in the garbage incinerator and smiles to hear it all flush away. Don't you wish sometimes, Emily?" He broke into a laugh. "Sometimes in the middle of the school year when everything's hectic, I pedal my bike to school and these guys driving trucks—cattle trucks—long hauls—go past me in a haze ripe with manure. And I tell myself how much I'd like to be them—to just get in the truck and go. Come home, eat supper, watch television, go to bed, and not worry about things—and in the morning just get out on the high road."

"Norm Visser, cattle trucker," she said. "Why not? You've got nothing keeping you here—"

"My parents."

"You can call them."

He held up his hands as if he were aboard a bike. "Or how about this? A Honda Gold Wing or a Harley—"

"A motorcycle?"

"I never outgrew Peter Fonda. You know, *Easy Rider*. Head out and look for the soul of America and all that."

"Leather jacket," she said.

"A babe on the back in a black T-shirt."

154

"Sounds like mid-life crisis to me."

"I wish," he said.

She reached out to him. "I'd be put away already if it wasn't for you," she said. "My kids would be wards of the state or something—I don't know." She took his right hand. "Promise me—don't get on that motorcycle until I say you can, okay?"

"Got a play to put on, remember?"

"You know," she said, "one thing that's really strange about all this is Meg—I mean that you were with her." She pulled her hand away and sat back. "Sometimes I tell myself that even with what you've already told me, I've got every reason in the world to hate you." She looked away. "Not hate really. I mean, I can't even think of hating you."

"Maybe that's why I'm here," he said, "the scene of the crime."

She took his hand with such force that he almost pulled away.

"I'm going to Omaha for you too," she said. "That's part of it, isn't it?"

He nodded slowly, as if the answer had to be found some place in him he'd not thought of before.

The prairies are what most people fly over, whether they're on a plane or on one of the interstates that drag unmercifully up and down an unending succession of sloping hills. Life in the towns that sit on these huge shoulders may be as plain as the landscape, or at least may seem that way to those who pass by, their car stereos filling the empty spaces with music or books on tape. Those who fly the jets that leave long ribbons across the sky likely take no notice of life down here at all; with their noses in some airport novel, they never consider the flesh and blood beneath them in such wide open spaces.

There's never been a full-fledged war on the plains. Most Indian skirmishes are long forgotten, except farther west where reservations exist in such isolation that the descendants of the old white settlers can keep history at arm's length. And there's no history of segregation, other than that once self-imposed by maybe a dozen ethnic groups—German, Bohemian, Norwegian, Dutch among them—communities now melting slowly into each other, as some long ago claimed they would. The whole incredible drama that unfolded on the Great American Desert, the whole space drawn and quartered by plow and furrow into the nation's breadbasket, happened so quickly that today it seems to have been almost effortless.

It may be the sheer size of the prairies that makes us think of them as empty, even today. Everywhere you look graceful rows of corn line the contoured hills. Fact is, though, the plains are empty, more empty at least than they were a century ago, the land itself shaking off those who can't maintain the rising cost of a viable existence.

Even though Emily Doorn was born on these plains, she didn't understand them. She was like the children of the Depression who, not having traveled anywhere else, never thought themselves poor during childhood. California had been a stark contrast, of course; and though several years of her life there were not without their joys, by the time she left LA, full of pain and sadness and failure, her goal was to return to the innocence that, had she not left, she would have realized never existed at all. She had returned home to find faith, but was losing it in the process.

Some of these thoughts rode with Emily the next morning as she set out for Omaha. She had left Neukirk at nine, the kids already a yard away and Norm standing at the driveway, not waving but smiling as she backed out into Main Street. As she followed the Missouri River south, the tall banks of Loess Hills like an engineer's set of miniature mountains beside her, she faced a despair deeper than the near hopelessness she had suffered through in the darkness of a failing marriage.

A part of her played devil-may-care with a kind of reckless abandon, much as she imagined her sister might have done in her years of rebellion. What did she care anyway what Marty Kamphoff might tell people? What did she care what he might say about her? Go ahead. It didn't matter to her. She knew what was true.

But enough of the old Neukirk was still in her to make her uncomfortable. She'd never considered having to live with notoriety.

But where would she go? Moving back to California would bring the kids closer to their father, but it would bring her there too, and she had no desire to be anywhere near Benjamin Forcier.

And there was her mother. But would she really know if her daughter left again? Did she even know that her daughter was there in the room? Occasionally the look in her mother's eyes offered a moment's possibility that things were going into that mind, but most of the time her stare was gray and cold as stone.

Traffic over the face of the rural Midwest flows predominantly east/west. People from Fargo vacation in Denver for the most part—or the Twin Cities—rarely in St. Louis or Kansas City. So the interstate she took to Omaha was as open as the plains themselves, the only traffic passing her, or being passed, bearing license plates from adjacent states—Iowa, South Dakota, Nebraska. Lots of trucks.

She'd grown up in a loving home in which her sister's life and death were simply not a subject for discussion. Everyone knew her parents to be remarkable for their graciousness and faith. "It's just amazing the strength the Doorns have, after what they've been through," people must have said. "Losing their daughter the way they did, yet so strong. Grace under the cruelest pressure known to faith—loss of a child." But in all those countless Bible passages they'd read after meals, in all the prayers that ascended from the kitchen table, neither her mother nor father had ever spoken of Meg on their own. Only occasionally she'd felt Meg in the silences.

Her picture stood on the shelf across from the desk in the dining room beside uncles and aunts, grandpas and grandmas.

Each year they decorated her grave when they went out to the cemetery the day before Memorial Day. And there was a picture of her—the same picture, a graduation picture—in the hallway of the old school, along with six others, all of them black-and-white—two of them in military uniform, none of them people she knew.

Some of the older teachers had asked her, when she was a freshman, whether she was Meg's sister. The question never bothered her. Of course she was Meg's sister. There were no other Doorns in Neukirk. Then they'd look at her and smile, as if it were a blessing to be related to Margaret Doorn—a smile she read eventually, however, as nothing more than sympathy.

She was thirteen, at a grade school music festival, when her Uncle Hank Mentink asked her what seemed an especially odd question at the time, "How are your folks doing?" She remembered Uncle Hank's question because it was the first time she'd ever considered that question to be something more than idle talk.

"They're fine," she told him, and Uncle Hank smiled, his broad arms crossed over his chest, his daughter's solo music clutched in one hand.

It wasn't until later, when they were standing in front of the judge—all of the grade eight choir—singing something (she didn't remember anything they'd ever sung), when suddenly it dawned on her that her uncle was asking her about her mother and father in a way that begged her to be mature and tell him—years after the accident—how, truthfully, they were doing. She stood there on the bleachers, back row—she'd shot up in the past year, towering over many of her classmates—behind all of the boys who otherwise never sang, and she felt something in herself she'd never felt before. It wasn't only that she had to think about her parents in a new way; it was also a discovery that maybe they weren't okay.

How are your parents?

She remembered that question now, driving down the highway. She bit her lips and looked at the clock. Interstate 80 was behind her and traffic had picked up, moving toward the city that sprawled out along the western bank of the Missouri. She saw a sign for the airport.

How are your parents?

Maybe I never knew them, she thought. Maybe the grief of a child dead, a child whose faith they weren't sure of, maybe the grief and the guilt—was her death somehow caused by something they did?—maybe all of that ended something in their lives, something more than the life of their daughter.

My parents are not fine, she might have told Uncle Hank, had she known. My parents hurt badly, she should have told him. My parents can't forget, she should have said. And what's more, they won't remember.

Something in them died when Meg did.

A flashing sign far down the street from the storefront where Mike Stellinga—Dr. Michael Stellinga now—listed his practice said it was 11:30. The sun turned the narrow street in the middle of the market district into a radiator. Emily stood on the sidewalk outside a music store with its windows full of black-and-white posters of rock groups whose names she'd never heard of; the door was plastered full of decals—Audubon, Nature Conservancy, Save the Whales.

It was a different world here, even though the prairie spread itself all around for hundreds of miles, just as it did around Neukirk. Omaha was the city again, full of people with spiked hair and earrings, ponytails, and sideburns halfway down the jaw. She recalled her childhood memories of Omaha. Sometimes they'd come here before Christmas to shop. The feel of heavy crowds struck such terror in her then that she'd never dared lose sight of her parents for fear that, once lost, she'd never again go back home. So many unfamiliar faces, so much to be afraid of.

She walked up the steps to the music store, then turned right up another flight to a floor where four offices stood behind a single secretary, who wore no makeup. Emily felt immediately out of place.

"Can I help you?" the woman said.

"My name is Mrs. Benjamin Forcier," Emily told her.

The woman swung her chair over to a side desk where an appointment book lay open, a capless fountain pen in the gutter. She tipped her glasses down on her nose and followed the register with her finger.

"I remember," she said, smiling, dropping the glasses once again. "An old friend of Mike's?"

Emily assented with her shoulders. "Friend of a friend, you might say."

The secretary twisted around fully and looked closely, not as if judging. "He wondered about it. Said he didn't know anyone by that name." She shook her head, defensively. "You know, not many women today use their husband's full name."

"I'm divorced," Emily said. "My name is Doorn—Emily Doorn." She had purposely not used her own name when making the appointment, in case he should try to prepare some story for her.

"Will this be a professional call?" the woman asked.

"Oh, no," Emily said. "I live three hours away. I wanted to see him about some things that happened years ago . . . years ago."

"Emily Doorn," the woman repeated, her eyebrows arched into a question.

"That's right," Emily said.

No one else was in the waiting room. Even though the place was a half day south of Neukirk, the office was much more LA, from the magazines on the tables—*Smithsonian*, *Audubon*, *American Artist*—to the print on the wall. There was only one, a Western motif with something Native American in the lines, but a strange, translucent sky that communicated a visionary experience—not at all realistic. It was signed, she noticed when she looked closely, but it was the only remarkable item in an otherwise featureless waiting room. A place, she thought, that tried to be nondescript—six elegant old upholstered chairs that didn't match, heavy with wood trim, and a round magazine table with a glass top.

She had no memory of Mike Stellinga, so there was nothing in her mind to direct her to what he might have become. What was clear was the fact that he'd not become the preacher he was in training to be during those six months he'd spent in Neukirk.

Emily felt in her skirt pocket for the note, the one Nancy'd found in the envelope pasted in the Bible. She'd worn her denim skirt and a soft cotton beige blouse, billowy and long-sleeved, that she took from a place in her closet she'd not touched since she'd come to Neukirk; there simply weren't that many occasions, other than church, to wear something other than T-shirts and jeans, not even to the bowling alley.

What were the chances of this man even remembering the note or Meg Doorn or her parents' concern after her death? He was already gone when it all happened. University of Illinois. What if he looked at the note and hunched his shoulders? He could lie, too, she thought. It would not be hard to claim forgetfulness—one note, sent years ago to a little town a couple hundred miles away that he probably wanted to forget.

She held her hand up before her, felt a kind of pride in the fact that it wasn't shaking, that fear or nervousness wasn't tensing her equilibrium. The fact is, she thought, this whole trip might well be meaningless. On the other hand, Mike Stellinga—Dr. Michael Stellinga—downtown shrink, could be a man who loved to reminisce. He'd almost be that age, she thought.

When he appeared at the doorway to his office, she was surprised to see a man so looming. He was considerably overweight, his thinning hair so long it seemed unkempt. He wore a desperado's mustache that grew down from the corners of his lips and spread almost to his chin. And the first little tic she saw in him was the way in which he toyed nervously with his bolo tie.

"I remember the Doorns," he said. "You're Emily?"

"That's right," she said, rising from the chair.

He cocked his head as if nothing were connecting.

"My parents were Benjamin and Vivian—Meg was my sister."

"Sure," he said, registering no sign of surprise or fear. "Salt of the earth, Sally," he said to his secretary. "The old shirt-off-your-back types. The kind of people that would put me out business." What he said wasn't meant simply for his secretary. "Listen, you want to have lunch with us? You're welcome to. We usually just grab a sandwich or something."

It was almost impossible to think of this man as a youth pastor; while he had to be late-fortyish, he looked fifty-plus. Even his face was paunchy. But there was a friendliness in him that warmed her.

"Whatever suits you," she said.

"Sweet," he said. "The kind of deference you never see anymore—at least *we* don't."

"I'm not really from Neukirk," she told him. "That is, I was born there, but I've lived in California for years. I recently moved back."

"You're bucking the trends, aren't you?" he said. "The whole Midwest is swarming the other way."

"Maybe I am," she said.

There was nothing officious about him really, even though she was somewhat uncomfortable with the way he'd thought of her as a type; but then she'd known more than her share of psychologists in California.

"We were thinking about the Spaghetti Factory," the secretary said. She pointed at him with her thumb. "He's got this thing for carbohydrates."

"I'm overweight, and let me warn you—I smoke," he said. "It's getting so today you're only worth your salt as a referee of other people's problems if you can draw up a list of your own. I sin to pay my dues."

"Lunch sounds fine," she told them. "I haven't eaten."

"Come on then," he said, reaching out his hand to her. "There's nothing quite so therapeutic as breaking bread—something I picked up on in my days in the ministry."

She took his hand, although he didn't mean to shake it formally, only to lead her, gentlemanly, toward the door.

"I got this thing about honesty," he said. "You're from Neukirk, so I better tell you right off. Sally's my secretary, but she's also my partner." He still had hold of Emily's hand. "We live together. I'm no preacher anymore," he said. "You can do what you want with that information, I suppose, but I'd just as soon be up-front."

She nodded. "I've been back in Neukirk for less than two weeks," she said.

"No wonder you're here," he said, smiling. There was this constant bit of condescension in almost everything he said, but it didn't come out in a way that seemed patronizing. She thought he was probably good at what he did.

Once they were out the door, he turned back and locked it.

"You know, Neukirk was really my first job," he said. "I mean, even though I didn't earn any money to speak of—it was an internship—it was the first time that I was out of school, and it's likely that I learned as much there as I ever did in seminary."

"In Neukirk?" she said.

Sally and Mike both waved to the man in a leather vest at the counter of the music store just across the hallway.

"About myself, I mean," he said. "Mostly that's what all learning is about, don't you think? About yourself? I mean, really."

"You sound egocentric," Sally said.

"I am," he told her. "You should know."

She looked at Emily and raised her eyebrows, pleasantly. "I threaten to leave him daily," she whispered. "But I've been an enabler for years—so has he."

"And she'd leave if we weren't living in sin," he said. "But she's just like the rest of us around here, another case of arrested development." Emily followed him out of the front door of the

163

building. "She stays with me because living in sin is too much of a kick for her, the old Baptist. You know, Emily, we're like Meg that way, all of us. I've often wondered what it's going to be like in South Florida in a few years with all the late-sixties folks going to seed. We're going to turn that place into a commune. Out with the shuffleboard, in with the Frisbees. Flower gardens and natural food and Bob Dylan on the boombox."

"We just use each other," Sally said, smiling. "We don't really love each other. It's just a matter of coming to terms with our respective pasts."

"You remember Meg then?" Emily said.

She started just a bit when Sally slipped a hand beneath her arm as they walked up the street, a threesome, Mike walking along on Emily's other side. "Meg's why you're here, I suppose," he said.

She was surprised to hear him say that.

"It was too big a story in Neukirk. They didn't have a way to handle it. Kids get drunk all the time there, Sally—there's tons of kids who guzzle beer. But Meg wasn't a drunk, and what she had her eyes on was something Neukirk didn't get." He reached his arm into hers. "I don't want to get into all that yet, not until I get my fix of pasta," he said.

Emily told herself that Mike Stellinga couldn't have known who she was by the name Norm had given when he made the appointment, her married name; and he hadn't seemed able to place her even when she gave him, through Sally, her real name. All these connections he was making had to have come up in the past few minutes.

"I suppose you've never been here before," he said.

"Not very often. And not since I was a kid."

"This is the Old Market area," Sally said, "because that's what it was—before IBP and whatnot other companies began going out to the farms instead of waiting for farmers to come into town. In the days of the stockyards. It's quaint, isn't it? We've got a few homeless, a couple dozen addicts maybe, and pretty much whatever's gay in the city."

"They're all alike," Mike said. "Like us. People with chips on their shoulders. Chips? No, more like boulders."

"From Omaha?" Emily said.

"Probably not. From Sioux City and Neukirk and Hastings and thirty-five dozen other places here and there on the open spaces. People who didn't fit."

"*You* didn't fit?" Emily said to him.

"I can tell you lived in California," he said. "Neukirk people wouldn't ask a question like that until they were in their cars and I was back in the office." He squeezed her arm. "But then, you probably have whatever grew in Meg too, I suppose."

"And what was that?" she asked.

"I told you—after I eat, please," he said. "I got a little of Neukirk in me myself, remember—out of sight out of mind. You're going to have to loosen me up with a little wine, I think."

People made a path for them as they marched down the sidewalk, people lugging shopping bags and looking, for all the world, like tourists at a quaint little theme park. There were a few street people too, of course, men and women hawking all kinds of paraphernalia—rings, earrings, stick pins—and dressed in T-shirts, body stockings, and other garb that begged attention.

"I hate to say it, but this reminds me of California," Emily said.

"Not so outlandish, though," Mike said. "It's the lot of Midwesterners to be derivative, I think. It's in the cards somewhere. One time or another, the Lord said, 'Let there be a Midwest, where nobody does much of anything original, where work is righteousness, where people keep a certain shine on their faces so the rest of the world can see they're from Nebraska—'"

"Or Iowa," Emily said.

"Or whatever."

"So why don't *you* live in California?" she said.

"We just brought a little bit of it here," Sally told her, gesturing with her free arm. "Besides, there's no pollution."

She'd been in Spaghetti Factories before, a chain, the kind of place where the junk that was standing outside of her garage might go well. She sat at the table across from Mike and Sally and told them that if she'd known they would be eating here, she would have carted a trailer full of stuff she'd cleaned out of the barn in her backyard, stuff she could have peddled here quite handily.

In the time it had taken for her to meet them and walk two blocks to the spaghetti place, their acceptance convinced her she could get the truth from Mike—whatever he knew—and that she would get it in a way that would be kind. The easygoing blend of sarcasm and respect he showed to the place where she'd grown up made her smile.

They ate well, especially Mike, even though Sally warned him about leaving the last dinner roll alone. While they ate, Sally talked about herself, not because she was brimming to spill all, but because Emily asked. And by the time they finished their salads, Emily found herself wishing this woman lived in Neukirk.

She was divorced, a native of Grand Island, the daughter of a man who once preached in a Baptist church but had quit the ministry—not unlike Mike—for reasons Sally never understood, her father being the kind of man who didn't speak openly about failure. She had been a teacher, third grade, for ten years, while her husband—her former husband—had driven a truck, a cattle truck, long distances. Their marriage had broken, she said, because there was no giving; her husband was nearly addicted to the long hauls (*addicted* was her word), while her frustration—she'd had three little children—grew. The money was good, she said, but there was no love; so she left her children and the small Nebraska town where they'd lived.

"I know what you're thinking," she told Emily. "Don't think that I haven't thought it myself."

"Do you ever see them?"

She nodded her head. "Yes," she said. "But all of them—this

was all years ago, of course, and they're grown now—all of them got really poisoned toward me for what I did, abandoning them. And maybe I did, I don't know. But I couldn't go on."

Emily pointed at Sally, then at Mike. "So you two met how? Doctor and patient?"

"Yep," he said. "Breaks every rule in the book." He raised a finger to his lips. "Promise you won't tell a soul."

"And now we both help people," Sally said. "Daughter of a fallen pastor and a fallen pastor, both of us broken up—it's a great story, isn't it?"

"The truth is," Mike said, "ours is the only profession that actually requires failure on a resume. I'm not kidding. You ought to go to a conference sometime—nothing but basket cases."

"Maybe I ought to apply," Emily said.

"Stop it," Mike said. "I left my meter in the office."

The way they talked together, Emily thought, was wonderful. "So why don't you get married?" she said.

Mike put down his fork. "I'm supposed to ask the questions," he said.

"This isn't therapy," Emily said. "I didn't come here for that."

"You didn't come to find out about me either. I don't even remember you. You must be a tail-ender—"

"Not much of a tail really, only the two of us," Emily said.

Sally had ordered the vegetarian plate, a small portion, and finished quickly. She sat back, both hands on the table, her right hand on her glass of wine. Mike faced her when he spoke, as if his intent was to review the past, what he remembered, what he knew, and Emily was only a kind of guide to bridge the gaps.

"What I remember of her folks," he said, "is that they were great people. And one of the things I could never figure out was where Meg came from. Meg was her older sister. She died a month after I left—maybe a little longer. But I could never understand where she picked up the edge she had—this appetite for politics, so unlike Neukirk in 1968—or today too, I suppose."

"'Unlike'?" Sally said.

"Somehow she flew into the whole antiwar thing. And she was only in high school. There were kids in that church who went off to college and never began to understand what was going on in the world they lived in."

He picked a pack of cigarettes out of the patch pocket of his shirt, slapped it up against the edge of his hand and took one out.

"I had this view then," he said, still looking at Sally. "You know, everything fit in those days for me, and sometimes I'd wonder—I'm not lying here—I'd wonder if maybe Meg was adopted. I even asked. And Daniels—he was the preacher— Daniels said that it was odd that I would ask. But he didn't know Meg that well because she seemed so, well, *practiced* at concealing what was on her mind, even though when she'd talk to me, I found myself trying to hold her back."

"Was she?" Sally asked.

"Was she what?"

"Adopted?"

Mike looked at Emily and shook his head. "No. Part of it was just the times, I think. But part of it was your parents too, whose devotion to God—that sounds so hokey, doesn't it?—but, Sally, you should have known those people—" He stopped abruptly. "They're gone, aren't they?" he asked Emily.

"My father. My mother's in a nursing home."

"I think now, when I remember them—and Meg—I wonder if maybe she'd picked up the same kind of tenacity or devotion that they had and merely brought it into politics."

"Good for her," Sally said.

"Sure, if she'd lived in the Market it would have been all right," he said. He'd pulled a pack of matches from the box at the register when they'd come in. He struck one and held up a hand as if there were a wind. "What do you know?" he said to Emily. "What do you know and what do you want from me?"

She pulled the note out of the pocket of her skirt, handed it to him.

"University of Illinois," he said, reading it. He shoved it at Sally. "I remember when I got the job there how important it was for me to use university stationary. I'm embarrassed."

"What happened to her?" Sally asked.

"I'm sorry," he said. "I didn't explain. It was a car accident, wasn't it?" he said to Emily.

She stopped for a moment. It was such an easy way of summarizing. "Yes," she said.

"I don't really remember writing this. Of course, things were wild on the campus at that time, and I wasn't thinking much about Neukirk." He dropped his hands. "I'm sorry," he said to Emily. "I don't want to sound crass, but that's the way it was. Neukirk was a kind of school for me, and a good one—well, maybe not a good one either. Only God'll settle that one, I suppose. But in Champaign at that time—1968—things were wild. Besides, I didn't want to go back—"

"What did they know?" Emily said.

"I don't understand the question."

"What did my parents know about Meg? About what she thought about things, about what she did. She was smoking— I've got that from a reliable source—"

"That was a crime in Neukirk?" Sally said.

"Dope," Emily said. "And it was a crime."

For the first time since they'd met, Emily felt a bit of condescension from them. "I'm no saint," she said. "I'm not here to put my sister in hell—that's not it. I could care less if she smoked anything at all back then, but I want to know what my parents knew about her."

"Why?" Mike said. "What did they tell you?"

"Nothing," she said. "It was not something we ever really discussed."

Mike pulled an ashtray from the edge of the table.

"Not that I couldn't have. I mean, I inherited a lot of her clothes, even though they were out of style. And I got her bike. Her picture stayed on the bookcase. It's not that they didn't ever speak of her. They did."

"Virtuously?" Mike said.

"Meaning?"

"Meaning, as in 'Meg would do this, you know—why don't you?'"

"Never."

"As in what?" he asked.

"As in, 'Meg never wanted to be held.' My mother would say things like that, reminisce. 'Meg never slept much as a baby.' That kind of thing."

"So what they didn't talk about," he said, "was Meg as an adolescent. Meg as a teenager."

"And never anything about her death."

Mike sat back from the table, folded one arm over his chest to hold the other one up, the one with the cigarette. "I remember telling them about the abortion," he said.

Emily grew cold.

"We met in the church. I was happier there, more sure of myself. It's like some people in the pulpit, you know. Once they get up there, it's like a drug, it opens them up. They get to feeling stronger because they have this sense that the Word of God is theirs."

"An abortion?" Sally said.

He held the cigarette between his thumb and forefinger, close to his lips. "I didn't tell Daniels because—well, because I thought of it as a failure. She'd come to me," he said, looking directly at Emily, "and she told me that she was pregnant and that she knew this guy who could line up an abortion—I think it was in Sioux City. I don't remember."

"That's before Roe v. Wade," Sally said.

"Sure," he said. "We're talking back alley here, although I'm not so sure that it was as bad as people make it out to be. I don't know. I really don't know what she went through."

"She told you?" Emily said.

"Yeah. One night she called and asked if she could talk. She told me she was pregnant—and she wasn't broken up. I had another one like that when I was there in Neukirk, another girl who got pregnant, and I could hardly keep her in Kleenex. Not Meg. I don't know where she got her steel."

"What happened?" Sally asked.

He took one long last puff, then doused the cigarette in the tin ashtray on the table. "I told her in no uncertain terms—and she thought of me as a friend, I'm sure, or she wouldn't have told me in the first place—but I told her it was wrong, it was sinful, it was against God's Word, and that it was even a sin to consider it."

"She did it anyway," Sally said.

He nodded. His eyes took on a dreamy quality. "Good gracious, I've not thought about that for a long time."

"How did you know she did?" Emily said.

"Because she didn't have the baby—it was that simple."

"Maybe she just missed a period—"

"No. A couple months passed, and I met her again one day. I was young and full of ideals. I cornered her in the church parking lot, in the back—you know, where they used to keep that burn barrel? And I said to her that I hoped it wouldn't happen again." He raised both hands up in the air. "By rights I should have reported them both to the church, you know, but I didn't. I thought like you did, Emily—I figured that maybe she'd just missed a few. My goodness, she was only seventeen, thin as a rail, pretty, beautiful girl—like you."

"She admitted it then?" Sally said.

"She looked right up in my eyes and she said that she'd had the abortion, that it was over, and that, yes, it—meaning pregnancy—wouldn't happen again."

"And you told all of this to my parents?" Emily said.

"I was just a squirt, and I had this great idea that a preacher could be a prophet and a priest at the same time—that I could deliver great sermons and still be compassionate to sinners." He looked at Sally. "But I couldn't."

"You took it personally," Sally said.

"You know," he raised both hands, "by rights—I should say, by the rules of the game—I should have at least told Daniels everything, my senior pastor. We're talking major violation of God's law here. I mean, the seventh commandment gets broken three nights a week in a place like Neukirk; but back then, at least, abortion was murder. Probably still is—probably worse today."

"You didn't tell anyone?" Sally said.

"Maybe because it was my failure—or anger. Probably anger. I remember walking out of that churchyard after she'd left. I remember going to my office in the church and opening the Bible, playing this silly game of just flip it open somewhere and expect that Jesus Christ will somehow walk out of the pages and spell relief. I don't remember what I read, but I do remember thinking that that girl had heard the Word of God directly from his spokesman on earth—me, the wet-behind-the-ears preacher —and simply disobeyed."

"But you told my parents," Emily said. "You said that you told my parents."

"I felt like the Old Testament God. I wanted to fling thunderbolts, you know, even though I loved that girl—and I mean that truly. I respected Meg because she was open and honest and she loved to discuss things with me, all kinds of things that meant a lot to me then—principles, you know, things the rest of the kids didn't care about."

"Why did you tell them?" Emily asked.

He waited for a moment, as if there were a variety of options in his mind. Then he pulled himself up and pointed. "Because I thought it was the right thing to do. They were her parents—your parents," he said. "And even if I didn't tell Daniels or anybody else in church, I thought it was the right thing to do, maybe a way of dealing with my own indecision. I hated the sin, you know—that's the way we were always told to think of it—I hated the sin, but I loved the sinner." He shook his head, laughed. "Listen to me, Sally," he said, "I still think it was the right thing to do."

Sally pulled back from the table and shook her head.

"They must have been destroyed," Emily said. "If I know my parents, they must have been really broken."

He reached for his water, took a drink. "They were just like Meg about it. I told them in my study, in the little cubbyhole Daniels gave me. I sat them down and I told them what had happened, and neither of them cried. I swear, neither of them."

"I can't believe that," Emily said.

"I'm not making it up," he said. "Maybe you were right when you said, before, that there were things about your parents you really never knew."

"It was anger," Sally said. "It was a kind of retribution on your part—"

"Don't analyze," he said. "We're not talking about caricature Christian parents here, Sally—the Bible in one hand, a bullwhip in the other," he told her. "We're not talking about abusers, religious fanatics. We're talking about good, good people."

"So you thought the home was the best place to work it all out?"

"I don't know what I thought exactly," he said, angrily. "All I know is I didn't tell the whole bunch of people I should have told back then. They were way too righteous. The only people I told were her parents because I trusted them, I believed in them. And it seemed to me then—twenty, what, twenty-five years ago—that it was the right thing to do."

"It was anger. She'd broken your trust—"

"Sally, this isn't a board game," he said. "We're talking about this woman's sister here, this woman's sister and her mother."

Everything stopped for a moment, and he reached across the table to take Emily's hand, laid his over it, then pinched her fingers lightly. "Look at me," he said, and she looked up into his eyes for what seemed thirty seconds, maybe more, before finally he said it. "You didn't know any of this, did you?"

She looked at Sally, then back at him, tightened her lips and shook her head.

He pulled his hand up to his forehead. "Wow," he said. Then he leaned forward, put both elbows on the table, and held his head with his fingertips. "It never dawned on me that you wouldn't know," he said. "I mean, I never considered the fact that your parents wouldn't have told you the whole story. I should have guessed. Nothing like silence in Neukirk—nothing so comforting as holding it all inside and thinking maybe it will all go away."

The waitress came around to ask if there was anything else and when all three were silent, she ripped the check off the tablet and laid it beside Mike on the table.

"I came here to find out exactly what you told me," Emily said as soon as the woman left. "There's no need for you to apologize." She stopped, inhaled deeply, had nowhere to go.

"It wasn't all that rare," Sally said. "I know others—"

"It's not the abortion I'm concerned about. I'm enough of my parents, I think, to know that there isn't much the Lord won't forgive."

"You got a gift, girl," Mike said. "It's something I lost somewhere—I don't know where, but sometimes I think it's gone."

"You mean about her—about Meg?"

"Oh, no, no. Don't misunderstand. I used to believe in principle," he said, laughing. "Now I guess all I believe in is making do." He looked down at the ashtray, pushed it around in small circles. "I'm sorry if I hurt you."

"I'm wondering what it did to my parents," Emily said. "I mean, what you told them."

"Sometimes I wish I was still there in Neukirk, you know—all that certainty about things," he told her. "The only thing I'm convinced of now is that I'm not God." He started to pull himself out of the booth. "Maybe I spent too much of my life thinking I was his hands, when I wasn't." He looked at Sally. "You mad at me?"

She smiled, shook her head.

He pointed at her and looked at Emily. "The only reason we're not married is that this way it's impossible for her to divorce me—that's the truth."

"I keep threatening," Sally said.

Mike picked a twenty out of his billfold and laid it on the

ticket, then shoved it to the corner of the table where the waitress could get it.

"You know, I've come to believe that sometimes in life it's a whole lot better not to know the whole truth," he said.

"It's not just that," Emily said. "I'm not really concerned with what Meg did or didn't do—that's not it at all."

"What is it then?" Sally asked.

Emily closed her eyes.

"Some kind of mystery or something? Something about her death?" Sally asked.

Emily shook her head. "I don't know if I want to tell you exactly," she said. "I don't know if I want to hear what you'll say." She looked at Mike directly. "Maybe I'm just crazy. Believe me, everything you've said is really helpful. I'm glad I know it all. I can live with my sister the way she was—whatever that was."

The waitress came and picked up the money and the check.

Emily had seen enough of these two to respect them, enough to know they weren't flawless. "My mother had a stroke," she said. "She can't speak. She can't do much of anything really, but she sits in a chair and she watches Main Street during the day, and sometimes I visit her and speak to her."

She stopped for a moment and looked into both of their faces to be sure nothing was there but openness. "I don't exactly understand her—my mother—or faith, for that matter. I found out about Meg since I came back to Neukirk—"

"Stupid gossips," Sally said.

"No, that wasn't it. It was the man she was with, the man who was driving the car when she was killed. He told me everything, and it was painful—"

"Everything?" Sally said.

"Except the abortion. I didn't know about that—I don't know if he even knew." She wound the napkin around her fingers. "My mother can hum a song—'Some Day the Silver Cord Will Break'—a hymn my sister liked, I guess, when she was maybe twelve. It's the only thing she can do, hum."

"I'm sorry," Sally said.

"You don't have to be. Sometimes I think it's the rest of us who have the trouble." She felt again as if she could cry. "Once I'd heard what Meg was like—and it was all new to me, all this rebelliousness, the politics—I thought neither Mom nor Dad ever knew anything at all about her. Norm said they didn't. He didn't think so."

She found it difficult to go on.

"I was bad in a way. I saw my parents living in a world that didn't exist—not at all—and I started hating them for it. Not *hating* them really—I'm not saying it clearly." She brought both hands up in front of her, palms together. "I thought their faith was blindness, see? I thought they were just living in another world, not the real world."

"And then you found this note?" Mike said, picking it off the table and shoving it back to her.

She nodded. "The song is the only thing that comes out of her. It's not even really recognizable. I don't know if the nurse is even right about which hymn it is, but she claims she's heard it often enough to figure it out." She turned circles with her finger as if that hymn were playing on a phonograph there on the table. "But it sounds different to me now," she said. "Not so much delusion, I guess, as hope. Not for my father, or for me, or for herself—but for Meg. I can't help but wonder how many years she's been humming it."

"That's all she has," Mike said.

"This maybe means nothing to you, but I'm wondering right now—and maybe I'll never know—just exactly how my sister's death affected my parents, how it changed their lives. Does it make sense that I would want to know? Even if nothing would change?"

"Makes perfect sense," Sally said, and Mike nodded.

IV

Just across the Big Sioux River, maybe a dozen miles west of Neukirk, two triangular signs stand beside each other on a lonely country corner where two gravel roads intersect in the middle of acres and acres of corn. Splashed across each of those signs is a large black "X," a warning to everyone who takes the time to look that sometime in the past an accident happened here, an accident that took two lives. "Think," those signs say.

Thus does South Dakota make moral lessons of its traffic fatalities. You'll find such signs all over the state, and they are effective, especially when they stand in clumps of two, or three, or four. There's nothing to indicate whether what happened was occasioned by drinking, by inattention, by mistake or sheer fate; but even if you don't know who or when or how, those signs create a story that has a definite conclusion, even if it has no beginning. They are intended to be, and they are, sermons; but they are also monuments, like cemetery stones, that make otherwise indistinguishable ditches into historical places.

But making object lessons out of highway fatalities seems, at least to some, in poor taste. Imagine Emily Doorn, on her way back from Omaha, taking a left at some unmarked corner of the highway, slowing down through the loose gravel of two miles of country road, coming up over a rise and crossing one of those old wooden bridges that still span gullies and washes, and then spotting an "X" where twenty-five years ago her sister was killed. "Think," it would say.

Or imagine her parents, like so many Neukirk people their age, having gone out for supper at some town's pride and joy supper club, and then returning, looking at the crops, taking a back road to get to the spot where their daughter was killed and finding the "X" still there. Wouldn't it be natural for them to climb out of the car and uproot that sign? Wouldn't they want it down?

On the Iowa side of the Big Sioux there are no such signs. So when Emily came back north from Omaha late that afternoon, when she felt the impulse to drive past that corner—she knew where it was, of course; the spot would be marked forever in her mind—she found absolutely nothing to say there had been an accident, nothing at all.

In fact, as she stood there at the eastern edge of the intersection, it appeared to her that this otherwise forgettable meeting of two county roads might look exactly as it did all those years ago. It was August, just as it was August on the night Meg died. Fields of tall corn stood on three of the four corners, and perfectly clean, straight rows of beans stretched away, waist-high or better, on the north side of the western corner. Shards of plastic and a flattened, decaying cardboard six-pack lay in the ditch grass. The only indication of this being a public spot, something other than simply a place where some farmer marked off his land and kept the corn from the beans, was a series of brightly colored signs, running one after another along the bean rows, announcing exactly what number seed someone had planted here in May—bragging, it seemed, as if the road were full of shopping farmers looking for great deals come spring.

There was no sign here, no "X," no brass marker with Meg's name and the date of her death in raised print. No tire tracks, no black strips where someone hit the brakes, no scalped grass in the ditch where the cars had rolled. It was as if nothing had happened here. And that seemed strange and painful. What she'd gone through since returning to Neukirk was caused by what had happened here; now the numbness of this spot made her loneliness even more torturous.

A tall, square house, recently painted, shining like a marquee in the afternoon sun, stood up on enough of a rise to be seen from the corner—the place Norm must have walked to, already knowing Meg was gone. A quarter-century ago. Even the people who lived there now might well have no idea what had happened here.

Norm and Meg had been driving north, toward Neukirk, up the road to her left, a perfectly flat stretch with a slight rise maybe a half-mile below the intersection, far enough away that no one would call this corner blind, at least not from the south. And the boys in the other car—she didn't know for sure whether they'd come from the east or west, but for some reason she'd always thought they were going towards the highway, east. That's the way she'd always seen it in her mind. Why? she wondered.

After the funeral, after the committal in the cemetery in town, after the gathering at the church for cake and punch and coffee, after everyone had left and they'd gone back home, the three of them, in her father's car—the green Buick, the one her father bought because it once belonged to the State Patrol and therefore had been well-maintained, he said—the three of them drove out here to this corner. Not until this moment had she remembered that trip.

Her father'd parked the car, just as she had—in almost the same spot—but they didn't get out. She'd been in the back seat, her arms up over the front seat between her parents. She tried to bring it back, to dig into that memory, bring it into closer focus. She tried to remember crying, but what she remembered was her mom and dad sitting on opposite sides of the car, and herself, her chin resting on her arms on the front seat, between them.

They didn't get out, and if there were marks here in this ditch somewhere, if there was grass flattened or sod upturned, she didn't remember seeing it, even though she was sure somehow that the boys' car—what did it look like?—had come to rest here beside where she stood, in the north side ditch of the road east of the intersection. Somehow she was sure.

What did they say? She remembered nothing, simply that she was there, and it was the afternoon after the funeral because she remembered having the dress on, the dress Mrs. Ferringa bought, the woman who'd taken her shopping in the days between Meg's death and the funeral. She was wearing that dress, navy blue with white trim and a square white collar down her back, and new shoes, patent leather. And everything was hot, terribly hot. She'd been in the back seat, all dressed up from the funeral.

She remembered her mother turning finally, resting her hand on the back of the seat, her mother's arm over her hands; she remembered her mother's eyes, clouded and red, as they were all through those days.

But nothing was said. Her father kept both hands on the wheel in the way he always did, looking forward, down the road where she was sure the boys had come.

No one had said anything. None of them had spoken.

Why? she thought. The silence grew into a way of life, some thin membrane stretching over the hurt. When she was older, when she could have listened to the whole story, understood something of their pain, it was impossible for them to speak, to pull away whatever it was that had grown protectively over the hurt. And so they never spoke, not that day after the funeral, and not later.

Was it right? she wondered.

Maybe they would have liked this corner just the way it was now—the corn and the beans and the ditch grass, the awkward, barren posts that still remained from the days when every parcel of land was fenced. Maybe they could have appreciated this silence, this almost painful disregard of quietness at the very spot where it had happened. The corner remembered nothing of the accident that had taken Meg's life. Yes, her parents would have liked the corner this way—no sign, no marker.

Not because they had forgotten. There was, after all, "Meg's favorite song—1962." Never forgotten, beneath that thin membrane. But what if they had spoken?

"We're all a bunch of basket cases," Mike Stellinga had said of his profession, but at least they listened to people who spoke.

From a mile away, maybe more, the thump of a tractor hitting road gear carried along through the flat tunnel created by cornfields. A dog barked. The sound of children, their voices almost distinguishable, brought a kind of life to the corner.

She started walking back toward her car, ill-at-ease about being spotted out here alone, not wanting to draw attention to herself. She put her hands in the pockets of her skirt and followed the ditch grass, as if she might find something. All she spotted was a few bunched plants of what her father used to call hemp, a weed—actually, marijuana—growing as densely as it always did. And she thought of Norm holding a plastic bag with what remained of the dope Meg had picked up at that apartment in Sioux City. Were these plants descendants of whatever fell into the ditch when he threw it all away, the traces of evidence?

But marijuana grew all over the ditches out here, she remembered, even when she was a kid. And she couldn't believe, not really, that these plants were somehow a ghostly legacy, because she didn't believe in a God who would commemorate what happened here with sprouting hemp that wouldn't die. She couldn't believe in that kind of God.

She got into the car, urged it into drive and crept slowly toward the intersection, then sat there looking up the road—south, then west, then north—and realized something she'd felt for the last three hours. She didn't want to go back to Neukirk. Not only because of what she'd learned about Meg, but because she didn't want to go back and have to speak, or have to keep silent. What she wanted to do, desperately, was refill all those half-emptied boxes around the house, throw the junk back into the barn, call up the movers, and leave. But for what? For LA, for Florida, for what place?

And she didn't want to return to what she faced in town, even without this new information. She didn't want to go back to Marty Kamphoff or to the bowling alley. She didn't want to speak to anyone about anything, not even to Norm, to whom she'd likely have to lie. What good would it do to tell him what Stellinga had remembered so clearly? Maybe the only place she could stay, where she could be as anonymous as she'd been in LA, was here, nowhere, the scene of the accident.

Was that what her parents felt? Was that why the only sound her mother could emit today was the strained notes of an old song that sometime, years before the accident even, Meg had chosen as a favorite?

She understood the comfort in being here for what it was—a merciless irony—but she didn't want to move; certainly she didn't want to go any further north toward town. She didn't want to go back. Her parents must have felt it, she thought, knowing what they knew. They must have felt the same burden, the same irony. Maybe witnessed in themselves the same kind of refusal to leave the scene of the accident because too much of them—their daughter, yes of course, their daughter, but so much more too—had died right there. They, too, must have felt that they simply couldn't go on. It was easier and it was even right, they probably assumed, not only to bury their daughter, but to bury themselves as well. Never forget, of course; but don't bring it up, not ever.

The radio was on and the air conditioner blew out cold air that threw a chill on her neck. Her windows were closed, so she didn't hear the tractor come up behind her, never saw it until the image jumped out at her from the rearview mirror.

And even though she knew that what she thought the instant she saw the tractor was Neukirk instinct—this odd guilt, the silly worry about what someone would think of her sitting out there—she couldn't stop the reaction. Her conscience flipped madly through alternatives. If she took off quickly, she'd look guilty—a BMW with California plates. If she stayed, she would almost certainly make him stop. And what would she say? Would she tell him why she was here? What other motivation could she have to be here, she thought? She was checking the crops? It was ludicrous. It was fear—Neukirk fear—at its worst.

It angered her to feel her own mind so much a victim of

small-town self-consciousness. She slapped her hands on the wheel, then turned off the engine, right there in the center of the intersection. She glanced in the mirror and saw the tractor, no more than a few car lengths behind her, slowing down. She reached for the latch and stepped out, not because she wanted to face this guy, but because she refused to be strong-armed by this Neukirk guilt that prompted her to run away, that caused her to worry about how her being there "might look." She closed the door softly behind her as the tractor came up, stuck her hands in the pockets of her skirt, and leaned back against the side of the car.

It was a kid, a boy, a teenager. He waved, then slowed to a stop and came out of the cab on the other side of the tractor, walked around the front. Big, strong farm kid in a surf shirt with the sleeves torn off, no cap, his hair bleached not only by the sun, but also by a thin coat of dust.

"Got trouble?" he said, smiling.

She looked at him and told herself that there was really no reason why she couldn't explain exactly why she was out here.

"You out of gas?" he said. "Our place is just up the road."

"I'm not in trouble," she said finally.

He was tall and strong, but she could see something in him that was reticent, even afraid.

"I thought I'd come out here," she said, and she plunged on, "because this is the place where my sister was killed—in an accident." She forced herself not to look away, and when it was out, when the words had passed, she pulled herself up from the side of the car, took her hands out of her pockets, and rubbed them together. "You wouldn't remember," she said. "It was long before your time."

He looked around as if he could find a trace.

"Did you live here twenty-five years ago?" she said. "I mean, did your parents live on that farm?" She pointed up the road behind them.

"We're a Century Farm," he said. "You know what that is? My great-grandfather farmed here. We've been here a hundred years. Got a sign by the driveway." He stuck his fingers in the back pockets of his jeans, turned at the waist and pointed with his eyes back up the road. "The state makes a big deal out of it."

"Maybe your father remembers," she said. "Margaret Doorn—that was my sister's name. She was called Meg. It was 1968, and it wasn't terribly late—around midnight."

His eyes squinted slightly.

"She was with a date." It sounded strange to her now to call Norm a date. "She was with this guy and they hit another car with some kids in it, some guys, and she got killed. The only one."

"My parents heard it," he said. "They've told me about it. They heard the accident. They came out here—"

"They did?" she said.

"Sure. Even now, sometimes, they'll talk about what kind of bad sound it made." He hunched his shoulders. "It was before I was born, but I know about it—I sure do. It's something they've talked about a lot."

"Really?" she said.

"A million times. I get sick of it sometimes. See those corners," he said, pointing. "Every year we put corn in there, we shave off the corners, instead of running them right up to the edge, here." He pointed at the ditch. "You know why?"

"Because of that accident?" she said.

He nodded. "I always hear about it in the spring, right when we're planting. I always hear that story then, when my dad reminds me not to plant the corners. 'Big crash,' he says. 'We were lying in bed and half asleep, but we heard it anyway, even though it was a quarter-mile down the road.' That's what he always says." He swung his shoulders toward the intersection. "And they can get real edgy about sounds in the night. It wasn't pretty I guess," he said, then he looked away.

"I'm sure," she said.

"You from California now?" he said, pointing toward her license plate.

"I moved there years ago," she told him.

He nodded at her, as if somehow it made sense.

"It looks silly, I suppose, me out here," she said. "But this is an important place for me."

"I don't know your family," he said, "but you know the guy who was driving—"

She shook her head yes.

"He was my teacher—Mr. Visser. Great guy. I mean, every kid that ever had him loved him. Kids look forward to being in sixth grade—I'm not kidding." He hooked his thumbs in the front pockets of his jeans. "It wasn't his fault—that's what my dad says. Now that I had him as a teacher, I don't think about it at all really. But when my dad told me once—that was years ago already—when he told me it was Norm Visser, I thought about it almost every time I'd see him."

"But no more?" Emily said.

"Now he's just a guy that used to be my teacher."

"Was it the other guy's fault?" she said.

He hunched his shoulders, pointed at the house back up the road. "Don't tell my old man," he said, "but I think that even to this day when he thinks about it, he blames himself. I know he does."

"Why?"

"'Cause of them corners," the boy said. "He shouldn't of planted all the way up. Sometimes I think when he remembers that sound the way he does, when he describes it, you know— the way it woke him at night and how awful it was—I think he blames himself."

"That's almost twenty-five years ago," she said.

"I know," he said. "Your sister—she was dead right away, wasn't she? She flew out of the car, I think."

"That's right," Emily said.

"But one of them other guys had a lot of bones broken or something, and the way they talk about it, there was a lot of screaming." He looked down as if ashamed himself. "I know that the neighbor up the road—" he stopped, as if wondering whether it was appropriate to give the name. "I know he came up in his truck and then went back to call the ambulance, but he never come back here," the boy said, pointing at the gravel beneath his feet. "That's part of the story my dad tells—how the neighbor never come back after calling because—"

"Why?"

"Because that kid had so much pain. That's what my dad remembers, I think, the sound of that kid screaming."

"It wasn't your father's fault," Emily said.

"The kid we're talking about doesn't live here anymore—it was Lonnie Rynders. He's a lawyer in Des Moines. Of course, you know all that—"

She shook her head to say that she didn't, but he didn't seem to notice. He seemed almost lost in the whole story, even though it was something that had happened years before he was born.

"You know, we got land down this road. My dad's got a forty just on the other side of that hill up there, and we got a couple of bins at the side of the field—maybe you seen 'em." He pointed at the tractor. "I been hauling grain to town today—we sold some from last year. I go by this corner an awful lot," he said. "And it doesn't happen every time either, but lots of times, when I'm in my car especially, when I come up here to where you're parked, you know?—I think about it."

"You're kidding," she said.

He shook his head as if it was silly of her to think any different.

"It's something I got from my dad, I suppose. He never forgets." He laughed lightly to cover the seriousness. "I'm going to tell him you were here. That's all right, isn't it? What's your name?"

"Emily," she said. "Emily Doorn."

"I'm Chris, but lots of people call me Bud—like my old man."

"Chris?"

"Chris Ellerbroek," he said.

Her memory held no pictures of a man named Ellerbroek.

"What's your father's name?" she asked.

186

"Harold?" he said, as if it might ring a bell. "Maybe you ought to talk to them sometime. My mother's name is Louise, and she's not from here. She's from Mason City, sort of, a small town around there. I think they'd both like it really—I mean, if you'd stop."

"Maybe I will," she said.

"I'll tell them I saw you out here," he said. "I got to pick up another load of grain up there, but when I get back I'll tell them." He seemed to wave to her before he half-turned. "They'll like that—knowing you were here," he said. "I'll tell them."

Once the wagon he was pulling—its triangular warning sign on the back—disappeared up the hill to the west, she turned north up the gravel, headed toward Neukirk. Way up ahead somewhere, maybe sixty miles north, a huge thunderhead rose from the flat prairie space like a solitary mountain. Ahead of it for as far as she could see, clouds, thinner and less defined, darkened the sky; but the storm, or at least its greatest violence, was at the end, though lightning still splashed frequently across its huge gray face.

She'd forgotten what it was like to watch storms, to stand out in the yard and see the way the huge clouds somewhere far away were bringing hail and rain, sometimes tornadoes, and always fear. Those storms appeared out of nowhere on days like this, when the damp heat brought sweat out on her father's face as he simply stood and watched the clouds. On days like that everyone knew that somewhere on the plains, somewhere close probably, someone would catch the violence—lightning, hail, or twisters. It was just a matter of fate—where it would all come down.

And then the wind would change and blow from the northwest and chase the moist heat somewhere south, back where it came from. The land would cool, and her father would be grateful, thankful they'd got rain, even though he'd know—and he'd pray that way too—that somewhere some farmer like him would walk out of his storm cellar and see a barn flattened or corn stripped or half a field of beans gone.

It would have been impossible for her parents to tell anyone in Neukirk about what had happened to their daughter, about an abortion. Even now it would be difficult for any parent there to admit; then, it was something that simply couldn't be said. So they'd lived with that knowledge buried within them, as deeply as the death that had come so unexpectedly and so untimely.

If only she'd known, she thought—even years later, when she was old enough to understand. If only they could have told her, opened it all up somehow. Maybe they could have breathed.

She followed the gravel back north toward town, one long and lonely mile after another, past a few farms and, on one corner of another intersection, a boarded-up schoolhouse, its yard full of hogs. Some of these farms she knew—the Tigelaars, the Hesselinks, the Kroons—big houses, most of them with porches and front doors that looked obsolete because all the traffic came and went through the back, the door closest to the machine shed. Big gardens, richly green, half potatoes. Barns, most of them run-down and sagging or pitched slightly, like the fun houses that claimed to defy gravity.

The whole business of farming had changed, of course; there were few dairies anymore, few pastures, few Holsteins. Where the cattle yards weren't overgrown with weeds, the farms themselves became acreages or hobby farms; cattle pens were immense, humped above ground level with manure— dozens upon dozens, even hundreds of cattle standing there as if useless in the muggy August heat, hogs down in the mud trying to keep cool.

She'd always found it hard to think of herself as a farm girl, so little she really knew about farming. She never understood whose decision it was, but sometime during her childhood there must have been an agreement that Emily, like Meg, wasn't going to do much outside the house. She never drove a tractor while her father scooped up hay bales on the wagon behind; never milked, since her father never had more than a few cows, and even those were gone by the time she was old enough to ride a bike down the road to the neighbors; never planted corn or picked it; never cultivated. What she knew about farming was its loneliness, although she'd never thought of herself as lonely; most of her playmates were farm cats willing to let her dress them or carry them around the yard.

How many times in LA, when she'd tell people she was born on an Iowa farm, had she been admired for being a farm girl? At how many parties had people wanted to know what it was like, as if growing up out here, where the air was redolent with manure, was really some kind of exotic joy? She imagined them picturing her on a stool, milking, or gathering eggs from the kind of henhouse you'd see in a cartoon, the kind where the hens could suddenly break into a song.

People in California seemed to have the notion that growing up on a farm was really beginning life in the way that God had intended, the way all kids should grow up: milking cows, watching the kind of prairie storms that swept Dorothy away to Oz, and sitting on the front porch swing, sipping cold lemonade wrung from real lemons. What a wonderful world!

The silly thing was, she thought, actually growing up under this wide open sky, subject to the violent Iowa weather—oppressive heat, deathly cold, overpowering storms of all kinds— *was* exotic when compared to suburban childhoods, where the kid places were not farm groves, little ditch creeks, or haymows, but shopping malls. After all, hadn't that been part of the reason she came back to Neukirk after the divorce—this belief she'd developed in LA that her own children, now missing a father, needed something of the freedom she'd had as a child, something of the values? Weren't there, in fact, more "values" here? Isn't that, at least partially, why people referred to all of this as "the heartland"?

She'd just wanted her kids to play in unfenced backyards, to ride their bikes all over town, to be safe no matter where they spent their afternoons. And she'd wanted to be near her mother.

She'd never once considered that in coming back to Neukirk she might learn things about her sister she didn't want to know or expose her children to someone like Jason Kamphoff. She'd never considered such things possible in heaven.

She hadn't expected Norm Visser either. And had she known that he still lived in Neukirk, so many years later, she would never have guessed he would become not only someone she could love and trust, but someone who would tell her what he did about her sister.

Her dead sister. A picture on the bookcase. A memory. A bad memory, really. Painful. A pain that was alleviated only when her name was left buried, in perfect silence.

She knew some parents made an icon of a child who died, an angel, a saint—even a standard for the other children. But it had never been that way with her parents. Her mother never said much about how Meg would do her hair or clean up her room or have her devotions. Her father never hauled out Meg's report cards or urged Emily to play the same piano pieces. When she died, Emily thought, Meg was buried and descended into wordless oblivion.

Because of the abortion? she wondered now. Because the sin was so great that there was no hope for her salvation? Because of the shame her parents must have felt, knowing their daughter had killed her baby? Because her parents had stepped in for God Almighty and aimed their oldest daughter toward damnation?

No, she thought. She knew of parents on these farms who would have done that, people who were so vindictive, so stubbornly committed to quarrelsome righteousness—but not hers. It wouldn't have been her father's way to write off his daughter, to give up hope for her soul and deliver her into the hands of the Devil. That wasn't him.

They must have put the whole subject into some kind of storage, in her presence at least. But maybe in their quiet moments alone, lying together in the heat of an August night, the anniversary of her death, maybe they spoke about it, in whispers.

Was it their faith that brought them the most pain? If they

weren't Christians, couldn't they simply have buried her and gone on? What had obsessed them—what still seemed to obsess her mother—was the uncertainty of Meg's salvation, something that must have made even the good days out there on the farm seem dark.

What good is faith, she thought, if it delivers nothing but dread?

She turned left, away from Neukirk, once she got close enough to read the name on the water tower south of town. She turned left, not to avoid going home, but because she wanted to drive out to the place where Ben and Vivian Doorn had farmed—the place she'd grown up.

The grove was thinner. Tons of ash trees must have died. Alongside the eastern edge of the place, where her father used to dump the garbage, the corn ran right up to the edge of the trees. The storage bin she'd painted still looked good; the braces her father had put between the walls to hold the place together when it was full of grain were still there, shoulder high.

Apples were hanging heavily from the two trees east of the house. Before long they'd be dropping to the ground. That was a no-no, of course, and for years her job. You let the apples rot and you'll ruin whatever grows for the next several years—the worms'll crawl up into the tree or something. She couldn't remember the theory as well as she could the job: "In the fall, Em, keep the grass beneath the apple trees clean."

She had slept alone upstairs after Meg was gone. There were two bedrooms up there, but her parents slept downstairs. Her father didn't care much about how things looked to others—neither did her mother, really—so they lived in a house that was small and rather randomly put together. No central air, no upstairs registers, only a grate in the hallway outside her room where warmth from the furnace would rise from the kitchen beneath.

When she saw the house again, she wondered why she'd never really been scared alone upstairs. She must have been shipped off somewhere when it happened, because she didn't remember them cleaning up Meg's bedroom, getting rid of the wall posters she could just barely remember, not for what was on them but because they were all over and made her sister's room exciting. When she thought about the other room upstairs, all she remembered was the waterfall furniture, a yellow spread, and a little plastic lamp that hung from the headboard. It was all older furniture, sort of late-forties, and she couldn't remember whether or not it was the furniture that was there when Meg was alive. It just seemed to her, when she thought about it now, that it was a nondescript guest room that rarely had guests.

She remembered bringing home a boyfriend from college—not Benjamin—and waiting until she thought her parents were sleeping (her dad wore a hearing aid that came off at night) before sneaking over to his bed. They'd slept together all night long, right above her parents' bed.

Did they even worry about her at all? Shouldn't they have worried about her more—after Meg?

She drove slowly past the old farm. The sky to the west was lit with a pastel that seemed almost peach, but beyond the grove there was already enough darkness to make whoever might have been inside put on a light. She didn't know who lived there.

The garage behind the house was empty, its door open. She saw no one in the yard, so she drove in the west driveway—there were two of them, one on either side of the house—and stopped the car.

New paint job. Somebody spent more time with it than her father ever did. The board along the roofline was done in charcoal, like the window trim and the front door. It was a cute home now—not cute maybe, but painted more attractively. Her father spent some summer evenings every few years throwing white paint up on the sides. She remembered painting too—and scraping the bubbles of ruptured surface that always appeared first on the east side, where the sun would bake the hardest.

Many of the buildings were gone, including the little shacks where her father kept hogs. The place was an acreage now, and it had all the earmarks: a wind sock on the mailbox, a couple of huge butterflies affixed to the siding near the front door, a plastic mother goose and her goslings on the lawn, a miniature wind-mill—splashy little decorations her mother wouldn't have liked at all and her father wouldn't have had time for.

She drove slowly around the back of the house. The trees made the whole place look different. The big maple was gone, the one whose limbs used to offer her a way of getting up on the garage roof. There were more small trees around—the kind that grew millions of orange berries, ornamental, offering little shade. The shrubs on the east side of the house were probably too big. They were woody and looked old, and she would bet—judging from the yard knickknacks—that someone had already mentioned that the time was coming when those shrubs would have to be dug out. Her mother had planted them, she remem-bered, picked them out at a lawn and garden store in Sioux City and brought them home in the trunk of the Buick.

The laundry poles hadn't changed. It was her job to paint them with that paint—what was it called again?—made for metal, aluminum in color, so bright in the sun when she was fin-ished that she could stand there and look at them for hours. To-day they were white. Here and there the rust had broken through.

And there was an air-conditioner, slightly off-balance, at the northeast corner, not new anymore. The grass grew a bit longer at its edges.

She could go to the door, she thought. Tell them she used to live here. Ask if she could see the house one more time. Were there any traces of her—of her family, even of Meg—in there anywhere? If you cleaned out the furnace ducts might you find an earring maybe? Somewhere, caught behind a baseboard or back in a closet or cupboard, would there be a slip of paper, a shopping list, a coupon, a recipe cut from a magazine? Would the pencil marks where Mom had measured her growth still be scratched into the side of the door?

It would be more horrifying to believe that there are no ghosts than to believe there are, she thought.

The police had come to the front door. It was not yet midnight. She'd heard the commotion and crept down to the bottom of the stairs, opened the door silently so she could see across the hallway and into the kitchen. The voices were too low to hear, but she knew it was something important because no one ever came to their house late at night. She came out of the stairwell into the silence. She knew someone was there but she heard no voices, and it was the silence that scared her.

She came out of the hallway and turned toward the living room. The preacher was there—she remembered that now. The preacher and the police. Her mother sat on the arm of a chair in her housecoat, her whole body jerking, Emily remembered; and then suddenly she'd pull a hanky up to her mouth, hold it there for a minute, perfectly still, as if thoroughly composed. Her father's grief was more open and voluble. So scary she turned away. She'd walked back down the hallway toward the staircase and opened the door as quietly as she could, then gone back upstairs, not to her bed but to the grate in the hallway.

It was hot. Summer pajamas. She sat at the grate above the kitchen, just outside of Meg's room, sat there cross-legged and listened. Nothing came up clearly, but there was enough in the sounds to make her know that it was something bad.

When she heard the footsteps come back toward the kitchen, she stood and ran to her bedroom and got into bed. They must have heard her footsteps over the wood floor, she thought. Her mother came up, but she had pretended to be asleep.

It was amazing that she hadn't thought this all through before.

She didn't remember the moment, the exact moment, she was told that Meg was gone. She didn't remember whether her mother had said *dead* or *killed* or *gone*. She didn't remember even seeing her mother there at her bedside. *Did she hold me in her arms? Or did she merely say it, standing beside me? Did she sit beside me and hold my hand or comfort me somehow?* She didn't remember. And she didn't remember how she understood death. She remembered the empty chair at the table, though, and the way they all stood at the cemetery.

Everything that happened after that was a jumble until later. How long? She couldn't remember.

Mrs. Ferringa had lain with her in bed, a woman she didn't really know at all, a woman who, she discovered much later, also once lost a child. Mrs. Ferringa didn't even go their church. She just showed up that day after the funeral, with all the others. The house was full of people, lots of them people she didn't know. Then Mrs. Ferringa took her by the hand and led her upstairs to bed, then lay with her on top of the sheet, lay there until finally Emily had fallen asleep. All night long that woman lay there, because Emily remembered waking up at times and finding that woman beside her, that woman's arm around her. It was something she'd never forgotten, that Mrs. Ferringa—who was around the house a lot in the days following the accident, but rarely after that—that this strange woman had slept with her throughout that hot night at the end of August, the end of the summer.

She'd circled the entire house now, coming out the driveway on the other side, facing north again. No one was home, she was sure. She could, if she wanted, walk up to the door, knock, and if no one answered, enter on her own and look around. She could walk up the stairs, look at her room, all alone up there. She could sit there at the windows overlooking the bean field on the east side of the driveway and remember how they'd look for Dad sometimes when the dinner was ready, how he'd nod as he came up the driveway on the tractor, nod and wave his cap.

She waited at the end of the driveway for a few minutes, then put the car in reverse and backed slowly up the gravel until she stood just beside the front door, where she put the car into park. No one would care, really. Even if they came home when she was there, if she told them why she was here, they wouldn't care, not really—not Neukirk people.

Just in the front of the house, in a corner between three little shrubs, recently planted, stood a ceramic deer, a doe, and her fawn lying on the grass beneath her. On the other side stood a wishing well with a thatched roof, someone's hobby project. The place was so different. Whoever lived there now lived as if the whole family were on display, as if everyone in town took time to ride by and admire the place.

Her mother would never have spent money on such silliness. She had flowers, of course, but each fall she'd collect the withered heads of the marigolds, store them in coffee cans in the cellar, and next year use the old seeds to turn the patches of dirt along the east side golden. She'd never bought anything for ornamentation; she didn't even like jewelry. When Emily was in high school, she had to take her mother shopping or she would have worn the same old styles year in and year out.

And it wasn't just cheapness either; it had nothing to do with putting money in an old sock or stuffing it in a mattress. Her mother just didn't have a public face, and neither did her father. There was church, of course, twice weekly, but little else—sometimes a meal in town on a Friday night. They simply never thought in terms of how they looked, of what others thought. It was a mark of their purity, their simpleness, that in some sweet way—built on natures that seemed, at least, remarkably content—they didn't think of appearances.

She could have gone into the house, but she didn't. Not that she lacked courage or gall. But it wasn't her house anymore. The same wood and the identical plaster walls were there under new coats of paint or wallpaper, but there was little there to remind her—other than the shape of things—that this house had been hers.

And besides, she was tired of moving backwards, tired of digging up so much old stuff, of learning things that really had, in some ways, made her life more miserable. The only person she felt at all comfortable with—Norm Visser—she really didn't want to see. And when she looked at the front porch, with its extra trim and its swing and the fancy little plaque that announced the name of the family, she told herself she didn't need any more of the past and that maybe her parents had been right in not speaking of it, that people can go mad chasing down events that are long past and best buried.

So she put the car in gear and pulled out of the driveway, turned right down the gravel and then left again toward town.

She hadn't asked for this, she told herself. She'd never imagined that if she moved back to Neukirk so much that she never knew would parade in front of her, as if the whole world of Neukirk had been sitting back patiently for these many years, waiting for her to return so they could present this pageant of something she'd never known.

That Meg had died was terrible. That she was with Norm and they weren't in full control was horrible. That Meg had lived some kind of invisible life apart from her parents, from her own mother and father, seemed tragic. But that Meg had taken the life of another human being, a defenseless child, was something Emily thought maybe she would have been better off not knowing.

She'd come here to give her kids the gift of a small-town life. Instead she'd found herself buried by stories that came so quickly she'd not had a moment to absorb them. And now there was more. Norm Visser had been a father, and her parents had known. If there was more to it she didn't even want to know.

She drove into town from the west, past the grain elevators tall as fortresses on either side of the street. She snuck in, as if afraid of what the place still held in store. She had no choice but to face Norm. Everything else she could bury, but he was sitting there in the old house she'd bought—it was so naive of her to think life would get so much better in one of Neukirk's old homes—and he would want to know.

Across the tracks, past the bowling alley, and up to Main Street.

In the three hours plus it had taken her to get back to Neukirk from Omaha, she hadn't considered Norm's part in all of this, weighed down as she was with so much that was so startlingly new.

197

Turn right up Main, past the old bank, the false-front stores on the first block of the business district.

How could he lie, she wondered. He must have known about the pregnancy—he had to know. Meg couldn't have kept it from him. But why hadn't he told her? What possible reason could he have had for withholding that part of the story other than guilt?

What else hadn't he told her, she wondered. What other parts did he conveniently leave out—and why?

For two nights he'd held her, comforted her, the only human being she'd trusted at that point, and now she wondered about him, what she could believe of what he'd said. After twenty-five years had he just somehow conveniently forgotten a pregnancy? An abortion? Sometimes people completely obliterate certain memories, she thought. Did he simply forget that once, long ago, he'd fathered a child that had been aborted?

Or did he simply lie?

Past the hardware, Mertes' Clothing Store, Rexall Drug, the little beer hall shack, a new place that sold Western wear, a movie rental place, and by the time she got past the Co-op on the right, the funeral parlor, the old school building become community center, by the time she finally turned into the driveway, she was not pitying him. She was angry that he could tell her so much, yet leave out the one part she was sure her parents hated most.

He was standing beside his pickup, one elbow propped up on the side, when she drove in behind him. He wore a droopy tank top that said "Drake Relays," leather gloves, Levis, and running shoes, and even from the end of the driveway she could see the way his hair was matted with sweat. The moment he saw her, he went into a dramatic fainting act to show her his near exhaustion. She parked the car facing the front end of the pickup and got out slowly.

"You're going to have to move that thing," he said, pointing. "I been at this half the day—you ought to take a look inside." He nodded behind him, toward the barn.

She reached into the front seat for her purse, then pulled the strap up over her shoulder before looking around for her children.

"They're off somewhere playing," he said. "Haven't seen them for a while, but they're all right. I spoiled them rotten."

She shut the car door softly, walked up the driveway toward the truck, afraid—not angry, but scared.

He pulled away from the truck as if he were going to come to greet her, but when she stopped at the front door, he put his hands up on his hips. "Tough stuff, Em?" he asked.

"Where are they?" she said.

He looked around again and hunched his shoulders. "They were here just a little while ago," he said. "They're all right—trust me. I'm the one that's scarred from trying to keep up with them. Look at me. I'm ready for the Home."

She put her hands in her pockets and faced him, even though she was shredded inside. She wanted to be angry with him, had every right to be, she thought, but still couldn't.

He wiped the sweat off his forehead with a rag from the back of the pickup. "The garbage guys told me I could save you some money if I flung some of the junk into a bin back of their place, so I got the truck—"

She turned away from him, looked out across the stretch of open backyards south to the end of the block and across the street to the church.

"Are you going to say something, Em, or am I going to have to guess at what's on your mind?"

She'd looked right past it at first, but now she saw, in her own backyard, a brand-new swing set midway between the house and the barn. "Where'd that come from?" she said.

"Whoever says you can't buy love doesn't know what he's talking about," Norm told her. "All day they've been on it. Just when you come home, they disappear."

"It's something Marty Kamphoff would do," she said.

"Okay, it was wrong," he said, "but I've been single so long I don't know what do with all my money." He took a step closer to her. "I can throw it in the pickup with the rest of the junk. Do it tomorrow, if you're mad."

She nodded.

"You want me to leave, Em?" he said.

She twisted her fingers in the strap of her purse. There was nothing left to be cute about, she thought, nothing left to say but what had to be said because for years there had been nothing but silence. And in all the times they'd been together since her return he'd not told her everything, not the whole story.

She didn't move any closer to him, but when she swung toward him she did so as if she were meeting an enemy, her face stern and rigid.

"How come you never told me about the abortion?" she said.

For a moment he stared, his eyes almost empty. Then he walked away toward the barn.

"Norm," she said, "don't quit on me. If I've got to face all of this, then so do you. You owe it to me—you do."

The doors to the right side of the barn were propped open by a pair of spades leaning up against them. He walked into the half-darkness inside, almost disappeared in the shadows at the front of the stall.

She followed him to the door and stood on the ledge, but he kept his back to her, hands up on the old manger.

"Mike Stellinga knew about it, Norm," she told him, "because Meg told him herself—"

"When?"

"Just before she had it."

He slammed his hands down on the wood. "Oh, man, I can't believe it," he said. "Emily—"

"It was yours, wasn't it?"

"Of course it was," he said, his back still to her. "She didn't sleep around, Em. I suppose it all looks really black, but I wish you'd have known her."

"Didn't you have the guts to—"

"Wait a minute," he said, turning. "I never knew myself. I never knew it, Emily. Shoot, what did I know about things? I was nineteen, sure that the whole world was a lie, but I didn't know anything. I never knew she was pregnant, and I really—honestly and truly, Em—I never knew she did it."

"What do you mean, *never*?"

"Not until she was dead, Em—that's what I'm saying. Not until your sister was buried did I find out that she'd been pregnant . . . with my child—"

"How?"

He came out of the darkness, stood before her at the doorway, where the lines in his face broadened in the slanted light from the window on the west side of the barn.

"That freaky music teacher," he said. "The guy didn't last two years in this town and then the board canned him—and they should have. He was a jerk, but he was messed up. He'd been there—Vietnam—and he was in no condition to teach."

"He told you?"

"I met him in a bar in Iowa City. After he got dumped here, he went back to school on the GI bill. He's the one that set her up, Em. He's the one that found her the address. He's the one that got it done. And she never told me."

"I can't believe it—"

"I'm sorry," he said. "It's the truth. He'd been there, Em. He was there in the jungle—out in '67. He told her what kind of life he'd lived over there, you see, because she'd listen—that's what she was like."

"He didn't get her pregnant—"

"I'm not saying it was his fault. I'm saying that other kids were scared of that guy, thought he was nuts—and in a way he was. He got all screwed up over there. But not Meg. She wasn't afraid of him, not at all. I'd come home from the university and fill her up with all the radical talk. But he was giving her the real stuff. He'd been there, and she wanted to know."

"And she never told you she was pregnant?"

"I don't know why not," he said. "Believe me, if there's one thing I wish I could ask her—even today, even all these years later—it's that."

"Why?" Emily said. "I don't understand why she wouldn't have told you. For heaven's sake, Norm, you were the father—"

"Independence maybe. I don't know. I've thought about it often enough," he told her. "But I think it was more that she didn't want her life—our lives—maybe her life alone, I don't know—she didn't want it complicated, didn't want to have to deal with everything a baby would bring—"

"Did you ask him?"

"I acted as if I knew, and it never dawned on him that she wouldn't have told me. That's why he brought it up the way he did." He turned toward the door between the stalls of the barn and put his hands up on the beams. "I'm sitting in this bar and there he is, Mr. Music Man. He comes over to me and he's half-tanked and slobbering all over, but for a minute I thought it'd be all right to talk to him. I knew him. He was here when I was a senior." He brought his hands down.

"He told you?" he said.

"'It's just the pits what happened to Meg. One of the class-iest chicks in Neukirk,' he says. 'That woman knew what's happening,' he said. 'I was sure glad to help you guys out.'" Norm looked up as if the man's face were above him against the dark wall. "I can remember him yet, what he wore and everything—a red T-shirt with a raised fist. Big beard by that time. He couldn't have had it in Neukirk in '68, but by that time he'd grown this big beard." He turned to her. "That's what he told me. I had absolutely no idea, Emily—really. I had no clue that's what happened. I didn't know a thing."

"What did you do?" she said.

"What could I do? Meg was already buried, Emily. I mean, this was almost two years after the accident, and I was two weeks away from marrying someone I never should have married—at least not after he told me that."

"You mean, that's why your marriage—"

"Who knows? If life were a puzzle, I think there'd always be a part missing. The marriage failed, flopped bad. It was a mess. It never was at all, Em, and I know this much. At least part of it was Meg—"

"You loved her?"

"I told you, I didn't know what love was. I still don't."

"You didn't love her?"

"After that guy told me what he did, everything turned black." He took a hoe off the nail in the wall where it hung, put the blade on the floor and leaned on it. "The way I saw it then, it was God telling me that the whole marriage thing—I didn't love *that* woman, Em, I swear—the whole marriage thing wasn't right. That's the way I saw it. Or else why did he throw me and this guy into the same place—why did God steer him over to my table with half a jag on, slobbering all over, and have him tell me that it wasn't just Meg I'd killed—"

"You didn't kill her—"

"But a child too."

"Don't say that."

"When I looked in the mirror, Em, I saw a double murderer." He threw his hands up in the air. "There, you want the whole confession—I killed your sister and a niece or a nephew you never had."

She came up behind him and put her arms around his neck, leaned her head against his back. "Why do we lie, Norm?" She felt the pressure of his breathing against her face, but he didn't move. Silence crept up around them.

He tapped the blade of the hoe three times on the floor. "Sometimes for the best of reasons."

"I suppose you never told her either," she said.

"Who?"

"The woman you married?"

He shook his head.

She lowered her right hand and held it against his chest. "So you didn't tell me because of Meg, I suppose—her memory. You just figured nobody knew—"

"What good is it," he said, "to bring up something that no-body on the face of the earth could do anything about?"

"You're protecting her."

"Maybe I am," he said. "But I owe her a whole lot more than protection."

"She's dead," Emily said. "For a quarter of a century she's been dead."

"But not gone," he said. "I got all I can do right now to keep from falling on my face."

She pulled him against her firmly, both her arms around his chest. "You thought nobody knew—"

"Except Mr. Music—"

"So you didn't want to tell me because there was no reason—" she said.

"No reason at all. Why, Emily—you give me one good reason why—even now? What good is it for you to know your dead sister once had an abortion? And if the good citizens of Neukirk knew—"

Norm pulled himself away from her gently, hung the hoe back on the nail, then went to the front of the stall, away from the open doors.

"My parents knew," she said.

"No." He shook his head firmly.

"Yes," Emily said. "Stellinga knew, and he told them."

"When?" he said quickly.

"When she didn't get pregnant—"

"Before the accident?"

"Yes, before the accident."

He kicked the wall angrily, slapped the doors shut on an old kitchen cupboard someone had moved into the carriage stall years ago, then pounded his fists down on the countertop.

"They knew," he said. "When I stood there in your house that night, after the accident . . . when I stood there and told them that that song—whatever it was—was Meg's favorite, they actually knew something I didn't." He turned quickly. "Oh, man, why didn't they say something?"

"Maybe for the best of reasons."

"So they knew it for all those years?" He put both hands down on the countertop. "I can't believe it."

"Silence is a good place to hide," she said.

Six years old. Her mother in a flowered housedress. Her father in his chair beside the register. Norman, a boy she vaguely knew as her sister's boyfriend, alone on the couch. Emily in the kitchen, listening. The crying, the tears. Who lied the most? Who knew everything?

"Did the whole church know? I mean, the council and everything?" he said. "I can't believe it—"

"Stellinga told me he didn't tell anybody, not even the pastor, Daniels—you remember him, the old one?" she said. "They didn't get along that well, I think, so he didn't tell a soul—"

"Except your parents."

"And now part of him regrets it," she told him, "because he says he thinks he did it out of anger. He'd told her not to do it, but she did anyway."

He held his hands in front of him. "Look at me, Em. I'm getting close to fifty, and all of this is so far behind me that there's grown up people in this town who don't even know what Vietnam was all about. But here I am, scared to death that somebody might know the whole story. What's the matter with me?" he said. "I should have never come back here."

"You think it's this town?" she asked.

"It's the only one I know," he said.

"It's the one you never could leave," she told him.

Some silence arises from a kind of necessity. There were moments she remembered, after Meg was killed, when the house had been full of people, none of them talking. What stretched between the two of them now, in the darkness of the old carriage stall in the barn, was that kind of silence. A silence that's not so much a lie as it is a comfort.

"Did they tell her they knew, you think?" Emily said.

"Maybe that's why she wanted so badly not to go back at all that night. Maybe that's why—"

"But you don't know?"

"If she'd have told me, she'd have had to tell me everything, Em," he said. "And she never did."

Out of nowhere, it seemed, the kids came running up. "Can we ride along to the dump again, Norm?" Sammy begged. Rebecca slid over to her mother's side and hugged her.

"I've been dumping some of this stuff. And I trimmed the bushes in the front, cut down some of the dead branches of those ash trees on the south side. Stuff you can burn," he said, "goes to the dump. I've been taking them along and they ride in the back of the pickup."

"Can we, Norm?" Sammy said. "Can we, Mom?"

Norm looked at her.

"Mr. Visser lets you ride in the back of the truck?" she said.

"He says we got to sit down the whole time," Sam told her. "He says not to move once he starts going."

She looked at Norm. "All right," she said, "if you do things just like he tells you."

The kids scrambled up into the bed of the pickup.

Once Emily backed the BMW out of the way, that's how they left the driveway: Norm driving, Emily on the passenger side, the kids in the back on the floor where they found a little nest amid all the junk, each of them with an arm up over the side.

She didn't talk to him, nor did he speak to her, all the way out to the dump. They rode up to the stop light on the north edge of town, turned left two blocks, and took the pitted gravel road, full of puddles from the rain they'd had in the last week, past what seemed a thousand junk cars, and went through a steel gate that stood open to a rutted path up to a pile of branches and stumps.

Norm slipped out the door, and the kids jumped off the back and took off into the field full of wrecked cars.

"May they do that?" Emily said when she got out of the other side and stood looking at him across the bed of the pickup.

He hunched his shoulders. "They're not going to wreck much I guess."

The place was a mess, a forest of tree limbs and gangly weeds already brown and dead, some of them flattened into the ground where other trucks had run their loads back deep into the pile. Norm started unscrambling the branches, one at a time, and heaving them into the pile.

"So now what?" she said.

"I'm empty," he said. "I got nothing left at all."

"You know I've got no one else," she told him. "You understand that, don't you? I feel almost as if you let me down, but you're all I got in all of this."

He reached for a bunch of branches, and what was left came up together. Beneath lay a whole stack of old screens she'd seen up in the barn—useless screens since the year somebody had put all-weather windows on the house and since the old Van Voorst place had been equipped with central air.

"Why don't you help me with these things?" he said, picking up one corner of a screen.

"You're throwing them?" she said, picking up her end, then letting him get his left hand beneath the center to spin the screen out onto the pile of branches and leaves.

"You're wrong, you know," he said. "About having only one person."

"Mom?" she said.

He nodded.

One by one, they took the screens out and threw them on the pile.

"I don't even know if she hears me," she said. "I don't even know if anything goes in."

"Maybe it doesn't make any difference," he said. "*Maybe* is all you got, Em."

When they were through, she called the kids back from an old wheelless school bus, its yellow sides blanched and faded, but thick black letters still visible on the panel beneath the windows: "Neukirk Public Schools." They complained about having to go. Rebecca had an old St. Christopher statue in her hand. "I got Jesus," she said. "I found him."

"I told her she shouldn't take it, Mom—it doesn't belong to her," Sam said. "It was in one of those cars."

"It's not Jesus," Emily told her, pointing. "It's a saint."

Rebecca's hand opened fully and she looked inquisitively at the figure. "What's a saint?" she asked. "Wasn't Jesus a saint?"

"I think she ought to put it back," Sam said, jealous.

"Where'd you find it?" Emily asked.

It was clear from the look on Rebecca's face when she turned back to the rows of cars that she didn't have a clue where it came from.

"Sometime I'll stop up there at the office and pay for it," Emily told them. "Sometime when I'm going by I'll stop in and tell them that you have it, Rebecca. That's what we'll do," she said. "Now you guys get in the back and we'll go home."

When she and Norm got into the cab, she looked at him as if expecting a reprimand. "Maybe I will," she said. "It wasn't a lie. What makes you think I won't?"

"Okay," he said, "I'll buy that."

The empty truck banged more as they drove up the gravel road. She could feel the way the kids bounced when they hit the biggest bumps.

"All these years," she said, "she's carried all of that alone." She put her hand on the dash when they got to the end of the road and Norm stopped to check the traffic. "I think the least I can do is tell her I know."

He turned left back to town.

"You think that's stupid?" she said.

"Telling your mother what?"

"Telling her I know—that's all. Just telling her I know."

"Why would that be stupid?" he said. "What could you tell her that she doesn't already know?"

That night Emily's ex-husband called. She was alone. She hadn't asked Norm to stay, not so much because she was angry at him—she wasn't—or distrustful, but because she didn't need him there, and she didn't want to need him.

She put the kids to bed, came downstairs, put water on for tea, and started to clean up in the kitchen. Norm had left the whole downstairs cleaner than it was when she'd left—no dishes in the sink, no clothes lying around, no toys beneath the kitchen table. The papers lying around the phone were neatly stacked, the pencils she'd left on the countertop arranged in a little box he'd found somewhere, the counters wiped clean.

Two moving boxes stood beneath the cupboards where she'd put the plates and other dishes they'd been using, both marked "kitchen"—one of them opened, the other still taped. It wasn't more than three weeks since she'd packed them—or helped pack them; the movers had done most of the work, with her supervision. What remained in the opened box were the kinds of utensils you don't use everyday—a yellow plastic strainer, wire whips, a triangular spatula for pie, an assortment of cookie cutters.

She took a paring knife out of the drawer beneath the counter across from the sink and sliced through the tape of the unopened box, opened the flaps, and found kitchen decorations: a wicker basket, some dried flowers in a delft teapot, and a piece of handwork her mother had cross-stitched, then mounted and framed before sending it to LA—"God bless our home," in red sampler print surrounded by a green border, a tiny cornucopia at the base.

She didn't like hanging pictures, didn't trust herself because she was often unsure, even after she'd put in the nails, that she would want something exactly where she'd put it first. But a nail already protruded from the wall, just beside the window, so she put the handwork there, backed away to check it, then left it there, even though she wasn't sure if it was too high.

Her ex-husband called right then, just as the kettle boiled and she went to make the tea.

"How's everything?" he said.

She told him everything was fine.

"They roll out the red carpet, I bet?"

She said they had—a whole work group from her mother's church.

"The kids?"

Fine. Adjusting. Lots of neighborhood space.

"Your mother?"

The same.

"Find a job?"

Not really.

"LA weather's been unbearable. Awful heat. You know how it is."

Hot here too. Doesn't cool off at night.

Silence.

"I want to see the kids," he told her. "I can grab a day or two next week. I know it's not in the contract, but I thought you wouldn't mind." When she didn't say anything, he kept going. "I can get a room somewhere close," he said. "I'm not asking for much. I just want to see how you're doing—all of you. I won't be a bother."

What kept her from saying anything was the fact that she knew there were no easy answers.

"Maybe Tuesday. I'll fly up on Tuesday, get in in the evening, spend Wednesday with you, and get a late flight back— barely twenty-four hours."

"Maybe you should wait," she said.

"Something wrong?"

"I've only been here what?—two weeks or so?"

"I miss the kids."

"They're fine."

"I'm not."

"What's the matter?" she said.

"I told you—I miss the kids."

"That's new, isn't it?"

"Emily."

"I'm sorry," she told him.

"Loneliness is no picnic," he said. "You've got dozens of friends there, I bet."

She tried to find a way around things. "I haven't been bored."

"Everything's fine?" he said. "You don't sound too mellow—"

"*Mellow*?"

"Tell me everything's fine," he said.

"Everything's fine."

"You're not saying much."

"Things happen," she said, "things we don't expect."

"For instance?"

She sipped from her tea. "Why don't you wait a week?" she said again.

"What's going on? Is it something with the kids?"

"They think they're in heaven," she told him. "They fall asleep at night—nobody wanders back downstairs. They're that beat. That's how hard they play."

"They have friends?"

"Tons."

"Good."

If she would even hint about Jason Kamphoff, he wouldn't wait until next week.

"Then what is it?" he asked.

"There's no problem," she told him. "Everything's fine. It's going well. I'm not moved in yet, at least not totally. There's boxes around here. I'd just rather that you waited a week or so—"

"You're lying," he said. "Don't lie to me, Emily. We did enough of that."

"Yes, we did," she said. "How's Sandra?"

He waited for a few seconds. "She's fine. Everything's fine here—"

"And so am I," she said. "But I've got all this clutter around here yet, boxes half-opened, nothing up on the walls, furniture in a jumble. I'm not ready for you. Don't come, all right?"

"Since when did you start worrying about a clean house?" he asked.

"Don't get hostile."

"I'm not. I'm trying to be nice—it was a joke."

"Jokes always come at someone's expense, don't they?" she said.

"I didn't call to argue," he said. "I miss my kids." He waited a few seconds. "It doesn't pay to go back into the old mess, does it? It wouldn't do anybody any good. There's some things you might just as well determine to shut up about and let them be, let them die."

"You're right," she said.

"Thank you."

Silence. She pressed the bottom of her spoon against the stained teabag on the saucer. She'd been picturing him in their house, in his office, leaning back in the big black chair, the phone cradled in his neck. But he wasn't there. The house had been sold, and he was in an apartment or at work. She looked up at the clock. It would be like him to work late now that she wasn't around, now that the kids were gone. Or he would be with Sandra. She listened to background noise and distinguished only violins. He was in his office at the university.

"Okay, I'll wait a week," he told her. "It's no good for anybody if I come and you're angry."

"That's right," she said.

"But you're not telling me things, Emily. Will you excuse me if I tell you that I'm worried?"

"Don't be," she said. "It doesn't help." She wanted it to end—and she didn't.

"It's a man?" he said.

Every last obscenity she'd chucked at the men in Tony's came back to her, but she restrained herself. "I won't dignify that with an answer," she told him.

"I'm sorry," he said, and when he didn't speak again for a while, she guessed that he was. "I got just this to say, Emily, and then I'll quit: I'm sorry for the mess I put you through—I mean, for my part in it. I am. I like talking to you—even *this* you, the one that's not telling me anything. I still do. I loved you, Emily," he told her. "I still do, I think, even though—"

212

"Even though what?" she said.

"Even though I'm willing to admit that what broke us up was more my fault than yours."

Who knows what love is really? Norm had said to her—twice, she remembered.

"You can't walk out of my life the way you left California," he said. "That's what I'm saying. Just moving back there, you know—there's no such thing as 'out of sight out of mind.'"

She held the phone with both hands.

"Don't take this wrong, Emily, but I want to speak plainly. I miss you."

She found herself at the edge of crying.

"I don't hate you," he said. "I mean, I know this must sound phony, but it's been hard since you've gone—you and the kids. You represent something—"

"I don't want to *represent* anything, Ben," she told him. "I don't want to stand for anything in your life—not order or peace or goodness—"

"I'm sorry," he said.

What she'd always loved about him was that he reasoned with her. He could be stubborn about some things—and so could she—but at times when they talked about important things, when they disagreed about something deadly serious, he would still listen; sometimes he would even accept the fact that he'd been wrong. He was not defensive at all—that wasn't one of his faults.

"I'll wait," he said. "But I'm coming, you can count on that, Emily. You hear me? You can put me off for a while, but count on it."

"I will," she said.

"I'll call," he told her, and there was an awkward silence then, neither of them quitting, until finally Emily did.

"Good-bye," she said, and put the phone back on the cradle, the only sound in her ears through the silent, empty house around her that one final word.

She slept, but not well, and awoke the next morning before the kids. She was scheduled that day to work the lunch shift at the bowling alley. Tony opened at six daily for breakfast, so he would be there already, she knew, and she could get him if she called. She looked up at the clock after she finished her orange juice and was nearly through her second cup of coffee.

When exactly, she didn't remember—maybe somewhere on I-29 to Omaha—she had decided that she wasn't going back to Tony's, not after what had happened over there. So she called Tony—but she got his wife, Ann, who told her that he was fussing around with the pin-setters when she really could have used him up front.

"I've decided not to come in," Emily said.

"Don't be thin-skinned," Ann told her. "Why don't you come in right now. Goodness knows, I can use the help."

"I'm not coming at all," Emily said. "What I'm saying is that I quit. I hope that doesn't leave you stranded."

"It does," Ann said. "Means I got to stay on myself here for lunch. That's what it means."

"I'm sorry," Emily said.

"As am I," Ann told her right away. "The funny thing about these guys is the way they want us all pretty to look at, but they love it when we beat on 'em too. It's stupid, isn't it?"

"What do you mean?"

"You're foolish to quit now. You just got their attention, Emily." Ann took a moment to bite on something that sounded crunchy, like toast. "They know you got hair on your teeth long enough to mow—and they like that."

"I shouldn't have said—"

"Come on. Too many people second-guess every last thing they've done. We got more people with migraines around here because they build this silly racetrack they circle around constantly—around and around—'should I of done this or shouldn't I?' And mostly they're women, too. I thought better of you."

"What do you mean?"

"*You* know what I mean," Ann said. "Fanciest thing in this place is the pool table. And then you come along—"

"Ann," she said, "I can't."

Another bite of toast.

"You still there?" Emily said.

"Tell you what," Ann said. "I understand, but let me lay this on you, if that's what it's going to take. Let me explain that come 12:30 or so I'm going to be angry because there's likely some law in this state that says a woman shouldn't work as long and hard as I'm going to have to just to make up for you and your precious feelings. Andy Vellinga had it coming—"

"Ann—"

"Okay," she said, "you're *not* coming in. You told me and I heard it. But you remember what I said."

When Norm came over, he had a beautiful and tall young girl with him, a blond, probably soon to be a seventh grader. She was already designing to have the whole nest of curls every Neukirk high school girl wore, not to mention the little chicken-butt front, and when she talked she made a habit of pulling her lips over her braces. Julie, her name was, the girl Norm had promised was the apple of the teacher's eye.

By then the kids were at the breakfast table over twin bowls of Captain Crunch. Neither of them backed off an inch when this girl came in, this stranger—they'd already built up a kind of trust in this place.

"We'll be back in an hour," Emily said to her kids, looking up at Julie. "We're going to visit Grandma."

"Is she all better?" Sammy said.

It was impossible for her to explain to him—to either of her kids—her mother's odd condition, alive but unresponsive. She'd taken them to see their grandmother three or four times, but finally concluded it wasn't in anybody's best interest to continue.

She sensed—who could know really?—that it was hard for her mother too, and the children seemed scared to death around their grandma. From the moment they saw her stonelike face, her un-moving body in the shiny braces of the wheelchair, they sat in that room as if nailed to their chairs.

"She's not any better, Sam, but she likes it when I come to visit," Emily said.

"When she gets better, can she come here?" Rebecca asked.

"When she gets better," Emily told them. "Now you guys listen to Julie, okay?"

She showed Julie the Kool-Aid in the refrigerator and where she'd stowed the cookies, and she told her the kids had made friends in the neighborhood and that they might want to wander a little, and if they did, she'd be happy if Julie would just keep an eye out. "I mean you don't have to play with them all the time if you don't want to, but I'd feel safer if you'd know where they are."

"I love kids," Julie said, with a Neukirk kind of embarrass-ment, as if it were the kind of open confession people somehow didn't make.

Emily looked up at Norm and smiled.

"You don't have to do this," she told him as they walked across the yard toward his truck. "I didn't intend for you to go along."

"If you didn't want me, you'd have told me long ago," he said.

She didn't get in. "Let's walk," she said. "I want to walk."

In a town that prides itself on cleanliness, on perfectly or-dered flower beds in weedless backyards, in a town that had curb-and-gutter a decade before any other village in the county, in a town where store owners sweep their front sidewalks every morning—even after rain—the hospital wing, by law as well as tradition, has always been the very essence of purity. Inside, everything glistens. Even the trays of pills, morning and evening, are set perfectly, the lines of small plastic cups as ordered as checkers on a board.

Now and then a grandchild will break the stiff stillness that ordinarily sits in the long corridor like a distinguished old guest. And some nights—and days—there are moans and cries to remind anyone nearby that this place is little more than a front porch to the great sepulchre of earth. But inside the rooms, where few of the patients have strength sufficient to move around themselves, nothing is ever amiss. If it can be said that the Neukirk elderly, steeped in the old-time religion, are already planning their lives in heaven, gearing up for the glory they see ahead, then it's only fitting that the wing seems to have so little of life's dirt and grime.

Obviously, the place is not without its sadness. There's a waiting list of people—families of the elderly and infirm—wanting to secure one of the fifteen rooms that line the corridor. But some of the patients hang on to life with the stubbornness of children who refuse to miss anything and won't close their eyes. Some cling even when everyone knows it would be much better if they'd just let go. And sometimes there's impatience on the part of family, of nurses, and even of residents themselves, who most vividly of all, when they are capable of understanding, realize how tardy they can be in leaving.

Nancy Greiman was sure that Vivian Doorn was one of those pained by the fact that she continued to live. She knew from experience that if patients like Vivian wanted to get better, if they willed it, sometimes they could regain something of what they'd been. And while Nancy thought she'd seen some eye movement she recognized as a sign of a functioning mind, she'd also noticed for too long a kind of sleepiness that meant Vivian would love nothing better than to pack up and leave for a home she'd looked forward to for a long time. But it did surprise her, given that Emily was here now and visiting almost daily, that Vivian seemed to be loosening her grip.

Maybe, Nancy thought, Vivian had reasoned that with her

daughter back home and safe it would be okay to die. After all, Emily—who'd had so much trouble in her life, the separation, then the divorce—was not surrounded by strangers anymore, but by good people in a place where her children—Vivian's grandchildren, her *only* grandchildren—could be happy and safe. Like that priest in the Bible who, on seeing baby Jesus, claimed he was ready to depart. Maybe it wasn't as much a defeat as a victory, Nancy thought—not as much a refusal to fight as an acceptance of the joy Vivian's faith had promised.

Nancy had missed Emily the day before but had seen no indication that Vivian had even noticed her daughter's absence—no irritability or anxiety, Nancy thought. She was convinced, of course, that she could see traces of those emotions and that she sometimes did. So when Emily came in that morning, Nancy was happy to see her. Losing patients, for any reason—whether by will or by forfeit—was nothing she looked forward to, even though she understood death as a given with this job.

When she saw that Norm Visser was with Emily, however, Nancy's first reaction was the kind of shock that comes out in muffled tones and irritation.

"You weren't here yesterday," she said when the two of them made it to the nurses' station.

Emily hadn't expected scoldings from Nancy—or cattiness, for that matter. "I was out of town," she said. "I was in Omaha all day."

Nancy deliberately looked up at Norm and nodded coldly.

"How is she?" Emily asked.

"Your mother doesn't change much—she's an old woman."

Emily went up to the desk and put her arm over the countertop. She spoke quietly but firmly. "I had this feeling you were different," she said.

"Different?" Nancy said.

"I thought better of you," Emily told her.

"I don't understand—"

"You're angry with me because I wasn't here yesterday?" Emily asked. "Is that it?"

"I'm sorry," Nancy said, averting her eyes.

In a tone subdued, but earnest, Emily said, "I'm not sleeping with him." She nodded toward Norm. "You can tell anyone you'd like—okay? Straighten it all out. I'm not sleeping with him."

Nancy thumbed through a couple dozen files, aimlessly, still refusing to look at them.

"Maybe I was wrong in trusting you," Emily told her.

Nancy stood, ran her fingers through her hair. "No," she said. "I'm the one that's sorry. I thought worse of you—I mean, when you came in like that, I thought better of you." She threw up her hands. "I'm not making sense."

"Even if I was," Emily said, "what business would it be of yours?"

Nancy put down the files and crossed her arms over her chest. "I cared, I guess," she said. "I'm sorry."

Norm grabbed Emily's arm. "Let's go see your mother," he said.

Gently, she pulled her arm away from his hand, still facing Nancy. "I would like you to hear this too—for Mom's sake, not for yours. For her sake. So she knows that you know everything. Come with us," she said.

"I'm sorry," Nancy told her. "It's just that the two of you—"

"It's all right," Emily said. "But I want you to come with us."

So all three walked to Vivian Doorn's room.

The story Emily had learned since coming back home, most people would have said, didn't need to be repeated to her mother, who already knew as much as she needed to know about her older daughter. After all, she was dying, and her ability to understand anything was highly questionable. But ever since she and Norm had had it all out, the whole story, Emily had been convinced that what she knew now—so much more than she'd ever guessed to be the truth—had to be told to her mother.

The story itself wasn't so important. Whether her mother knew what kind of shape her daughter was in the night she was killed was immaterial; after all these years, she didn't have to know everything. But Emily believed that by telling her mother the story as she knew it, by letting it out into the air—even the stale air of the hospital wing, by bringing truth to where there had been only years of silence, she could give her mother, maybe for the first time, the opportunity to breathe, to release her from the prison of her well-meant silence.

Emily walked into the room and saw the outline of her mother's shoulders against the back of the wheelchair. She looked at Norm, who nudged her on with a nod. He walked in front of her and took a chair on the left, within her mother's line of vision. Nancy leaned against the dresser, behind her mother, where she could look straight at Emily.

Emily pulled the wooden straight chair, the one she always sat in, up close enough to allow her to hold her mother's hands.

"I missed coming yesterday, Mother," she said.

Her mother's eyes continued to stare straight ahead, blankly.

"I went to see Mike Stellinga—he lives in Omaha and he helps people," she said. "You probably remember him. He was just a kid when he was here, an intern in our church. He worked with the kids here years ago." She didn't dare bring up Meg's name. Not yet.

"He told me everything, Mother, everything about what happened years ago. Everything about my sister, Mom. Everything about what happened, about what he told you, about her."

Her mother's nostrils flared so slightly that Emily didn't dare think it was anything more than an involuntary movement.

"Norm Visser is here too, Mom. He's sitting right there. And he told me things too, things I didn't know, things you and Dad never said."

She took each of her mother's hands in hers, folded her hands around them.

"I remember Meg's picture, and I remember the night that it happened, the way Mrs. Ferringa stayed up in my room, and

I remember all the tears, of course. And I remember the way you and Dad and I drove out to the place where it happened—after the cemetery, after the little get-together at church. I remember that all very well," she said.

Any movement—even a blink—caught Emily's attention.

"You know the people who live in that farm near the corner—they're still there. They've been there for a hundred years," she said, laughing politely. "I met a boy out there, and he said that ever since that accident he hears about it every year, even though it's so long ago. He said his dad always keeps the corners clean now because—" she hesitated, wondering quickly what she had to know, "—because he still remembers the accident."

She looked up at Nancy, not as if she needed approval but as if she had to know that someone was here.

"I know the whole story, Mom," she said. "I know about the abortion, about you knowing about it, and I know you must have worried—both of you, you and Dad—how you must have worried about Meg, about whether or not she was—" it was hard for her to say it, "—about whether—you know, about her soul, Mom. Because I know you. I knew Dad. You were always wonderful, and I understand, Mom—you have to believe me—I understand what it must have been like for all these years to wonder about Meg—about whether or not she's with the Lord."

She looked up at Norm and understood why he had lied the night he came to talk with them—how safe it must have felt to lie, how almost blessed.

"I know everything, Mom, but I don't mean that I know anything about Meg's soul—none of us do . . . well, maybe Dad does now, I don't know. But none of us know anything, do we? You can think the worst or think the best, I suppose, can't you? And maybe I'm not as strong as you are, either—I mean, in faith. You and Dad were so strong. But I want you to believe me when I say I don't worry like you do—I really don't."

A twitch in her mother's lips, a tightening.

"That isn't why I came," she said. "I can't say you shouldn't worry. I wish I could, but I can't."

Her mother's eyes dropped just slightly, as if she'd determined to look toward the window to Main Street.

"There's things we can't know, I suppose. There's things we can only hope," she said. She looked at Nancy, then at Norm, as if maybe there was something they could say. "But I'm not telling you this because I think you were wrong in not telling me." She squeezed her mother's hand. "Mom, please. Do something to show me that you hear me. Please?"

She looked up at Nancy, who shook her head and then walked over and stood at thewindow.

"Do you, Mom?" she said.

The look in her mother's eyes seemed oblivious—vacant.

Emily looked at Norm.

"Keep talking," he told her.

"Mother, squeeze my fingers if you hear me," she said, but there was no movement in her hands.

"Mom, the kids are fine," she said, straightening her voice as if it were a garment, wrinkled. "They're at home now, playing. You should see them, Mom—they love it here. They really do."

A fraction of an inch, maybe. Just a slight rise in the position of her gaze.

"Sammy's getting so big. He protects his sister, too. You should see them. Some kids fight like cats and dogs, you know—brothers and sisters—but they get along so well, really."

She reached up for her mother's cheek, held her right hand against it lightly, then dropped her hand slightly and swept a small drift of silver hair back up behind her ear, then dropped her hand back to her mother's lap, retrieved her mother's fingers.

"You don't have to hold this alone anymore, Mother," she said. "I wanted to tell you only this much—that you don't have to carry all of this burden alone. I know everything now, everything there is to know about Meg, everything anyone can know, I suppose, except God."

Was there any slight movement, any openness, any glint of recognition in her eyes?

"I know it all, Mom," she said, "and now you can rest because there's no reason for you to hold on to this whole thing any-more—no reason at all. I can do your part, Mom. I know."

Her mother's face looked neither braced nor contorted, seemed to carry nothing of the pain that must have made its life in her through all those years of silence.

"And I think the way you did it was the best way you knew how." She pulled her mother's hands off her lap. "I can take it now, Mom," she told her again. "You aren't alone. I can carry some too." She put her mother's hands back down, released them, folded them into each other, then straightened her house-coat. With the backs of her fingers she followed her mother's forearms down over her wrists and began to hum, very quietly, the old hymn marked as Meg's favorite in the hymnal.

But there was nothing on her mother's face, no indication that even a bit of what Emily had thought so important had be-gun to fill the silence.

Norm stood, stepped over and stooped beside her mother. "I'm sorry, Mrs. Doorn," he said. "I'm really sorry."

Emily reached for his hand, hoping with such force that she thought she might will God's miracle herself. But even though the three of them waited together there for what must have been another five minutes, Emily found no trace of recognition in her mother's face, no brightened eyes. She seemed to be, already, in some other world.

"She's tired," Nancy said, finally.

"Who knows what she's hearing?" Norm said. "Nobody knows what's inside."

Jerry Staats was once maybe one of the toughest kids ever to grow up in Neukirk. He lives in the house just south of the hospital. Jerry's father lost his life when he was canoeing by himself down the Big Sioux, in April, of all times, when the wa-ter eats away at the banks and sucks in huge old cottonwoods like so much cheap timber.

223

Mrs. Graven lives in the next house south of the hospital, as she has for fifty years. When her husband was alive, he built a kind of park in the backyard, complete with fountain and a huge screened-in aviary he stocked with goldfinches and a few exotic breeds he needed to take in during the winter. But that was years ago. Mr. Graven had a heart attack in 1965, and she's been alone ever since.

Nobody gets out as much as Edna Westerbeke, who lives in the house on the other side of Mrs. Graven. The only attribute they share is chronological age. Rumor has it that she's been asked to marry four times since her husband died, but she loves her freedom. Last year she and a friend she picked up at some nunnery (she's as Protestant as anyone, but she's never stopped wanting to learn about things) went off on one of those Love Boats and you should have heard what people said when she came back wearing the broadest possible smile.

The hardware store has been in the hands of the Banks family for almost eighty years, and business has never been better. Fred Banks, who's in his early fifties now, lives just south of Edna Westerbeke, hustled a wife right out of Neukirk when his first mate, a plump southerner who never quite made Neukirk her home, died unexpectedly at thirty-five. I can't tell you how happy people have been for him. They do wonder how Shirley Navis, who's forty and had never been married, is going to tolerate Fred's hunting madness. But already this year, during pheasant season, he turned down an offer to go to South Dakota.

Picture the two of them, then—Norman Visser and Emily Doorn—walking down Main Street past those houses, each with its own story; but on this day the two of them were as oblivious to what was there on the street as Vivian Doorn seemed to be to her daughter's desire to share the burden she must have carried for all those years.

Old pictures of Neukirk show Model A's parked diagonally down Main, close to downtown. But it's been years since anybody's parked diagonally. There is no parking, in fact, down Main Street, not even two blocks farther north, where the stores begin. Main Street is really a highway, not just some flat, dusty, prairie road from an old Western movie.

It may be difficult for you to imagine that, after hearing so much about Neukirk, but we're not quite as rustic as you might believe. I've said before how cattle trucks run all night long on Main because the highway is a major shortcut between Omaha and the Twin Cities. Even though most of Neukirk shuts down completely after midnight, there's always people on Main.

The morning Norm and Emily visited the wing was almost perfect weather. The sun shines a lot on the Plains. Say what you want about the beauty of Seattle or the Great Lakes or even the Northeast, but nothing is more beautiful than the sun shining on our broad blanket of cropland. And it was shining that morning when the two of them left the hospital, weary, as you can imagine, but not at all joyful.

You need to know about the weather because it was so perfect that the two of them could walk easily and slowly down the sidewalk that's becoming bumpy here and there from the protrusion of roots from nearby maples. Picture them there, walking down Main Street, both of them looking down, not so much because of the cracks and shifts in the sidewalk as in mood. All Emily had wanted was some sign she'd eased her mother's burden of silence—a sign she never received, even though she'd prayed right then and there, her mother's hands in hers.

You need to know about the weather because it wasn't much past ten o'clock that morning, and it was perfectly bright, so there was no reason that all of those folks from Neukirk, the ones in cars and the ones in trucks, couldn't shift their eyes from the double-lane highway that runs straight through town. They all saw Norm and Emily walking down that sidewalk.

And those who were there at precisely the moment they passed Edna Westerbeke's saw something they thought remarkable, something worth mentioning again and again, even though they might put it into a sentence in no more noble place than a modifier. "Who do you think was walking—together—down Main Street?"

That's the news that got out that morning. That's what people saw when the two of them were maybe two blocks south of the hospital's side door, the one they'd exited a few minutes before. A lot of people claimed to see it—the moment Norm Visser stopped walking, stood in the middle of the sidewalk, looked directly at Emily, the most beautiful woman most people had ever seen, and took her in his arms, the two of them standing there like a statue, right there in broad daylight on Main, holding each other.

And then they walked, people said, hand in hand, back home to a place the whole town will likely call the Van Voorst place for about another thirty years.

Norm Visser, the man who'd driven the car in the accident that killed Meg Doorn a quarter century ago and lived alone after that, and Emily, Meg's little sister—such an unlikely couple, and yet so right too, considering their burden—had walked down the sidewalk in plain view of the whole town, arm in arm. What a story.

Nancy Greiman never told anyone what she'd heard—well, only her husband, who's the kind of rock she's learned to trust. So they were the only people in town who didn't wince when they heard the story of how those unlikely two were walking down Main in plain daylight, middle of the morning, arm in arm, after a hug that lasted much too long, people said. But Nancy said nothing at all.

Neither Emily nor Norm spoke much during that walk home. They walked slowly, in silence, until Emily told him, "I can't live this way. I can't live not knowing whether anything got through. I can't."

They turned up the driveway and started toward the back of the house.

"What do we know about what's in there?" she said.

"In where?"

"In her," she said. "I don't know what my mother holds inside."

"And she never knew what was inside her daughter," he said.

Emily stopped and pulled her hand away from his. "How could she do that?" she asked. "I can't begin to imagine how my mother could live that way—not knowing."

"Sure you can," he told her. "You know your mother. Everybody knows your mother." He shrugged his shoulders. "She believed," he said.

"Sounds so easy," she said.

"You know better," he told her.

Nobody in the bowling alley expected to see Emily Doorn back. Ann was grousing, of course, because she wasn't looking forward to so much work when she was—"years ago already," she claimed—far too old to take care of so many men for so long in one day. Ann hadn't told them about Emily's phone call that morning. The regular customers just assumed she wouldn't be back, despite the attempt that some of them had made to bring peace. It's characteristically Neukirk to think the worst but hope you'll be surprised by joy.

And they were. Emily appeared, maybe a bit late, but still early enough to help out with most of the lunch hour.

She did her job, and she did it well, people said. And while she might have taken the edge off the flirtatious giddiness she'd once put on, she was—as the men were to her—kind, gracious, and appreciative. Her tips skyrocketed.

Unlike stories, people's lives go on beyond the back cover.

Benjamin Forcier came to visit a few weeks ago, as he'd promised over the phone. Everyone knew he was there because of the rental car in the driveway, the motel room he'd rented at the Colonial, and the fact that he was seen—this stranger dressed to kill—at least a dozen times in town.

Some people have started to think that once her mother dies, Emily'll go back to him—maybe because she's just too eccentric for Neukirk, her beauty too much an odd commodity. But they don't know there's more to the story of Emily Doorn, and it's unlikely they ever will, even though it happened right under their noses and it's all written down here. Maybe the best place to hide things in this town is in a book.

After all, Emily may stay. Her children are happy here, and she likes the house. Marty Kamphoff never shows his face around the Van Voorst place, but she's got Norm Visser and Nancy Greiman, and she has something she didn't know she was missing for all her years growing up here and even those years she was living, happily, in California. Right now she has as much as she needs, and probably as much as she'll ever know, of the truth, enough to set her free. It's truth that can be terrifying—as it was to her—but is, nonetheless, the truth.

And in Neukirk, as anywhere I suppose, that's no mean commodity.